PRAISE FOR

THE BODY UNDER THE PIANO

"Pure delight—brimming with adventure, mystery and fun. I loved every character, every clue and every page. Now that I know all the answers, I have only one question left: why did this book have to end?"

—Rebecca Stead, author of
Newbery Award winner *When You Reach Me*

"Mystery lovers, you need to check it out!"

—Kristin Cashore, author of the Graceling series

"Heartfelt, funny and suspenseful, *The Body under the Piano* is an excellent beginning to what is sure to be a pleasantly gruesome series."　　—Starred Review, *Shelf Awareness*

"A remarkable, cool, and likable detective."

—*Kirkus Reviews*

"A solid dose of tart wit makes it an extra-enjoyable read."
— *Horn Book Magazine*

"[A] compelling, splendidly surprising murder mystery."
— *Booklist*

"A delightful mystery."
— *Bulletin of the Center for Children's Books*

"Jocelyn offers an enjoyable entrée to the Queen of Crime and to the genre; the narrative's arch tone, the girl's vital grandmother, and the novel's surfeit of extravagant teas should please." — *Publishers Weekly*

PRAISE FOR
PERIL AT OWL PARK

One of CBC Books' Best Middle-Grade and
Young Adult Books of 2020

"Aggie's wit, character, and warmth are ever engaging as she matures, and Jocelyn maintains a pleasing pitch of humor, feeling, and historical realities throughout."
— *Toronto Star*

"*Peril at Owl Park* is just as engaging and appealing as *The Body under the Piano*. Aggie has emerged from her shell while her interests in murder and her creative imagination continue unabated."

— *Historical Novel Society*

AGGIE MORTON
MYSTERY QUEEN

THE SEASIDE CORPSE

MARTHE JOCELYN

WITH ILLUSTRATIONS BY ISABELLE FOLLATH

tundra

Paperback edition published by Tundra Books, 2023
Previously published, 2022

Tundra Books, an imprint of Tundra Book Group,
a division of Penguin Random House of Canada Limited

Library and Archives Canada Cataloguing in Publication

Title: The seaside corpse / Marthe Jocelyn ; illustrations by Isabelle Follath.
Names: Jocelyn, Marthe, author. | Follath, Isabelle, illustrator.
Series: Jocelyn, Marthe. Aggie Morton, mystery queen ; 4.
Description: Series statement: Aggie Morton, mystery queen ; 4
Identifiers: Canadiana 20220453128 | ISBN 9780735270848 (softcover)
Classification: LCC PS8569.O254 S43 2023 | DDC jC813/.54—dc23

Published simultaneously in the United States of America by Tundra Books of Northern New York, an imprint of Tundra Book Group, a division of Penguin Random House of Canada Limited

Library of Congress Control Number: 2021949164

Edited by Lynne Missen with assistance by Margot Blankier
Designed by John Martz
The text was set in Plantin MT Pro.

Printed in Canada

www.penguinrandomhouse.ca

1   2   3   4   5   27   26   25   24   23

Penguin
Random House
TUNDRA BOOKS

For my writing compatriots,
the Misanthropic Stabbers,
a lovely set of friends

Aggie Morton

Hector Perot

Everett Tobie

Grannie Jane

Sylvia Spinns

Sergeant Harley

Arthur Haystead

P.C. Ronnie Gull

Chapter 1

A Novel Adventure

THAT SECOND WEEK IN JULY was full of surprises. Lovely, mysterious and ghastly surprises.

Plus, one that broke my heart in two.

Meeting my very new nephew was the marvelous beginning, even if he lay in my sister's arms and rarely woke up, except for nourishment, during my four-day visit. Once, he considered me with such gravity that I was convinced his navy-blue eyes were attempting to read my mind. How he might interpret such a briar patch I'd never know, as wee Jimmy was only eleven days old.

Mummy would stay on at Owl Park for two weeks more, to help my sister Marjorie learn to be a mother while I went off to my next adventure. This began with my first-ever ride in a motorcar! (Admittedly, a tad more thrilling than watching a baby sleep.) Marjorie's husband, James, had purchased a brand-new Peugeot a few weeks before his son was born. Today he was practicing his new driving skills by taking me to Lyme Regis, beside the sea.

"It's a fine day, and we're going a distance of twenty-nine miles," James told Mummy. "The drive won't take much longer than an hour. I shall be back before tea if Hector's train is on time." We were to pause at the railway station in Axminster to collect my best friend before driving five miles more to our destination.

I peered at the row of mysterious brass-rimmed gauges set into what James called the dashboard, just above my knees. These bobbing needles next to the steering wheel told James the quantity of petrol in the tank and the speed at which we were traveling. The wooden panel itself protected us from the noisy whirr and oil splatters produced by the engine.

James opened a compartment under his seat and pulled out a folded map and a pair of smart leather gloves. "The wood of the steering wheel warms up and begins to sweat at this time of year." He buckled the clasps at his wrists. "The gloves provide better grip." He handed the map to me and started the engine. We lurched backward before he adjusted our position to drive out through the courtyard gates.

"Take off your hat," he added, "if you care to keep it.

The wind will think it's a gift otherwise, and carry it off." I removed my hat and tucked it into the lunch hamper in the back seat.

The rush forward into a shimmering afternoon shook loose a burst of laughter.

"Oh, James!" I had to shout because of the warm, whistling wind. I patted the gleaming wood of the dashboard to tell him, *How beautiful!* In his beam of pride, I saw a glimpse of the boy he must have been before he grew up to be Lord Greyson. And a peek at the boy my teeny nephew might become?

"This motorcar is the prettiest thing in my life," James said, at a half holler. "Aside from your sister, of course."

I leaned over to punch his arm.

"Hey! Not while I'm driving!"

I snatched my hand back and held down the map fluttering on my lap. How foolish to tease the person at the helm of a machine roaring through the countryside faster than a cantering horse!

"You'll be at Camp Crewe four nights before your grandmother arrives on Friday for her weekend at the hotel in town," said James. "Are you nervous to be without family for so long?"

"Hector will be with me, so I shan't be nervous," I said. "Though I've never slept in a tent before. I expect that will be odd. I'm more curious than anything else."

"No other Morton female has ever slept in a tent," said James. "Not your sister, or mother, nor your Grannie Jane. That's quite an achievement. Add to that being part of a rare fossil excavation, and you may claim uncommon scientific endeavor!"

"Especially now that they've uncovered something so grand to excavate," I said. "The remains of a creature lying unseen for all of history."

"Our timing is indeed fortuitous," said James. "We had no idea, when the arrangements were made, that Mrs. Blenningham-Crewe would trip over a spectacular find. This sort of undertaking usually leans heavily on guessing and luck."

"Guessing and luck is what makes fossil-hunting and paleontology so like detecting," I said.

James flashed me a smile. "Just your cup of tea, eh? But here's a chance to apply that curiosity to a subject more savory than human corpses, do you see? At the governors' meeting for the museum, when this notion of encouraging young scientists came along, I jumped at the chance to have you and Hector be part of it."

"They didn't mind that I'm a girl?" I said.

James concentrated very hard on the road for a minute, but it was a sham. Not so much as a field mouse in our path.

"Truth is," he said, after a bit, "there are occasional advantages to being Lord Greyson and on the board of governors. I suggested that the Natural History Museum must embrace the twentieth century and allow girls to learn about science. You're a bit of an experiment, do you see? Best foot forward, and all that."

Well, *humph*. I could summon good behavior when necessary, and Hector was as polite as a vicar on Sunday.

"What you mean is that I mustn't let you down," I said.

"No chance of that," said James, in his nice way. "I have utter faith that you'll hold your own with the boys, Hector and the other two. The Young Scientists League, the governors are calling it. They've even come up with a—"

"Slogan," I interrupted. "You said already. I've got it memorized. 'Introducing inquiring youth to the facts and the mysteries of Mother Earth.' Right?"

James nodded. "Professor Blenningham-Crewe and his wife have quite a reputation in the fossil world," he said. "I expect that this, this . . . whatever its name is, will be their ticket to fossil royalty. Some sort of swimming lizard—icky-something . . . quite unpronounceable."

"Ichthyosaur," I said. James had read us the letter from his friend Mr. Everett Tobie, who was part of the team at Camp Crewe.

"You see?" said James. "You're a natural."

"So, you fixed it for Hector and me to be part of the Young Scientists League, and you fixed it for your school chum to be the photographer, and—"

"No, no, I had nothing to do with that," said James. "It was Everett who informed me about the Blenningham-Crewes to start with. His contribution is drawing the specimens and taking photographs on digs. He's a real artist."

"How did he learn to do that?"

"He was always sketching, even at school. Cartoons of the masters, still lifes of the breakfast table, anything that caught his eye. He was born abroad, where his father was running a British outpost. His mother was Moroccan. Mr. Tobie met her out there and surprised himself by getting married. Sadly, she died early on, and his father brought Everett home to England."

I decided I liked Everett for this reason alone. My own Papa had died one year and six months ago. *Hello, Papa,* I still said to him most days. I thought of him for the smallest of reasons—when I put extra honey on my toast, or calculated a sum, or watched Mummy brushing her hair. What would he say about me riding in a motorcar? On my way to dig up fossils and to stay with strangers in a tent? So many things he would never know about my life!

"Will we get there in time?" I said. My nose and cheeks were tingling from sun and wind.

"Plenty of time." James reached over to tap the map. "Just don't steer me wrong."

I'd not had many opportunities in my life to follow a map but found it an appealing exercise. Quite simply,

I became a bird. Suddenly the world expanded in every direction, farther ever than a human girl named Aggie might see. The lines and dots on the page took on a meaning that outshone even words when looked at from the sky. I directed the driver admirably, my wings swooping this way and that, my fingertip tracing the miles.

The redbrick railway depot at Axminster had a roof that sloped to a high peak, like a gingerbread house with drippy icing. James stopped the motorcar nearby and we climbed down. My legs, and indeed all of me, wobbled a bit after the abundance of jouncing.

"Nice to stop shouting for a minute," said James. "You look a bit pink, Aggie. Put your hat back on while we're standing here. Your mother will give me a dreadful wigging if you start sprouting freckles."

"How long before the train comes?" I said.

James pulled out his watch. "A quarter of an hour, I should think. Let's see what Cook packed for our lunch, shall we? I'm mad with thirst." He opened the hamper and pulled out bottles of lemonade and a packet of cucumber sandwiches laced with dill from the kitchen garden at Owl Park. I kept one wrapped for Hector, as he was always hungry.

"How many minutes now?" I asked, as we tidied things away.

"We should hear the whistle any moment," said James.

We strolled along the platform, nodding hello to a porter who waited in the shade.

"Oh, look!" A bright poster was pasted to the station wall, showing a dog on its hind legs, wearing a ruffled collar. "There's a circus in Lyme Regis this very week!"

We read the list of attractions printed in gold and scarlet letters.

CLOWNS & TUMBLERS!!
DANCING DOGS!!

BICYCLING TRICKS!!
FAMOUS FIRE-EATER!!

Feats of Physical Fortitude by the STRONGEST MAN in the World!!

← OTHER RARE & REMARKABLE SIGHTS →

I mustn't get my hopes up. We had come to Lyme Regis for a more elevated purpose than visiting a circus. But wouldn't it be thrilling?

We heard the blast of the whistle. Hector was nearly here!

Certain works of literature referred to a steam engine as an Iron Horse, but it seemed to me more a mythical creature. Hot gusts of steam were *the fiery breaths of an angry dragon.* The ground trembled a little as the train approached, *like a Minotaur knocking down trees.* Thundering wheels screeched against metal tracks, *like cries of angry harpies.*

The beast shuddered to a stop. Carriage doors popped open along its length, releasing passengers from their compartments onto the platform. A slight fog of steam lingered as I looked madly back and forth for Hector.

There! James strode toward him, two paces ahead of me, but I darted past his elbow to make certain I was first.

"Hector!"

He wore a sailor suit, light blue for summer, and held his case in one hand while keeping a straw boater in place with the other. Was it because he came from Belgium that he looked so small and foreign? None of the hurrying adults paid any attention. Only I knew the prodigious friction of his brain cells, and the capacity of his heart for true friendship.

My unladylike greeting knocked him off-balance, but he withstood my embrace with good cheer. James scooped up the suitcase and hoisted it to his shoulder as if it were a loaf of bread.

"Did you bring your torch?" I said. "And your magnifying glass? I expect that will be especially useful, don't you, for looking at old bones?"

"Yes, and yes," said Hector. "Also, the vicar lends to me his binoculars. I am equipped to see both near and far." We hurried to keep up with James.

"And now!" I said. "The motorcar! Wait till you feel it purring and chuckling all about you!"

Hector came to a halt, suitably impressed. "A Peugeot Double Phaeton, monsieur?" he said. "Manufactured in this year of 1903?"

"You are correct." James patted the motorcar as if he'd built it himself. Hector ran his fingers over the gleaming bonnet, polished with industry by James as he could not bear to relinquish the task to a servant.

"We'll be a bit squished in back with the luggage," I said, "but I want to sit together, don't you? You won't believe how fast we go!" It was to be Hector's first time riding in a motorcar as well. "And let's never go anywhere without each other again," I said. "Never ever."

"And may we agree"—James tucked Hector's case

under the lunch hamper—"that this particular excursion will not include the discovery of a dead body?"

"I'm afraid we cannot make that promise." I grinned at Hector. "Can we?"

Foolishly, I was thinking of giant reptile bones.

CHAPTER 2

A VERY BEST FRIEND

MR. EVERETT TOBIE HAD INSTRUCTED James to find the church of St. Michael the Archangel in the village of Lyme Regis. We drove over cobblestones, peering about, until an old man with a barrow pointed the way to the helpfully named Church Street, and there we were. We parked the car in the shade of the rectory and found ourselves over-looking the cemetery. Beyond rows of gravestones were the rolling waves of the sea. This part of Dorset shared the same coast as my hometown in Devon, the next-door county, but it seemed much wilder here.

"Look how high we are above the water!" I jumped from the back seat and attempted to smooth wrinkles from my linen dress.

James plonked my hat onto my head and scooped up

our cases. "Everett says it's still a bit of a walk from here," James said. "Look for the footpath off that way . . ." He pointed to where the cliff took a jagged turn, forming a steep rocky backdrop to the crescent-curved shoreline far below us to the east.

"Ahoy there!" A hatless man in shirtsleeves waved both arms from the very path we sought.

"Everett!" James raised his hands, each holding a case, and waved a clumsy greeting in return. Mr. Tobie had thick black hair, dark golden skin and a smile as bright as the sunny afternoon.

"The one and only Everett Tobie," said James. Mr. Tobie doffed an imaginary hat and performed a sweeping bow. James put down our luggage, and the men embraced with quick slaps on each other's backs. Hector bowed in his elegant Belgian way.

I said, "Pleased to meet you, Mr. Tobie," and began a small curtsy, but was prevented by a firm shake of his head.

"I appreciate the effort," he said, "but we are *very* informal, as you will see. Lord Greyson here would be horrified if he knew the truth of it. You're to call me Everett and we all muck in as a team, right? That works best while camping. Save your fancy manners for the cook, if you know what's good for you."

That sounded ominous, but I could see he meant it in jest. We followed him on what he called the short route, winding through the small cemetery. I stopped to look at the stone for *Here Lies Eliza Wembley, Beloved Wife*, and *Timothy Martyn, Not Forgotten*, who had carved birds above his name. What better place to linger? Surely those who rested here deserved a few moments of consideration? Their time on earth—and their absence from it— were noted in so few words.

"It is a promising sign that you like graveyards," said Everett. "A paleontologist must be drawn to the deep, dark past." He paused beside a weathered stone marker. "Here's the one you'll want to notice."

To the memory of Joseph Anning, it read, *who died July the 5th 1849. Aged 53 Years*, and then, *Also of three Children who died in their Infancy. Also of Mary Anning, sister of the above*. Her death date was inscribed as well, *March the 9th 1847. Aged 47 Years*.

"That's a crowded grave," I said.

"Joseph and his sister Mary were the first people to discover an ichthyosaur," Everett explained. "The very first in the *world*, so far as anyone knows. She was twelve years old. And here we are, nearly one hundred years later, uncovering another on the very same beach."

Hector and I, also twelve, lingered to stare at the historic marker.

"*Ichthys*," said Hector, "is Greek for fish. And *sauros* means lizard. That's where the name came from. Fish lizard."

14

Everett's eyebrows lifted. His first peek at Hector's superior brain! "A scientist in the making!" he said. "I anticipate exciting days ahead."

The walk was nearly twenty minutes, but neither James nor Everett complained about carrying our cases such a distance.

"There is a track that comes from the main road directly to camp," said Everett, "but it's used by wagons rather than fancy motorcars, and has ruts as deep as ditches."

We arrived at an encampment of round canvas tents in a small meadow, a tiny village that made me think of Crusaders and jousting. A young woman with rosy cheeks and fluttery yellow hair came out to greet us. This was Helen, daughter of the cook and also his assistant—and now a childminder as well. Not that we needed minding!

"Hallo." She bobbed her head at James but seemed more curious about Hector and me, examining us with friendly gray eyes. Helen was what my Grannie Jane called *pleasingly plump*, healthy and bosomy. She wore a flowered dress under her apron, sewn by herself, she told me later. Hector made his adroit little bow, but I only smiled. I'd been taught not to curtsy to servants or helpers.

"And this is Arthur." Helen introduced the lanky boy lurking behind her. "Arthur Haystead." He glanced at Hector and attempted his own bow in the direction of Lord Greyson, though he looked rather like a pecking rooster.

"Arthur is the third member of our Young Scientists League," said Everett. "He lives in the village, but he'll be staying with us at Camp Crewe for the fortnight. He submitted an informative essay on hagstones when he wrote to request a place with us."

What was a hagstone? I felt a prickle of shame. Hector and I were here merely because James suggested we come, not for any knowledge about fossils.

"Hector," Everett was saying, "you'll be in a tent with Arthur and our other boy when he gets here, if that suits?"

"The pleasure is mine," Hector lied.

"Oscar Osteda is from America," said Everett. "He and his father arrive tomorrow."

"Master Arthur, you'll show our new friend where he's to kip, right?" said Helen. "You're with me, Miss Aggie. Thanks to you being a girl and needing a companion, these next two weeks will be like a holiday for me. I'll be sleeping a few extra minutes in the mornings, instead of going back and forth to town with my father." She picked up what she correctly guessed to be my case.

"Go on," said James, seeing me hesitate. "I'll take a look about with my governor's eyes while you put your belongings away."

The girls' tent was circular and made of white canvas, low around the perimeter and high in the middle.

"Leave your shoes out here." Helen slipped hers off, and obediently I did the same. "Less sand and grit inside that way."

The tent seemed smaller within than it looked from the outside, and the air was stifling. The dome reached well above our heads, but our cots were set off to the sides where the slope of the roof made us stoop.

"Not to fuss about the heat," said Helen, with a breathy laugh. "We won't be in here much during the day, and the warmth is obliging enough to stick around at night. It's cozy, but it's nice that we're only two. The boys are three in the same space."

I pinned on a smile. I had not shared a bedroom, except with my dog Tony, since Marjorie went away to school five years ago. And here I'd be with a complete stranger!

"I made yours up." Helen smoothed the dull green blanket that lay over a turned-back sheet and thin pillow. Two folded towels sat on the end of the cot.

"Thank you."

"It looks worn, but it's clean," said Helen. "My mam is the laundress for the camp, and plenty of others in town. I'll tell you one thing I don't want to be, and that's a laundress. Nor a cook, really, either. But I'm seventeen already, so if I'm not promised to be married soon . . ." Her voice trailed off.

Which of the thousand possible ways had she meant to finish that sentence? *If I'm not promised to be married soon, I shall become an old maid with nine cats. If I'm not promised to be married soon, I shall run away to sea . . .*

"Do you have a beau?" I whispered. Not a question one usually asked a stranger, but it seemed to be what she wished for . . . As if I'd dropped berry sorbet on a tea cloth, her face went pink that quickly.

"I do," she said, "but you mustn't say, not ever. My dad . . ." She wagged her head and widened her eyes. "He expects I'll be helping him till I'm forty and toothless. I won't be mentioning my Ned till it's a sure thing, you hear?"

"I'm good at secrets," I assured her. *If I'm not promised to be married soon, I'll be chopping onions till my teeth fall out.*

Between the beds was a small packing crate in use as a table for a lantern, a speckled tin cup and a notebook with a pencil attached on a ribbon.

"Are you a writer?" I said.

Helen's cheeks became rosier still. She moved the book from the crate to a place under her nubbly blanket. "That's my diary," she said. "Mostly twaddle, my mam would say, not that I'd ever show her."

I began to pull my own notebook out of the pocket I'd stitched to my skirt especially to hold it, but a voice outside interrupted.

"Helen? Are you there?" It was the boy, Arthur Haystead.

"Lord Greyson wishes to say goodbye to Aggie," said Hector.

"We're coming." Helen hopped up and I followed her into bright daylight. Arthur and Hector were mismatched sentinels: one tall and gangly, the other short and perfectly poised. Arthur's sandy hair stuck up like summer grass, while Hector's was as shiny and flat as new paint.

James and Everett were emerging from the biggest tent. The work tent, Helen called it.

"I have been with your hosts," said James. "You will have an illuminating time of it here."

"Thanks for the commendation, my lord," said Everett, not in the least bit respectfully. James laughed and pretended to cuff him. Everett pretended it had been a fierce blow and reeled backward.

But then James turned to me. "Do let us know, won't you?" he said. "How things are going? Marjorie and your mother will love to hear the news."

"Yes, James," I said, "I will write letters. And you needn't add the bit about being good children and obeying our elders."

James tugged on my plait. "Consider all instructions left unsaid. Except for the one about taking care not to fall into the sea. Look after each other. Your grandmother will arrive on Friday, for a weekend of sea air, and I shall collect you in a fortnight for another glimpse of the world's best baby."

He gave me a hug, and Hector a clap on the shoulder. Even Arthur received a salute. Then he strode off along the footpath toward the church and his lovely motorcar. He turned for a final wave, and I realized it was the first minute of the first week of my life when I would have no family within shouting distance. Hector pressed my hand. He'd been living in a whole other country from his parents and sister for nearly a year! How dare I make the slightest complaint? My mind spun back through the million hours Hector and I had shared during his time in England, a few of them scarily dangerous. For one night full of those hours in particular, he had shouted his throat raw with no one hearing.

I squeezed his hand in return, an optimistic promise that no such calamity would strike during this bright-skied, summery week.

CHAPTER 3

A New and a Very Old World

EVERETT DIRECTED ARTHUR to show us around, while Helen went to help her father with making our tea.

"If you please," said Hector, "the Grand Tour."

"I've been here since yesterday," said Arthur, "so I know it all." The Grand Tour meant that we stood on the grass in the center of a circle of tents as Arthur pointed to each in turn, naming its function.

"The biggest is the work tent, but I won't show you inside right now. They're still consumed," he said. "Till the light goes." He pointed to the next one. "Everett stays in the littlest tent, as he's alone. Then ours, and the girls', which you know already. The Blenningham-Crewes have the green one, over there by itself." There were perhaps a dozen paces between each tent, and the

21

length of a cricket pitch between us and the cliff over-looking the sea.

"Oh," said Arthur, "and Nina says that repeating 'Blenningham-Crewe' fifty times a day is a waste of breathing time, and that we should call her Nina."

"And monsieur le professeur?" said Hector.

"He's Mr. B-C, or just B-C. His wife calls him Howard."

"It is most unsettling," said Hector. "Such familiarity with strangers."

"We'll be thinking of ways to avoid calling them any-thing," I said.

Arthur laughed.

"What's that canopy near the hedgerow?" I asked.

"That's the shop yard," said Arthur. "Two men from the quarry were hired on to build things, like crates for packing and tables for the samples. The cook tent is the other big one." He led us in that direction. "It's jolly clever."

Helen leaned against a trestle table, sawing a loaf of bread into slices.

"Hallo again!" She waggled the bread knife and smiled.

"Everett says we eat at the tables under this awning, whether or not it's raining," said Arthur. "The cooking fires are on the other side, where the smoke won't bother anyone. There's an ice chest indoors and they've got stores of food and a place to chop things up." He might have been giving us the tour of the Royal Armoury, his enthusiasm was so keen.

"The food is good?" said Hector in a low voice.

Arthur hesitated. "Well, there's lots of it," he said.

"Oh dear," said Hector.

Helen had switched to a butter knife and was working her way down the stack of raggedly sliced bread. A large man was visible through the drawn-back flap of the tent behind her. Helen tipped her head toward him. "That's my dad, Mr. Malone. But everyone calls him Spud."

Hearing us, Spud came to the doorway to say hello. I could not help but think that his nickname was well chosen. He was shaped like a potato, bulging and lumpy, his head a second little potato precariously balanced up top. Tufts of hair sprouted from behind wizened ears beneath a white cook's hat. He nodded gravely and returned within.

"He's not in the best humor," whispered Helen. She kept up a steady pace of buttering the bread. "The mutton stew is more of a bean soup, thanks to the butcher not showing up today."

Hector sighed.

"I'll ring the bell when tea is ready," said Helen. Her buttering became even more slapdash for the last few slices.

"We'll go and wash, shall we?" said Arthur.

"Yes!" said Hector. "The journey leaves me . . . you say in English, grubby?"

Arthur led us to a small rough-hewn shed backed up against a patch of shrubs. To one side was an enormous tank, sitting on a wooden platform. A spigot and a trough below turned it into the camping version of a basin with running water. The loamy aroma told us clearly what purpose the shed itself was meant for. Hector's cheeks paled.

"It's a bit primitive," said Arthur, "but a good sight better than finding a tree to duck behind."

I turned the tap and wet my hands. Arthur stepped up and quickly shut off the flow.

"The soap is there," he said, "in the china cup. But you mustn't let the water run while you're sudsing. Every drop counts. Fresh water is brought out in these drums, by pony cart. My cousin Gordon loads the carts at the spring, only he's away this week. Gone with my mum and dad to Cornwall, to visit my sick grandpa."

"We'll be careful about conserving water," I said. "It's an ingenious setup, isn't it?"

I hoped that Arthur did not notice Hector's mortified silence while he washed his hands and shook them dry as I had, there being no towel.

"Hereabouts we call it a backhouse," Arthur said. "As outdoor lavatories go, this one is not so bad. They've dug the pit pretty deep under the bench."

Hector squeezed his eyes shut. I could almost see his stomach clenching. On our way back to the circle of tents, I noticed that the path was edged with white stones. Would they glow in the moonlight to show the way?

Everett joined us at the tea table. We still had not seen the Blenningham-Crewes.

"Oscar will arrive in the morning," Everett told Helen as she put down forks and spoons and napkins, "so we'll have another hungry boy for meals after that."

"But not the father, right?" said Helen.

"Mr. Alonso Osteda is staying at the Royal Lion," said Everett. "I don't imagine that American millionaires are well-suited to camp cots or backhouses."

"Not only millionaires," Hector muttered. He stirred his bean soup without bringing the spoon to his mouth.

"Mr. Osteda has an estimable collection of dinosaur bones," said Everett. "He was thrilled to hear about the ichthyosaur discovery, knowing he'd be here in time to see it. Nothing is settled, but a wealthy collector is never a bad friend to have!"

When we finished eating, we heaped our dishes in a tin tub. Another of Helen's chores was doing all the washing up.

"I'll fetch a jersey and meet you lot by the work tent," Everett said. "The Blenningham-Crewes will be finishing up now that the light is fading. We can say hello and then walk over to the cliff to watch the sun go down."

"A warning," whispered Arthur, when Everett had gone. "I expect in Torquay you'll have met women like Nina, but around here she's . . . well, she's *different*. She uses bad words, and calls people names. She dresses oddly. My mum thinks . . . well, my mum says she's no lady. Not a lunatic exactly . . . but strange." He tapped the side of his head. "You'll see."

As we neared the work tent, a man's raised voice made us stop in our tracks.

"Like it or not, if you want your research published, it will be under my name! The Royal Society—"

"The Royal Society," came a female voice, "is as stuffy and narrow-minded as a priest. If cowards like you accept the rules, and women back down without putting up a fight—"

"You risk being a thorn in their side more than a respected scientist." It must be Professor Blenningham-Crewe, speaking with his wife.

"The purpose of science," she said, "is to ask questions and to avoid assumptions. My question is, if women are not excellent scholars, then why are men like you willing to take credit for our work?"

Arthur signaled that we should retreat. Hector and I had begun to inch backward when the tent flap whipped open. Out came a man whose face blazed with fury.

"Who are you?" he snapped. "Lurking about, listening at keyholes."

We scuttled aside as he barged past. A woman appeared in the opening. Light auburn hair and flashing hazel eyes in a pale face.

"Not a bloody keyhole in sight," she said. "Come in, please. Don't be afraid of the wicked wolf. You must be our new Young Scientists. My name is Nina."

She wore a loose linen tunic the color of toffee. This was not *so* remarkable, though the garment was more like a gentleman's nightshirt than anything a lady would normally wear. Over it, she wore a man's canvas waistcoat, its several pockets bulging with tools of her trade. This seemed wonderfully practical. Her lower half held my attention for a moment longer than was polite. Loose trousers were buttoned below her knees, like a pirate's knickers. She wore no stockings and, indeed, *no shoes*! She welcomed us into the tent as if it were a shrine and she the guardian of holy relics.

Two long, low tables stood against the canvas walls, each covered—truly *covered*—from end to end and from corner to corner with lumps and knobs and rocks and shards, most between the size of a doorknob and that of a dinner plate. The first impression was of strewn rubble more than a valuable contribution to science. A closer look showed that the larger items were each painted with a small white square, while the smaller pieces had white cards tied on with string. A few lines of careful printing in india ink cited the date and location of discovery, the finder's identity and the name of the species to which the specimen belonged.

"You find all this since you arrive in Lyme Regis?" said Hector.

"Yes," said Nina. "All this in three weeks. Though every lovely ammonite and belemnite now sits woefully ignored because of Izzy! That's what my husband calls the giant fossil I fell over last week. I am still shivering in awe. The size alone!" She tapped her palm several times above her bosom, to mimic an ecstatic heartbeat.

Everett had come in while she was talking. "Our Young Scientists can help us catch up with these smaller things, starting tomorrow, eh? We'll get them goggled and wielding hammers first thing."

Yes! We were eager to feel part of the team.

"Has Miss Spinns gone home?" said Everett. "Will you come with us to see the sun go down?"

"Miss Spinns left ages ago." Nina glanced at a table in one corner that held a typewriter on a bit of a slant, and a tidy stack of envelopes. "She left letters for me to approve, being the efficient secretary that she is, and I now must go through and sign them all. Say goodnight to the sea for me."

28

"Watch out for adders during the day," said Arthur, as we walked toward the edge of the cliff to wait for the sunset. "They like to warm up in the sun as much as we do."

"Adders?" Hector's voice was nearly a squeak.

"Long gray wriggly things?" teased Arthur. Snakes were very low on Hector's list of worthy members of the animal kingdom. He found a stick and began to smack the long grass with every step.

"The beach disappears completely at high tide," said Everett, as we neared the edge of the cliff. "Six hours and roughly twelve minutes later, the water is as low as it ever gets. And then it turns and starts back in again. Over and over and over. Right now, it's on the way out."

Pale violet clouds scudded across a glowing orange sun, with the silvery sea shimmering gently to the horizon. It didn't look as if it raced back and forth all day and all night.

"This is called Back Beach," said Arthur, pointing to the curved stretch below us.

"Not much sand." I foolishly said what we all could see.

"Mostly stones and pebbles, it's true," said Everett. "Not very welcoming—unless you're looking for pre-historic treasures."

Arthur was bent on instructing us. "Those flat lime-stone slabs are underwater half the time. They're called the ledges. When the sea pulls back, like now, the spaces between them make excellent rock pools, for crabbing or finding good fossil bits."

"And do you see that pile of black stones a little beyond the ledges?" Everett pointed to a spot dozens of yards out from shore.

Yes, we could see.

"Nina collected those stones and made that heap to mark where Izzy lies," he said. "And *has* been lying for an uncountable number of years."

I considered what *uncountable* might mean, as the very, very old sun sank a little lower in the old, old sky.

"And along the beach?" said Hector. "What is this, where the cliff face is spilling down?"

"That's called a landslip," said Arthur. "My dad's grandpa lived here when that one happened. Great chunks of the cliff broke loose in the middle of the night after days of rain. Tons and tons of earth slid down to make a new foothill. Whole houses are in there somewhere. And a field of sheep."

"Not to mention prehistoric bones," said Everett. "A landslip is a fossil-hunter's happiest disaster, uncovering lots of surprises."

"Cazelty weather we call it in Dorset," said Arthur. "A tide swollen by the storm. Banging waves weaken the cliff foundation, and boom!"

Hector shuddered. But the scene before us was the opposite of cazelty. Wet sand freckled with clumps of seaweed glimmered faintly as the sun sank over the nearly still sea.

"The main thing to remember," Everett said, "is that the beach down there is engulfed at high tide, no matter the weather. You must never imagine that you can run more quickly than the English Channel."

CHAPTER 4

A GROWING CAST OF CHARACTERS

I AWOKE TO AN EXOTIC LIGHT I had never known before.

Last evening the canvas walls seemed close and rough as they rippled slightly in a steady breeze from the sea. Our lantern flickered from its spot on the makeshift table between the cots, casting spooky shadows as we undressed and put on nightclothes. I pretended that Helen was my cousin, for the purpose of not being worried about her seeing me in my underthings—or me seeing her in hers.

But the white canvas glowed in today's early sunshine, making it seem that I had slept inside a seashell. The rolling murmur of waves was as steady as blood through a vein. Helen was still sleeping, the faint burr of her breath moving a lock of hair that had fallen by her mouth. I dressed carefully, not wishing to wake her, thankful for buttons up the front of my dress instead of at the back. I carried my hairbrush outside and sat on a hefty tussock of grass while carefully detangling and rebraiding my hair. Helen slipped past after a bit, heading to the cook tent, but I watched terns and gulls diving for their breakfasts as the tide drew back. What a delicious way to greet the day!

"Bonjour, Aggie." Hector's sailor suit was a little rumpled. He'd smoothed flat his hair, but under his eyes were gray shadows.

"Hullo. Did you not sleep well?"

"Crickets," he said. Before I could laugh, he listed more woes. "The relentless muttering of Arthur Haystead. The snoring of the professor. Even from a distant tent, it is most insistent. Noisy water crashing against the cliff. The anticipation of adders slithering beneath the edge of the tent. Also, I think there is a bear creeping nearby. One thin piece of cloth between myself and certain death."

"I don't think we have bears in Dorset," I said. "Was it a badger, perhaps? Too bad Tony isn't here to bark at intruders! Did it snuffle?"

Hector shuddered. "This I do not know, as my head is under what they are calling a pillow but truthfully is a towel folded in half." He plunked himself down with an enormous sigh but then hopped up to check the backside of his trousers for grass stains.

"But look." I waved my arm across the magnificent vista of sky and sea.

"I look," he said, still gloomy.

Under the canopy beside the cook tent, Arthur was at one end of the table, while two strangers sat, hunched over bowls, at the other end. They wore workmen's garments, dark in color and ill-fitting about the shoulders. One of them, with sun-scorched cheeks and a stubbled chin, had removed his cap and set it beside his mug on the table. The older man had a fuller beard, ragged and laced with gray, and great creases about the eyes.

"Good morning, Mr. Jarvis," Helen said to the younger one. "And Mr. Volkov. Miss Aggie and Master Hector have joined Arthur as fellow Young Scientists."

Their return greetings were nods and soft grunts, hardly interrupting the business of eating porridge. When Hector produced his customary bow, they stared at him and then at one another, truly startled.

A stack of buttered bread showed that Helen had been hard at work. Tea, milk and honey—for putting on the porridge or on the bread or even in the tea. That was breakfast, plain and simple. We served ourselves from a big iron pot that held the cooked oatmeal, and joined Arthur. After a night of breathing salty air, with a breeze blowing in over the water, I was *as hungry as a bear awakening in spring, as famished as a sailor on a long sea voyage, as greedy as a hummingbird in a flower shop.*

Mr. Jarvis and Mr. Volkov took last gulps from their tea mugs and attached tool belts to their waists. I enviously examined these leather aprons slung with loops and pockets that held chisels and hammers and awls. How convenient for carrying a notebook and pencils and a sharpener, or a magnifying glass and a torch for detecting in the dark. Which might I prefer, a tool belt or a pocketed waistcoat?

"They're from the cement factory, t'other side of town," Helen explained, after the men had gone in the direction of the shop yard. "Quarrymen know how to cut rock better than anyone. Missus hired them for digging out the fossil she's so excited about, but they build things too."

"Good morning!" Everett's hair was damp, as if he'd generously splashed his face. He poured tea for himself and dropped onto the bench beside me.

Helen cleared the dishes left by the quarrymen. Arthur refilled his bowl with porridge.

"Did Nina eat breakfast?" asked Everett. "Or just the men?"

"You know her," said Helen. "She likes to walk out inches behind the tide with a mug of tea in her hands."

"Barefoot," said Everett, laughing.

"How she goes over those stones without boots, I can't think," said Helen, shuddering. "And that's before she wades into water that's barely melted ice."

"I'd meant to get you all out to look at Izzy this morning," Everett said to us, "but low tide was so early! And we should be here anyway, to greet our American visitors, Oscar and Mr. Osteda."

"Speaking of," said Helen, "I'll nip into the boys' tent. Make certain it's tidy enough to receive our new guest. I won't be doing this every day," she assured Arthur and Hector. "You'd best learn to do for yourselves, or what good will you be in the army, without a mother or a wife in sight?"

In the work tent, we met the secretary, Miss Spinns. An older lady, she was neatly dressed in a peach-colored blouse under a brown wool jacket and skirt, making my skin itch to look at her. Her hair, mostly silver, was tightly pulled back into an old-fashioned net snood. Thick black-framed spectacles rested crookedly on her pointed nose. Her eyes bulged with a look close to horror at the sight of three children, before she quickly ducked her head. The light was bright and pearly in this tent too, making even the bumpy rows of fossils look like treasures.

"Did you collect the post this morning, Miss Spinns?" asked Everett.

"When have I not done that, Mr. Tobie?" she said sharply, in a thin voice.

Everett sighed. "Thank you. Was there anything of note?"

"Not the one from the Natural History Museum that you're all so eager to receive." She turned her attention to the page in her typewriter, but then looked up again. "I'm sorry to say there has been a breach in the privacy of your endeavors, Mr. Tobie." She patted a folded newspaper that lay on the table beside her. "An article today announces that Mr. Blenningham-Crewe has discovered an item of scientific note."

"Oh dear," said Everett. "We'd hoped to keep things quiet until the specimen is actually extracted from the seabed."

"Too late for that," said Miss Spinns.

"Let's keep the newspaper well out of sight unless it is asked for," Everett suggested.

Miss Spinns tucked away the offending object just as Mr. B-C arrived. It was our first glimpse since yesterday's mortifying encounter.

"Children!" he boomed. "Forgive my bad manners on our previous meeting." His eyes twinkled at us, fully expecting his apology to be accepted. He was a different man this morning and wished to be our friend. "Welcome to our dragon's lair of keepsakes! Have you had a look around?"

"Yes, sir," said Arthur.

"Not everything yet," I said.

"Always take a collecting sack when you go down to the beach," he said, pointing to where several heavy muslin bags were hanging from a coatrack near the entry to the tent. "You never know when you'll spot a prize to bring back to camp."

"Good advice," agreed Everett. He showed how the sacks had a long strap to be worn over one shoulder and slung across the chest, leaving hands free to pick things up. An embroidered crest embellished the bottom corner of each one, with the letters *B* and *C* entwined, for Blenningham-Crewe.

"And when you arrive in camp with your sack full of crusty lumps," said Everett, "each one gets labeled with the date and place where you picked it up. When it comes time for cleaning, you'll select a small chisel or a pick and begin the careful work of revealing what you've found." He distributed goggles and rock hammers and chisels, and showed us how to hold the tools.

"Since you haven't yet been down to collect your own samples," Everett said, "you can practice today on ours." We crept around the tables, looking for the perfect things. "Best to start with one of the bigger pieces," he suggested. "You won't be so likely to break it to bits."

I chose one whose label read:

→ *JUNE 27, 1903* ←

MONMOUTH BEACH, LYME REGIS, DORSET
NINA BLENNINGHAM-CREWE
ANDROGYNOCERAS AMMONITE

Everett soon had us noticing glimpses of a rippled formation under the encasing layer of ancient stone. He demonstrated where and how hard to tap the chisel with the hammer, to slowly chip through to what lay beneath. Within minutes I was utterly absorbed, as the world shrank to the tip of a small tool nudging its way through to the mysterious skeleton inside.

"Have we heard an exact time for the Ostedas' arrival?" Mr. B-C's voice broke through the quiet *tap-tap* of our chiseling.

"After breakfast is what I was told, sir," said Miss Spinns, "though what that means to an American, I cannot say."

"This fellow is from Mexico originally," Mr. B-C told us. "As a young fellow, he was on a team that discovered a Baptanodon, in America. The state of Wyoming, I believe.

That hooked him! Then he had some luck in Texas a couple of years ago. I think they call it an oil gusher. But he's still a keen collector of prehistoric bones! We're hoping he'll direct some of his fortune our way."

"I don't think Izzy is actually for sale," said Everett. "Nina is very keen to get it into the museum."

"Plenty of time to change her mind about that," said Mr. B-C.

"What, please, is a Baptanodon?" said Hector.

"It's a kind of ichthyosaur, much like ours," said Everett, "but with even bigger eyes and a fishier body."

"*Ours?*" Mr. B-C looked at Everett in a not-friendly way. "You've become an owner overnight?"

Everett flushed. "Any of you youngsters ready for a change of scene?" he said. "Let's go along the cliff and meet Nina coming up from the beach."

We scrambled to follow him, away from his suddenly cranky boss. But we'd scarcely reached the cliff path when we heard a motorcar rumbling down the rutted track and coming to a noisy stop. Mr. B-C greeted the American guests and waved at us to hurry back. Mr. Osteda was brown-skinned with a black mustache and a wide-brimmed straw hat pulled so low that his eyes were nearly hidden. He wore a white linen suit and soft green leather shoes that surely had not been made for treading on stones or seaweed. Mr. B-C, in his loose beige trousers and matching shirt, appeared creased and shabby beside the elegance of his guest. The boy, Oscar, loitered off to one side, looking glum.

"He wishes to be anywhere but here," murmured Hector.

Oscar picked up a stone and hurled it high into the air as if he might fell a bird out of the sky. His bronze coloring was similar to his father's, and his dark hair so long that it flopped over his collar. His eyes were the color of wet sand.

"Hello, and welcome!" Everett managed to sound cheery. "I am Everett Tobie, the project photographer and artist. Mrs. Blenningham-Crewe will be here in a few minutes." He glanced toward the cliff path, as if willing her to appear.

"I was telling Mr. Osteda," Mr. B-C said, "that we missed our chance to visit Izzy this morning, with low tide come and gone. The next low water is this evening, when it will be too dark to see properly."

"Tomorrow will do!" said Mr. Osteda. "The marvel will wait, will it not?"

"Ha!" said Mr. B-C. "The marvel has waited over a million years or more, by our guess. I think we can depend on her staying in place for another night without floating away."

"Welcome to you too, Oscar," said Everett. "We've looked forward to your joining our company."

41

We each said our names, but when Oscar's turn came, he said, "You already know my name. He just announced it." Grannie Jane would have bitten off my nose for such a retort! Eight words to be rude instead of one to be polite!

But Mr. Osteda was hurrying on. "We would have been on time, but we got caught behind a parade of circus wagons. Flags flying, dogs yapping, trumpets blaring! At this time of day!" His accent had an American twang as well as a lilt that I took to be Spanish. He clapped his son on the back and beamed. "We followed them to the site—a mile or so from here—where they are pitching a gigantic tent. The ticket booth was not yet open, but that didn't stop me! I have secured us a box for the matinee tomorrow!"

CHAPTER 5

AN EXTRAORDINARY VISITOR

THE CIRCUS! TOMORROW! I wished I were five years old and could hop up and down while squealing and clapping my hands.

Arthur's face shone. "A box!"

"Where else?" said Mr. Osteda. "The view is best from a box beside the ring."

"We haven't taken an afternoon off since we got here!" said Mr. B-C. "What a treat. Say thank you, children."

We needed no prompting to thank him with giddy enthusiasm.

"Mr. Osteda?" said Mr. B-C. "Shall we walk to the cliff to intercept my wife on her return from the beach? She has been looking forward to your arrival."

"Aggie? Boys?" said Everett. "Help Oscar get settled, will you?"

"This will be my first time at a circus," I confessed, as we led Oscar to the boys' tent. "Once there was a real elephant on the Princess Pier in Torquay, with a lady standing up on its back. And another time I saw a man push a sword down his throat without choking, but—"

"I've been to the circus hundreds of times," said Oscar.

"Hundreds?" said a skeptical Arthur.

"You'll see things you've never seen before," Oscar promised. "Your eyes will pop right out of your heads."

"And the circus will sell tickets for a spectacle of popping eyes?" said Hector. This was not particularly funny but Arthur laughed until he snorted.

Oscar tossed his suitcase onto the cot that would be his. "There," he said. "That's me settled. I'd better go back to say goodbye to my father. He's staying in a hotel while I'm stuck out here."

"It won't be *so* bad," I said, thinking to cheer him up.

"Ha," Hector muttered.

"Maybe lunch is ready," said Arthur.

But it wasn't, quite. Worse, in the time it had taken to drop Oscar's case, Nina had returned, and discord crackled under the kitchen canopy.

"Nina. Dearest." Mr. B-C was nearly wheedling. "Mr. Osteda is offering a jolly diversion for the children. For all of us. An hour at the circus can hardly dent the schedule too seriously?"

"I'll stay in camp to assist Nina," Everett volunteered.

"It is fortunate," said Nina to her husband, dropping words like hot coals, "that your presence is not crucial to our success."

Ouch!

"If you'll excuse me, Mr. Osteda," she added, "I am preoccupied with the endeavor we've undertaken. I understand you're excited to know more about it? Low tide tomorrow morning is at six minutes before eight o'clock. I'll be heading to the site half an hour before that, should you care to see an ichthyosaur before the clowns and the dancing dogs." She gave a curt nod and marched to the work tent.

"I'm looking forward to it," called Mr. Osteda to Nina's back, "with great exhilaration!" He clapped a hand on Oscar's shoulder. "Have you got everything you need? I will baby that hired car back up the worst road in England."

He climbed aboard and turned the motorcar in tiny increments on the bumpy drive. He would have driven away but for the arrival of another vehicle.

"I say!" cried Arthur. "It's a Runabout!" Hector and Oscar ran after Arthur with the gleeful squeaks of boys in the presence of modern vehicles. It was an open carriage with four rubber tires that looked as if they belonged on an oversize bicycle. I went along because pulling the

Runabout was a darling white pony with big brown spots all over its coat. The driver dropped to the ground with a nimble hop and turned to us with a wide smile. He was not tall, but sturdy and muscular, wearing a striped suit that enhanced the breadth of his chest. His bowler hat was a bit dusty from the ride, its ribbon bright scarlet. He smoothed his pointy mustache, while his laughing brown eyes seemed to say, *Ha! What do you think of my scarlet ribbon, eh? And what of my polka-dot horse?*

We all were a bit dumbstruck. Mr. Osteda slipped out of his motorcar and rejoined us. This was too astonishing to miss!

"That last stretch," said the new man, "was as bumpy as riding the rapids on a Canadian river!" He pointed to where the buggy wheels had flattened grass in wild zigzag lurches all the way down the track from the main road. "Good thing I skipped breakfast, eh?"

As Everett and the professor sidled up behind us, the visitor pulled the hat from his head and bowed low. "A good day to all," he said, as if speaking from the stage of a theater. "Do I have the pleasure of arriving at the encampment of the Blenningham-Crewes?"

Mr. B-C stepped forward as if summoned by a schoolmaster. "I am Professor Blenningham-Crewe. And you are . . . ?"

"You're from the circus!" blurted Oscar. "Aren't you? Your face was pictured on the side of one of the caravans!"

"By gosh, he's right!" said Mr. Osteda.

"Indeed, laddie, you'll go far with eyes so sharp as yours," said the man. "My name is Cavalier Jones, and those painted caravans carry my Cavalcade of Curiosities."

We still were mostly speechless, but Everett managed to suggest that Mr. Jones might like some refreshment after his drive.

"A glass of something cold would please me very well," said Mr. Jones.

I wanted to stamp with frustration that no one yet had asked his business! We shuffled like a brood of ducklings to sit in the shade of the kitchen canopy, where Helen was summoned to fetch lemonade for everyone.

"Oh!" said Helen, staring at the circus man. "It's Mr. Jones!"

"Miss Malone!" cried Cavalier Jones.

"But why are you . . . ?" Helen began, and stopped as she flushed pink.

Her father appeared in the entry to the kitchen.

"Lemonade," said Helen, suddenly loud. "They're wanting lemonade." She nudged her father inside and followed him.

"I heard this very morning!" Mr. Jones addressed

Mr. B-C, but smiled again at his rapt audience. "About the digging!"

Helen was back, pouring lemonade into tea mugs, there being no glassware in the camp kitchen. How odd that Helen should be acquainted with this extraordinary person! Hector's eyebrows told me that he was thinking the same thing.

"If what the newspaper says is true," said Mr. Jones, "you've found a dragon older than the very cliffs and you're digging it out of the sea!"

Mr. B-C was caught with a mouthful of lemonade and swallowed with a small choking noise. "Newspaper?" He had not yet seen the one that Miss Spinns had hidden!

"This very morning! Wait, where is that—" Mr. Jones patted the large pockets of his striped suit jacket and came up with the torn-out page of a newspaper. He quickly found the item and began to read aloud. "'Lyme Regis has long been noted for . . .' Mmm . . ." His finger skipped across the page. "'Discoveries by Miss Mary Anning . . .' Mmm . . . Ah! Here it is! 'The town welcomes renowned paleontologist Mr. Howard Blenningham-Crewe (44 yrs.), and his petite wife, Nina (27), who is responsible for uncovering an ichthyosaur of a size somewhat bigger than she is.'"

He paused to survey our company. "Mrs. Blenningham-Crewe is not here?"

"My wife is working," Mr. B-C said. "Preparing to recover the fossil five days from now, on Sunday, when the moon is full and the spring tide allows us a few extra minutes. The remains are very near the low-water mark, making the whole endeavor much more challenging."

"And how big is it?" said Cavalier Jones. "This sea monster from the depths?"

"A rib or two under nine feet," said Mr. B-C. "And seems to be all there. Impressive indeed. But how the dickens did the newspaper get ahold of the story? It's meant to be under a blanket of secrecy!" He turned abruptly to stare at Oscar's father. "Is this your doing, Mr. Osteda? Have you let the cat out of the bag?"

"No, no!" Mr. Osteda put up his hands to protest. "I wish for privacy as much as you do, Mr. Blenningham-Crewe, until our deal is signed and sealed."

"Mr. *Osteda*?" cried Mr. Jones. "You're mentioned here too!" He ran his finger down the page and quoted, "'An American collector vying to own the remarkable treasure is Mr. Alonso Osteda, a millionaire with Mexican heritage . . .'"

Mr. Osteda said a word that should not be said in front of children. Not in England, anyway.

"This worries you, to have your business in the news?" said Cavalier Jones. "Ah, but most secrets pass quickly from lips to ears! Usually thanks to money changing hands. No harm, really, is there? In my world, the louder you trumpet what you've got, the more people want it!"

"That is precisely the trouble," said Mr. Osteda. "When it comes to a fantastic fossil, I want to be the first one there, with nobody else behind me. The price goes up if there's a crowd." He stopped himself with a cough. "Not that I have any intention of offering a low price, sir," he said to Mr. B-C. "Simply that I'd rather not compete with latecomers to the game, you see what I mean?"

Mr. B-C clapped him on the shoulder with an uneasy chuckle, and Mr. Osteda's smile flickered like a candle in a draft. All was not so jolly as it seemed.

"You intrigue me more and more," said Cavalier Jones. "The discovery of a spectacle that no one has ever beheld?" He pounded a fist against his chest. "It stirs the blood, does it not? I live for moments like this! To shake people out of their familiar caves for a few hours, to offer a thrill of astonishment! To exhibit the peculiar! There is nothing I like better than a secret waiting to be exposed. When is the next low tide? When may I come to see your treasure?"

TORQUAY VOICE

JULY 7, 1903

WOMAN MAKES HISTORIC FOSSIL FIND ON DORSET BEACH

by Augustus C. Fibbley

Lyme Regis has long been noted for its history of
extraordinary fossil finds, from the remarkable
discoveries by Miss Mary Anning some ninety-
two years ago, right up to this month. The town
welcomes renowned paleontologist Mr. Howard
Blenningham–Crewe (44 yrs.), and his petite wife,
Nina (27), who is responsible for uncovering an
ichthyosaur of a size somewhat bigger than she is.
Mrs. Blenningham–Crewe, once a student of her
professor husband, is a promising scientist in her
own right, and this discovery should be the first
giant step in her chosen career—if the Royal Society
would simply recognize the extensive and laudatory
contributions made by women in this field across

the globe. Although the matter is under discussion, the Society does not yet permit women to be Fellows or to present scholarly papers. This is a loss to their collective knowledge and to their honor, in the humble opinion of this reporter. Certainly, there is a persistent rumor in the world of paleontology that the last several papers presented by Professor Blenningham–Crewe were, in fact, authored by his wife.

Paleontology, a newly defined branch of science, is the exploration of prehistory (life before mankind) through the analysis of fossilized bones. Certain churchmen adhere to the biblical version of God creating the world in six days. They dispute the claim made by some scientists that the fossils discovered along the coast of Dorset and Devon could be millions of years old. The ultimate destination of the Blenningham–Crewe ichthyosaur is still in question.

An American collector vying to own the remarkable treasure is Mr. Alonso Osteda, a millionaire with Mexican heritage, who owns dinosaur remains unearthed in the United States. Will Britain allow an American to remove historical artifacts for private display?

The nine-foot ichthyosaur, scheduled for recovery this week, appears to be a nearly intact specimen of what has formerly been termed a sea dragon. Will this extraordinary discovery nudge the Royal Society to change its "No Females" policy? Will these prehistoric bones further the discord between church and science? Will this incomparable specimen thrill every person who sees it? This reporter believes so, on every count.

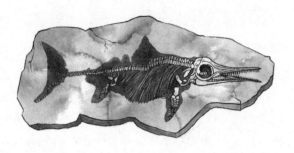

CHAPTER 6

A MIND-BOGGLING MONSTER

A LITTLE AFTER SUNRISE on our second morning, I awoke to newly familiar sounds—the rumble of the sea, the breeze riffling dry grass, peeps and trills from the other side of the canvas wall, the distant clink of spoon against bowl, a whiff of fire-toasted bread, and Everett humming on his way from tent to teapot. All telling a story that I happily understood.

As we'd quickly learned, the tide decided the daily schedule. Low water this morning was a few minutes before eight o'clock, meaning that the fossil would be exposed for twenty-four minutes before that, and for another twenty-four minutes following. Helen was up early to serve breakfast to all the men. Mr. Jarvis and Mr. Volkov were leaving as I came along, Everett and the professor still finishing. I heard boys' laughter by the spigot.

Nina hovered beside the trolley, awaiting a fresh pot of tea. Miss Spinns arrived from the village as I spread marmalade on buttered bread.

"A piece of post," she said, "given to me at the top of the track by a scrawny boy with a bell on his cap." She passed the envelope to Mr. B-C.

Hector and Arthur appeared, and began to heap breakfast onto plates.

"Oscar, he is not so . . . what the English say . . . perky," Hector said.

"Well, this is a rum thing." The professor's eyebrows lifted in surprise. Miss Spinns turned her face away but seemed to be watching sideways. Had she peeked at the note inside? There was no seal to crack, only a tucked-in flap. The word *sly* came to mind.

"Have a look, Nina," said Mr. B-C. "What do you say to that?" He held it out for her to see.

"Just tell me what it says, will you?" Nina drizzled honey into her teacup.

"'My dear Professor Blenningham-Crewe,'" he read. "'A great pleasure to meet you yesterday. This is to let you know I shall accept your invitation to visit this morning, early enough to see your marvelous sea dragon and to meet your clever wife. Yours in anticipation, Cavalier Jones.'"

Nina stared at her husband. "What new promise have you made for us now?"

Hector's eyes met mine. Mr. Blenningham-Crewe managed to nettle his wife at every turn.

"It's the circus chap who showed up yesterday," he said. "He'd, er, heard some news in town about Izzy and realized how close he was. I allowed that he might take a look for himself, since the Young Scientists are going down today anyway. He is an expert, after all, in rare sights."

Nina's face remained without expression but her words became sharper as she spoke. "Your first guest, the American, is meeting me on the beach in twenty minutes, so I must hurry. My morning will be spent appeasing him rather than the *sea dragon* that I actually care about. *My* sea dragon, since *I* found it. I identified it. *And*—blast and dammit—it will be *me* who recovers it, come hell or high water."

Miss Spinns gasped, and Nina laughed. "Miss Spinns, surely you are accustomed to my salty language by now?" She attached her tool belt and stood before her husband, chin tipped up and eyes smoldering.

"As enthusiastic as Mr. Jones may be, his presence will complicate my morning, will it not?" She plucked her hat from a bench and patted the various pockets of her waistcoat to be sure they contained what she needed. "I'm off. Are you coming, Everett?"

"Yes," he said. "Wait!" But Nina was already stalking across the yard. Everett scooped up his own hat and sketching pad.

"You can't run off and leave me with . . ." Mr. B-C's voice dwindled, but we knew he meant us. The dreaded children. Now four of us, because a bleary-eyed Oscar had joined our company.

"They won't bite!" called Everett, hurrying away.

We happily occupied the work tent and took up our chisels. Mr. B-C's tenure as childminder was brief, watching us chip stone from fossilized bone. Minutes later, we heard the rumble and creak of the Runabout, announcing the arrival of Mr. Jones. He again wore his striped suit, but also a tall pair of Wellington boots and a straw hat. Helen slipped out of the kitchen to give Oscar a jam sandwich as a carry-along breakfast.

"Time and tide wait for no man," quoted the professor, getting impatient. We set off at a brisk pace—though I did see Mr. Jones press a folded paper into Helen's palm before she went back to washing our dishes.

Mr. B-C was cheered to find Nina chatting cordially to Mr. Osteda when we arrived at the site of the ichthyosaur. Mr. Osteda narrowed his eyes on seeing the circus man, but merely said good morning to his son and urged him to watch the artist. Everett knelt on the wet sand, murky stains spreading over the legs of his trousers. He held a sheet of rice paper firmly against the rock with one hand and a black Conté crayon in the other. An image appeared under even strokes, the crayon catching every ripple and knob. Oscar rocked from one foot to the other, peering over Everett's shoulders. The emerging rubbing showed a skeletal jawbone holding a row of vicious teeth. Papa and I had made many rubbings on visits to Torre Abbey, but only of crypt lids or door details—never of teeth! Never of an extinct creature that once was alive and swimming in this very sea!

I followed Hector around to where the view held more than the artist's back and the bouncing Oscar. Truthfully, my first impression was disappointing. All this fuss about an oddly ridged chunk of stone? But, as with the little ammonites, a closer look showed how odd it really was. Further along from where Everett was working, the ridges were attached one to the next in a series. Ribs! Embedded in a sweep of rock that curved out of the shale like the spine of an enormous fish. Near the top end of the rib cage, where a human's arms might be, lay what I realized to be a fin, about the size of an oval platter.

"God's teeth." The occasion was grand enough to deserve a curse.

Everett looked up, and Nina barked a laugh. "I said something akin to that when I tripped over it," she said.

"But those gnashers surely do not belong to any god I've heard of. Are you done yet, Everett? The children would like to see the head."

"As would I!" cried Cavalier Jones, in his theatrical voice. "A moment like this makes life worth living!" He stood with his shoulders thrust back and one foot forward as if he were declaiming to a tentful of spectators.

Mr. Osteda muttered, "Pompous show-off!"

"Ssh, Dad!" said Oscar.

"Nearly done," said Everett. "Let me finish this one bit . . ."

"Hurry up, man!" Mr. B-C clearly wanted the wonderful thing revealed in all its glory. A quick study of the men's faces showed that each was thrilled by what lay, half hidden, at his feet—but also greedy for it. The science professor, the American collector, the circus man with a dramatic flair and the devoted artist . . . all bristled like hungry cats around a fish head. And what a fish head!

Everett deftly ran the Conté crayon over a final ridge to finish the delicate impression of a long and menacing jawbone. Oscar's father sighed loudly in admiration. Everett grinned and scrambled to his feet, holding the drawing high to avoid damp or sand. Now we could see the real thing. The snout was longer than that of a porpoise, fully the length of my arm. Each dangerous tooth was about the size of a man's thumb.

"These rubbings preserve the exact size." Everett slid the paper into a folio that Nina held open for him. "I've made lots of drawings from various angles, but it helps to have precise tracings as well. Along with the sketches and photographs, we are well armed to tantalize the museum people."

"The museum people?" said Mr. Osteda.

"A museum?" said Cavalier Jones.

"But why consult a museum at all?" Mr. Osteda turned to Mr. B-C. "I've seen enough. We can settle our arrangement at once! Avoid the headache of a museum and let me ship the damn gorgeous thing home to Texas! I can't wait to watch the coyotes scatter when they catch sight of it guarding the terrace!"

"Mr. Osteda, excuse me," said Nina. "If my husband has made such a promise—"

Mr. B-C reached a calming hand toward his wife. "Mr. Osteda has been so generous as to—"

Nina ducked away from the hand.

Mr. Jones stared at Oscar's father. "You plan to display the skeleton in the private garden of your American ranch? Where only the coyotes and members of your family will see it?"

"That's the idea," said Mr. Osteda. "It will join a *verrry* impressive collection."

"But, sir!" Cavalier Jones clapped a hand to his

forehead. "Should not this superb creature be shared with the entire world?"

Nina's face, as she turned to him, held the radiance of a person who has finally been understood. "Why yes, Mr. Jones," she said. "The entire world is closer to my dream than a few coyotes, I must confess."

Mr. Osteda's eyes flew back and forth between husband and wife, struggling to understand what he was hearing. "Professor, sir, my friend," he said. "I was under the impression we had a deal—"

"Museums?" Mr. Jones interrupted. "I love them!"

I had the poetic notion that he'd seen the crack in Nina's window where warmth poured in, and was unwilling to waste a single ray of sunshine. He put a hand on his chest.

"Museums bring to light what we do not know we wish to know," he said. "I like to think of my Rare Sights exhibit as a traveling museum." Mr. Jones smoothly covered the bleat of protest from Mr. Osteda. "More people pay a penny to come through my doors in one week than the Natural History Museum receives in a year! We set people's minds *afire!*"

Mr. Jones took one of Nina's hands in both of his own. "Cavalier's Cavalcade is offering a home to your magnificent creature. It should have its own caravan, and ride about the country like a king of the sea! I will let you think about what payment you would accept," he said. "I must hurry back to help complete the installation of our curiosities for today's crowd."

"We'll be there," said Oscar. "We're coming to the circus this afternoon."

Mr. Jones beamed. "All of you? How delightful!"

"In a box," said Arthur.

"Even better!" said Mr. Jones. "And will you bring along the girl who works so hard in the kitchen?"

We looked at Mr. Osteda to see how he felt about inviting another person.

"Of course, of course," he said. "But, Mr. Blenningham-Crewe! Please tell the man! The fossil is already spoken for, and not for sale."

"All this can wait," said Mr. B-C, trying to calm a rising storm. He glanced at the flow of the sea, which had turned and now was inching in toward us. "We could have a drink in town. Talk it over among men. What do you say, Mr. Osteda? Mr. Jones, you come along after your performance this evening. How does that sound?"

"Among men?" said Nina.

"I don't think that's the way to settle—" said Everett.

"I am overjoyed to drink with friends at any time!" said Cavalier Jones. "This minute, however, I must be off, or my circus will think I am shirking!"

"Hector," said Everett. "Will you be so good as to accompany Mr. Jones back to camp and to his vehicle?"

Hector bowed. "I may guide you, monsieur?"

Mr. Jones chuckled. "Guide away, boy."

"We are so fortunate as to be in your audience this very afternoon," I heard Hector say, as he set out for shore with the burly man.

Did Oscar's father regret having secured us a box for the matinee?

He said only, "Wily snake."

CHAPTER 7

A SPLENDID MATINEE!

OUR SEATS AT THE CIRCUS were two steps up, like a front porch overlooking the circle of sawdust marked by a low rope barricade. While the crowd was gathering, six men and a lady with a flute marched around the ring playing a thumping tune. From afar, their scarlet jackets with gold epaulets were showy and splendid. I liked even better when they came so close that we could have touched their sleeves—if we'd been brave enough to lean over the barrier. Dents in the bright brass instruments, patches on the uniforms, sweat stains on the rims of their muffin-shaped hats . . . I liked how these teeny details showed the dirt and zeal behind the shiny, noisy show. The lady must mend her stocking after the matinee, the drummer's front tooth was missing, the young trumpet player's trousers were too short and his socks did not match.

Helen, beside me, pressed herself forward with eyes glittering in the roaming spotlights. It took a moment to see what she found so captivating, but then . . . the russet-haired trumpet player looked directly at her, lifted his eyebrows and winked! She laughed out loud, glancing about to be certain that no one was watching. When she saw that I was, she flushed.

"Is that Ned?" I asked right into her ear because the band was making so much noise. She nodded ever so slightly. A secret romance playing out before my very eyes! She put a finger to her lips to seal my promise and settled back in her seat as the band moved on.

Mr. Osteda seemed to have put aside his resentment of Cavalier Jones for now, joining his son and the boys in clapping along with the jolly music. When a man came by with a tray of cakes and sweets, Mr. Osteda bought a stick of pink rock candy for each of us, and fizzy ginger drinks.

The cymbal player clanged his cymbals and the crowd hushed. I held my breath, as Helen and Hector each squeezed one of my hands. Into the spotlight strode a man with a sharply pointed mustache, wearing a top hat, a deep purple tailcoat and shining black boots up to his knees. Our new acquaintance, the ringmaster Cavalier Jones!

"Hear ye, hear ye!" He strode around the ring, inciting the crowd to roar. The cymbals crashed, the bass drum thundered, the music brayed and my heart went bumpety-bump! The Cavalcade had begun! A pair of tumblers cartwheeled into the ring, with a chimpanzee bounding up and down between them. The men somersaulted and walked on their hands and sprang forward and back, as if brothers with the ape. A troupe of clowns ran in, with painted faces, billowing trousers and hats that might have fit kittens. They played tricks on one another with bouquets of paper daisies and pitchers of water while the trombonist made rude sounds on his horn. Then came the two ladies on a bicycle who were pictured on the poster, dressed in spangled bloomers. One rode on the seat, the other on the handlebars. They traded places—while still in motion—until one sat, and then *stood*, on the other's shoulders and threw sweets to the children standing behind the rope. After that, six dogs with ruffs around their necks pranced on their hind legs and jumped through hoops and even barked and howled in chorus, conducted by the flute player.

And *then*! A crescendo in the music accompanied the reappearance of Cavalier Jones wearing very different clothing. He'd traded his ringmaster hat and coat for a spotted animal skin, his muscled arms and hairy legs fully on display for a tentful of staring strangers. I heard Helen giggle.

Scarcely bowing to the clamor of applause, Mr. Jones set about doing one marvelous thing after another.

His opening feat was to climb hand over hand up a rope fixed to the roof of the tent, all the way to the top in the beam of a spotlight. He dangled there by one powerful arm, urging the audience to count the seconds of his triumph. Who knew a minute could take so long to pass? While our eyes were fixed on him, the clowns wheeled in a tub full of water and placed it at the base of the rope. When lights revealed the waiting bath, the crowd cried out. No person could fall from such a height to land in a tub so small! And yet, with a gallant wave and a perfect swan dive, Cavalier Jones did just that. The applause made my ears ring! Onstage to greet him with a towel was one of the lady cyclists, balancing the bicycle on its back wheel while Mr. Jones patted his arms dry, until . . . he *lunged*, grasping both tires in his hands and lifting the bicycle over his head! The lady perched upon the seat and smiled pleasantly, as if from the window of a carriage.

Oscar and Arthur hooted and clapped. Even Hector threw his arms in the air. Before the cheering faded, Mr. Jones set the lady down and watched her ride through the exit tunnel. He looked about in puzzlement, shrugging his shoulders as if wondering what to do next. It was all part of the act, for in trotted the Spotted Pony with a feathered headpiece framing her dear dotty face. The strongman did a full turn, his gaze on the trotting pony while his eyebrows waggled up and down in anticipation. We all laughed and clapped and held our breaths again. Did he really mean to lift a *pony*?

Yes! Yes, he did! But first . . . he called to the animal, who pricked her ears and came right to him. The strongman fed her a lump of sugar, which the pony seemed to expect, and then hooked a finger around one of the saddle straps and led her *toward our box*! The strongman's eyes were on Hector.

"Will you assist, young man?" he said.

If he had been addressing me, I would have fainted in a heap of dust, but Hector stood up without hesitation. Arthur and Oscar gaped in speechless envy. Cavalier Jones put his hands under Hector's arms and swung him over the box railing as if handling a pigeon. Plunk, onto the saddle of the Spotted Pony. Hector sat tall, clutching the saddle horn and looking daft with surprise. The crowd cheered—and kept cheering—as Cavalier Jones knelt to hoist the horse and the boy onto his shoulders and into the air. Hector's face went quite pink. I felt pink all over! The band struck up a waltz and the strongman twirled in slow, careful steps, quite as though he were dancing. Finally, he placed the pony's hooves back on the sawdust, while the audience continued its wild applause. Hector blinked in relief. A moment to never forget.

Instead of returning Hector to our box, the Spotted Pony carried him around the ring for the closing parade. As the band went past, the trumpet player sent another wink our way. Cymbals, bicycles, dogs, tumblers, flags and clowns . . . the procession seemed endless—and then, it was done.

"I don't know what to say," I told Mr. Osteda. "I loved every minute. Thank you for bringing us! I'm only sorry it's all over."

"It's not over," said Oscar. "We still have the Rare Sights exhibit ahead of us! That's the best part!"

Hector waited at the entry to an area that worked as the backstage to the main tent. Over his shoulder we saw performers shedding their costumes, wiping makeup from their faces and putting away their instruments. We applauded a grinning Hector all over again. Oscar and Arthur behaved as if he had won a race at the Olympic Games in Paris, so noisy was their appreciation. Helen kissed him on the cheek! Even Oscar's father and Mr. B-C insisted on shaking his hand.

Eventually, acclaim for the hero subsided, and we looked about for the exhibition of Rare Sights.

"I'll not come inside," said Helen. "Those sorts of things make me squeamish. I'll walk about by myself for a bit, maybe pat one of those dogs."

"You'll come, won't you?" said Oscar to his father.

"Wouldn't miss it for the world, my boy!" Mr. Osteda said. "Nothing I like better than seeing something I've never seen before . . . except maybe owning it!" He laughed a deep, happy laugh.

The Rare Sights tent was not much bigger than the work tent at Camp Crewe, set up like a museum, with curiosities displayed on pedestals, and a label identifying each one. A jar with six human eyeballs floating in dark brine. An army of shiny beetles mounted on pins, waving wee arms in the air. A bloodstained blade supposedly from a guillotine used during the French Revolution. A bird called a laughing kookaburra from Australia, stuffed and sitting on a branch inside a domed glass case. Alive in the cage next door was a gigantic green snake, identified as a green anaconda from Trinidad. This species was not, apparently, venomous, but was known to be the heaviest snake on earth, and simply squeezed the breath out of its prey. Hector shut his eyes and missed two or three other items in his rush to leave it behind.

At the end of the circuit was a peculiar taxidermy creature shaped like a hunchbacked hedgehog but covered all over in bright scales that formed an armor, and with a long, striped, ratty tail.

"This must be pretend," said Arthur.

"No," said Oscar. "See?" He pointed to the label: Armadillo. "It's from Texas. We see these nearly every day.

We even squished one with our car last summer, driving to Mexico to see my abuela."

We stared at him, aghast.

"It was horrible," Oscar agreed. "The shell crunched under our tires."

"Next time," said his father, "we'll ship the carcass to Mr. Jones and let him make a few dollars. This place is so run-down, it gladdens my heart. He can't possibly afford to buy the ichthyosaur."

CHAPTER 8

A MAN WITH FEW FRIENDS

HELEN APPEARED FROM WHEREVER she'd been—and I was fairly certain from her extra-rosy face that it was not a dog with whom she'd been visiting. Mr. B-C bought us all ice creams and Mr. Jones came to say goodbye.

"The Spotted Pony has never received as much applause as when you were on her back," he told Hector.

"I am honored," said my brave friend, with a farewell bow. "Even if it is merely the circus ballyhoo," he added in a murmur to me.

To protect the undercarriage of his car, Mr. Osteda dropped us at the top of the track to Camp Crewe. He and Oscar were going to visit Mary Anning's grave in the cemetery, and then to spend the night at the Royal Lion

Hotel. The rest of us walked to camp, still abuzz with the afternoon's marvels.

"Not so certain I want our Izzy to be part of a circus sideshow," said Mr. B-C. "People might think our authentic scientific discovery is part of the flimflam. I'd be laughed at."

"The armadillo and the anaconda aren't flimflam," I said. "They're as real as real."

"Too real for me," said Hector.

"I hope our tea is ready," said Arthur. "I'm famished."

"It'll be done in a tick," said Helen, "as soon as I'm there to help."

"Might we be of assistance, mademoiselle?" said Hector.

"You think I'd ask the star of the circus to spread butter on bread?" said Helen. "You should have seen him, Mr. Tobie! Sitting up there, being whooshed about, not a flicker of fear."

Everett sat outside the cook tent, his drawings spread out on the table in front of him. He asked about every detail of our excursion without sounding wistful at having missed it. He'd separated the illustrations, one pile to be discarded and the other slipped back inside the precious portfolio.

"Where's my wife?" Mr. B-C sat with us, and Helen soon brought out platters of cooked fish and stewed tomatoes.

"Nina is dictating notes before Miss Spinns leaves for the day," said Everett. "She doesn't want to interrupt her flow of thoughts for—" He broke off to stare in dismay at the white slab on his plate. Any of us would choose flowing thoughts before overcooked haddock.

"She's not the only one working here, you know that, eh?" Mr. B-C poked at his food and then sniffed it. The fish was awash in pale pink juice from the tomatoes. "It may look like a day at the circus, but what I'm really doing is trying to arrange for an infusion of funds to our project. It is part of our task to be nice to millionaire collectors who might—" He paused and changed direction. "I think Nina might acknowledge that, without money, she wouldn't have her fancy work tent and her—"

"To be fair," said Everett, "she is very good at—"

Mr. B-C put up a hand to stop him. "Don't spoil my appetite. Who's paying your wages, sonny boy?"

Everett flinched. The professor pushed his plate of uneaten fish to one side. Helen appeared with a tray of puddings.

"You've made my favorite, haven't you?" said Mr. B-C. "Bring me two, will you?"

"Here you go, sir." Helen carried over two bowls. "Rice pudding with currants and cinnamon." She collected the plate of rejected fish as Mr. B-C picked up his spoon.

"I've got a wife so sour she puts lemons to shame!" he said. Everett looked up sharply and opened his mouth to speak, but the professor was still talking. "And here's this pretty thing making me rice pudding," he said with a wink.

Helen startled and fumbled the dish in her hands before catching it again neatly. She hurried to dump it in the washing-up tub, her face ablaze.

"Oi! You!" Helen's father stood in the opening to the kitchen. He was pointing a cleaver at the professor. "Don't you be pestering my girl!" he growled.

Mr. B-C froze, spoon dripping rice pudding halfway to his mouth. Spud stepped closer, the cleaver waggling in his hand.

"No, Da!" said Helen.

The angry father, I imagined, *raised the freshly sharpened weapon and advanced upon the trembling professor. With the practiced stroke of a man accustomed to butchering lambs, the cook aimed for the neck, and the blade cut swiftly. A full second passed before the scarlet fountain began its torrential rain . . .*

"If you get cheeky with my daughter again," said Spud, "I'll take your nose off. And maybe I won't stop there."

Goodness! No wonder Helen worried about keeping Ned a secret! She lifted the skirt of her apron to cover her face. Mr. B-C dropped his spoon and half rose to his feet.

Everett set his mug carefully on the table and spoke as calmly as if he were approaching an ill-tempered bull.

"Now then, Mr. Malone," he said. "You'll be wanting to put away the blade, I think? You're scaring your daughter."

"Da?" whispered Helen. "You hear?"

The cleaver came slowly down and we all exhaled. Helen let her apron fall, and tucked her arm through her father's, easily taking the weapon away from him. She reached inside the kitchen to put it out of sight.

"There now," she said. "All done with that, eh?"

Spud glared at Mr. B-C. "Warning stands," he said.

"Don't fuss, Da," said Helen, patting him. "It were nothing."

"T'ain't right," said Spud. But he let Helen coax him aside.

Hector and I bugged our eyes at each other.

"That was close," muttered Arthur.

But Mr. B-C was not ready to let the matter rest. His florid face scowled. If he'd been a dog, we'd have seen the fur bristling.

"I don't like being threatened," he said. "And certainly not by someone who works for me."

"B-C." Everett laid a hand on the professor's arm. "Leave it, I beg you."

Mr. B-C shook him off and picked up a pudding dish. He thunked it down on the table with such force that it cracked in two. Helen squawked in protest as her father jerked around, fists upraised to defend against attack.

"You are finished here!" roared Mr. B-C.

"Don't be ridiculous," said Everett. "Spud is not going anywhere."

"Oh yes, I am," said Spud. "My daughter being insulted is enough reason—"

"No, Da!" said Helen. "We need the work! Please, cool your temper."

Everett again offered a calming hand to Mr. B-C. Again, the professor wrenched himself away. But Miss Spinns was suddenly there.

"This way, sir." She took the professor's arm as firmly as the most rigorous nursemaid and led him toward the work tent, where his wife was waiting. Nina could not have missed the hullabaloo.

"Come on, you great lummox," she called. "The cook is the last person we send away!" Amazingly, she allowed him to enter the tent without kicking him—as I may have been tempted to do.

"Helen?" said Everett. "Will your father be all right?" Spud was now deep inside the cook tent.

"Oh, aye," she said.

"And you? Are you . . . insulted?"

Helen coughed a bark of laughter. "It were nothing," she said. "No father likes to see things like that, is all."

"No," said Everett. He excused himself and went to join the Blenningham-Crewes. I had the notion he didn't like to leave Nina alone in a cave with a pacing bear.

"Will one of you help round up the laundry?" said Helen.

"Aggie will," said Arthur. "Laundry is girls' work."

Hector winced under my glare, but let Arthur drag him away toward the shop yard.

A cart came on Wednesdays to collect and deliver the washing to Helen's mother, so we gathered the piles left especially. Miss Spinns emerged from the work tent, blue coat buttoned, bonnet tied firmly under her chin and a battered satchel tucked under her arm. She hesitated, seeing our arms full of bedding and kitchen cloths.

"She won't go in the cart with us," Helen murmured. "She always walks both ways, out from town and back again. She's pretty sturdy for a lady her age." As she laid out a sheet on the ground to hold the other soiled items, we heard a noisy dispute. "What now?" said Helen.

Miss Spinns edged away from the work tent, as if too close to a raging fire.

"If you think," came the professor's voice, "that I'll put up with this—"

"Howard, no!" said Nina. "You're not thinking prop—"

"I'm *thinking* that Everett has forgotten who's in charge of this operation. Forgotten who can fire him as easily as snapping my fingers!"

Everett's voice was lower, and did not carry so well to eager eavesdroppers, but we heard a few words: ". . . tremendous effort . . . in fairness . . . your wife . . ."

"That's another point you keep forgetting," roared Mr. B-C. "She's *my* wife, not yours!"

"Oh, for Heaven's sake!" said Nina.

This time we heard Everett clearly. "Will that be true forever, sir? If you keep treating her this way?"

"Lordy," said Helen.

A beat of silence. How awful were the looks on the faces inside that tent?

"Until death do us part," said Mr. B-C.

"It need not come to that!" said Nina, in a ragged effort to sound lighthearted.

"Indeed." Mr. B-C's voice sounded suddenly reasonable. "We must get back to work. Which will best occur without your constant interference, Mr. Tobie."

"What are you saying?" cried Nina.

"I'm telling Mr. Tobie that he is no longer in our employ," said Mr. B-C.

"Nonsense," said Nina. "Ignore him, Everett."

"First the cook, and now me?" said Everett. "And how will you—"

"Pack your things and leave the camp by morning," said Mr. B-C.

"Everett can't leave!" I whispered to Helen.

"He won't," said Helen. "It's the Mister being bullish. He gets in a tizzy and can't get hisself out."

"You're being unreasonable," came Nina's voice. "Can we—"

"I'm going to town," growled her husband. "I've had my say." The flap of the work tent shifted and out he came, a collecting sack over his shoulder and a look of fury on his face. Helen and I bent over, making busy with the corners of the laundry sheet. Miss Spinns pretended to help, pushing a stray pillowcase into the bundle. Helen caught my eye over the secretary's head and we shared a silent laugh. Mr. B-C strode to his tent, retrieved his ugly yellow hat and set off up the track that led into Lyme Regis.

"Thank you, Miss Spinns," said Helen, "for your assistance." Miss Spinns ignored the sarcasm and gamely hoisted a share of the oversize bundle to help lug it to the cart.

I heard murmurs as we passed the work tent. Nina and Everett placating each other, I supposed. What would happen to the Young Scientists if Everett left Camp Crewe? And what about the Izzy endeavor itself? Everett's drawings and photographs were a vital part of the scientific record, crucial to satisfying a museum or anyone else who might pay money to the Blenningham-Crewes.

Miss Spinns asked us to pause, and noisily cleared her

throat before calling out, "Excuse me, Mrs. Blenningham-Crewe? Mr. Tobie?"

Everett stepped outside. "Yes, Miss Spinns?"

"I am leaving for the day," she said.

But Everett must have seen the mortifying truth on our faces. "I suppose you overheard a little of the drama?" He looked to me because Helen and Miss Spinns were suddenly fascinated with the linens in their arms. I nodded, my stomach twisting.

"Let's get that load delivered to where it's going." Everett lifted the whole enormous bundle out of our arms. Spud was securing a crate of empty milk bottles in the back of the cart, and Everett dumped the bundle right on top.

"It'll stop the rattling," he said. Helen climbed in and tucked the laundry more snugly around the glass bottles.

Arthur and Hector showed up right then, pleased with themselves for having made a checkerboard of sorts from a scrap piece of wood.

"We collected light stones and dark ones, for checkers," said Arthur, holding up a bulging sock.

Miss Spinns tugged straight the brim of her bonnet and scuttled away up the track, like a blue beetle. When Spud drove the jolting cart past her a minute later, the secretary stepped aside and gave a brusque wave. We were still watching as the horse caught up to Mr. B-C, many steps further on.

"Spud's going to knock him down!" cried Arthur. The professor jumped out of the way. He lost his footing and staggered before righting himself to shake a fist at the driver.

"The old grouch," said Everett. "He almost deserved that."

"Oh, Everett!" I said. "What will happen next?"

"Next, you must scour about for kindling," said Everett, pretending to misunderstand. "Thanks to Spud leaving early, I can nick some wood and coal from the kitchen. Let's get a bonfire going. We'll have a picnic supper of sandwiches and biscuits, as none of us could stomach that fish."

"But really," I began. "Mr. B-C said—"

"Don't fret, Aggie," Everett said, putting a kind hand on my shoulder. "He's mostly bluster. It will all be better in the morning. Now, you see over there, where the stones are laid in a circle? That's where we'll have the fire." He made a small salute and headed to the cook tent.

"Well then." I turned to Hector and Arthur. "The professor has argued with three people this afternoon. Who do you suppose is on the list for tonight?"

CHAPTER 9

A JOLLY BONFIRE

A CHAFFINCH TRILLED and another returned the call. A strengthening breeze carried the rumble of the sea. The sky was more cloud than sky, gray and billowy. Calm settled over the camp. *Like pollen on a bee's wing, like dew on summer grasses, like sugar dusted over a tea cake.* How peaceful, when Mr. Howard Blenningham-Crewe was not among us to make noise!

But such peace hid simmering secrets. While we wandered and gathered sticks, I told the boys what Helen and I had overheard, the argument that ended with Mr. B-C telling Everett to leave Camp Crewe. Hector and Arthur stared, sticks in hand forgotten.

"This is most alarming," said Hector.

"But Everett is not behaving like a man who has lost his job," said Arthur.

"He tells us to make a bonfire," said Hector.

"He doesn't seem to believe it," I said. "He thinks the professor will change his mind."

Waves crashed at the base of the cliffs, though high tide had passed and the churning noise softened as we carted our few bits of wood to the site of the bonfire. Neither Hector nor I had built a bonfire before, which allowed Arthur to be Mr. Know-All. We determined the direction of the wind—coming from the sea, so onshore—and laid down the blankets on the side that would be less smoky once the fire was lit. Everett was impressed at how Arthur had constructed the pyramid of kindling. Nina brought ham sandwiches, left by Spud under a tea cloth. I went back with her to the kitchen to help carry bottles of fizzy lemonade and ginger beer.

"Will Everett really have to leave?" I asked, when we were alone.

"Certainly not," Nina said. "He's too important to the project. More important than Howard, if we're being honest . . ."

Everett let the boys strike matches to light the fire. Dark clouds bundled at the horizon, disguising the moment the sun went down. Any light in the sky faded quickly after that. Everett had nicked lots of wood from the cook tent, and we kept it burning through supper and beyond. We made up limericks and ate a whole packet of chocolate biscuits from Spud's pantry. It was a smashing evening, to use Arthur's word. I was not alone in wondering when Mr. B-C might turn up to spoil the fun. Nina looked over her shoulder into the darkness and then back at Everett.

"Is he making me worry on purpose, do you suppose?" she said. "Or is he stumbling home, completely squiffy, and likely to end up sleeping under a hedge?"

"I have a torch," said Everett. "Shall we walk up the track to see if he's in sight?"

Nina agreed that she'd feel better if she at least tried to find him. The moonless night soon swallowed them, though torch beams mingled with the blinking of fireflies. Our conversation idled until Arthur struck on a topic dear to all our hearts. Murder.

"I heard Everett tell Nina that you two found a corpse on Christmas morning," he said. "Is that true? At Lord Greyson's house?"

"True indeed," said Hector.

"In a puddle of blood," I added, upholding my reputation as a girl with what Mummy called a Morbid Preoccupation.

"It is not the first body that Aggie discovers," said Hector.

"Nor the last." I tried not to sound smug. "We stayed in a hotel last April and found a dead man in the garden."

"But that's shocking!" said Arthur. "I hope your room was free of charge!"

"I wonder if Grannie thought of asking," I said.

"Woooo! Woooooooooo!" We were interrupted by someone's feeble attempt to imitate a wailing ghost.

"Oscar," said Arthur, with derision.

The boy appeared from the direction of the cliff path, with a dirt-smeared face and a little out of breath. Flickering shadows cast by the flames turned him into a specter.

"Why aren't you with your father at the hotel?" said Arthur.

Oscar crinkled his nose. "I wanted to come back," he said. "It was boring in the hotel room by myself."

"Sit," I said. "We can add another log to the bonfire."

"Where's Nina?" said Oscar. "Did she go into town?"

"She and Everett have gone up the track, looking for Mr. B-C," I said. "He went off in a pique hours ago. He was meeting your father, wasn't he? But it's getting late and he hasn't come back."

"They won't find him on the road," said Oscar. He finally plunked himself down, on the smoky side. After a minute, he crawled around closer to us. Something fell out of his pocket and bounced toward the fire. Arthur scooped it up.

"Why are you keeping a random chunk of stone?" he said. "Did you think it was a fossilized tooth? Something valuable?"

Oscar reached out to take it back. "Give it here."

"It's nothing," said Arthur. "I thought you knew about fossils." He tossed it toward Oscar, but purposely not *to* Oscar. It landed closer to Hector, who passed it along without comment.

"Thank you." Oscar returned the stone to his pocket.

"Why did you say they won't find Mr. B-C?" I said.

"My dad was meeting him at the pub, like you said," said Oscar. "It's called The Crow's Nest."

Arthur made a snorting noise. "My cousin Ronnie is a police constable. He says the men at The Crow's Nest on a Saturday night are the ones who don't make it to church on Sunday morning."

"Lucky them," said Oscar. He picked up a stick lying near his feet and jabbed it into the heart of the fire, sending up a shower of sparks. "Anyway, it's Wednesday, not Saturday." Jab. Jab. "I saw Helen too. In town. On a street near the hotel. She'd be stopping for a nice long visit with her mum, she said, before she comes back tonight." More jabbing, more pretty sparks. But he wasn't smiling.

"Wasn't it awfully dark?" I said. "Along the cliff?"

Oscar said yes, not even a moon. We all looked up to where the moon ought to be and saw a faintly glowing cloud. We told Oscar about Everett's quarrel with Mr. B-C, and he told us about seeing Mary Anning's grave.

"If her headstone were for sale, my dad would have bought it," said Oscar. "He's a fiend for treasures that no one else can ever own. I thought it was a bit creepy, how Mary and her brother share a grave with three other little siblings, all stuffed in there together. My dad loved it. He went looking for the vicar of St. Michael's with an offer to remove the shabby old gravestone and buy them a new one."

"How did you stop him?" I said.

Oscar sighed. "I didn't. Luckily, the vicar wasn't home."

"If he were my father," said Arthur, "I wouldn't go about telling that story. You can't use gravestones as decorations."

Oscar only sighed again, inviting a cloud of gloom.

"Enough." Arthur took charge, sprinkling sand from a bucket over the smoldering fire. Then all three boys were pouring sand and water, stirring up smoking embers and hooting as the firepit became a cauldron of sooty soup. Watching them be silly together made me feel peculiar, and solitary. I was going back to an empty tent.

"Well, goodnight," I said. Hector stopped his shenanigans for a moment.

"You will be lonesome?" he said. "Helen is not yet here."

"I'm too tired to be lonesome," I pretended. "I will be asleep before you've all managed to wash the smut off your hands." Hector, of course, had one smear of black on his thumb, but the others had gleefully got themselves grubbier.

The shadowy corners inside my tent seemed to double in size without Helen to brighten them. Had she chosen to stay with her mother overnight rather than walk from town so late? More hooting from the boys as they used the tap beside the backhouse and squeezed themselves into their tent. A while past that, I heard Everett's voice saying goodnight, I supposed to Nina. They'd returned without a drunken professor.

The pull and drag of the sea on stones lulled me finally to sleep. I woke up to hear Helen come in, whispering sorry, she'd been to the backhouse, she hadn't meant to disturb me. Moments later, I heard the lullaby of her gentle snoring. A night with many wakeful moments that turned eventually into a Thursday morning never to be forgotten.

CHAPTER 10

A GHASTLY FIND

BY THE MORNING OF SPUD'S third breakfast, I knew that bread and butter was the most dependable item on the menu. Helen said the eggs were fresh from Middle Mill Farm, so I agreed to one of those as well. Soft-boiled. Hector had two and Arthur had three, plus ham. Oscar was sleeping late.

"Low tide is before nine today," said Helen. "I expect Everett will have you lot down there early for your fossil-hunting expedition."

Spud poked his head out to peer around, and then again two minutes later. Was he on watch for the professor?

"Is Mr. B-C so afraid of your father that he's skipping breakfast?" I whispered to Helen.

"Dad's been practicing how he'll say he's sorry," she

whispered back. "But I expect Mister is sleeping late, if he . . . well, if whiskey were involved."

I saw Everett raise his eyebrows at Nina as she waited for the tea to steep. She gave her head the faintest shake. The missing husband had not arrived home in the middle of the night. Mr. Jarvis and Mr. Volkov, at the small side table, seemed to be having a competition to see who could eat a bigger bowl of oatmeal and how quickly.

"I'm going out to the site," Nina told them. "I'll come to see how you're getting on with the Izzy-barrow when I get back. We'll need to test it with as much weight as we can load on."

"Aye, Missus," they said, and kept eating.

Miss Spinns arrived, with a fistful of envelopes. "Post for the professor," she said.

"I'll look at letters later this morning," said Nina. "Howard will have other things on his mind." She gave us all a wave and set out toward the waiting ichthyosaur. Miss Spinns poured tea for herself, holding her mug as carefully as if it were a baby chick. But then she abruptly dropped a letter on the table beside *my* plate.

"From Grannie Jane!" I tore it open and read. "She arrives on Friday, as planned," I told Hector. "That's tomorrow already! She reminds us that we're to spend the night with her at the Royal Lion."

Hector beamed. "A pillow! Perhaps even a bath!"

Oscar appeared, with just enough time to snatch up a piece of toast before Helen cleared the table.

"Well, team?" Everett carried his dishes to the bin. "The seashore awaits, but the tide does not. Let's head down, shall we?" The clouds were puffy white meringues in a pale blue sky. It was warm and breezy, but the sea— on its way to low tide—was calm.

Hector's shirt was nearly the color of the sky, and my dress two shades paler, a faded delphinium. We both wore sturdy boots and wide-brimmed hats, and carried collecting sacks. Everett and the other boys, behind us, stopped at every rock pool. Oscar was on the lookout for crabs. Arthur was delighted to have a new—if uninterested—listener for his vast store of information about limpets and sea urchins. The flat slabs of limestone forming the seabed along this part of the shoreline, Arthur said, were called Broad Ledge. Way out, Nina circled and poked her ichthyosaur.

And I was finally alone with Hector.

But Hector was itchy. He'd been bitten by a mosquito exactly where his collar met his neck, and the chafing was unbearable. His new boots were causing blisters on the outside edges of his baby toes. Arthur had dreamt very noisily last night, but not so noisily as to drown out the relentless peeping of an inconsiderate insect. The one mouthful he had tasted of this morning's porridge still sat like a stone halfway down his—

"Excuse me for interrupting," I said. "My dearest Hector. I have devised a new rule. For your own good, really. You may name five things each day—but *only* five things—to express your unhappiness with out-of-doors living. This way, I will know what worries you most, as you will be forced to choose among the dozens, and you will not feel ignored. Is that agreed?"

My edict was met with a silence so extended that I stood still and put hands to hips like a stern nanny. He finally allowed his eyes to meet mine.

"I am abashed," he said. "I agree to your new rule. Let us find something more compelling to discuss than my woes."

"We'll keep our eyes wide open," I said, "for surprises."

It was rough walking over black, knobby rocks and chunks of shale on the beach. We didn't know quite what to look for, but we didn't quite care.

"Surely there are enough lumps and bumps on tables in the work tent to keep a person occupied for weeks, and that doesn't include Izzy," I said. "Need we collect more? Though I suppose it is nice to find one's own."

Some yards farther on, I said, "Hullo, what's that?" A shape like a collapsed tent lay on the pebbles, a large waterlogged brown thing. "Is it a fish? It doesn't look like a . . . Or . . . goodness . . . could it be—?"

Hector sucked in his breath. The sound confirmed my guess. Not a fish, nor a shark, nor a dolphin.

A body was stretched out upon the ground ahead. The form became more defined—and more *human*—with every step we took. Skittering over slippery stones and swaths of kelp, we came close enough to see a person lying facedown and apparently drowned, one arm above the head—*his* head, for he was wearing trousers.

"Is it—?" said Hector.

"I think it is."

How awfully, gruesomely dreadful. His putty-colored safari clothes were drenched and dark. His hat was missing, and a circle of balding scalp gleamed on the back of his head.

Professor Howard Blenningham-Crewe.

He was on his belly with his face turned to one side, puffy and bruised. The eye we could see was more like a jellyfish resting in the socket. Sand and strands of seaweed matted the thinning hair, as if the professor wore a crown. I'd not ever seen a drowned person, despite living for all my twelve years near the sea. I had not known quite how a body might expand like a sponge, taking in water and changing its shape.

Everett and the other boys were still beyond shouting distance. They'd stopped by a rock pool, where Oscar poked at something with a stick. Way out on the ledges, where the sea would be when the tide came in, Nina was hunched low next to her big find. But what Hector and

I had found—this still and sodden man—seemed even bigger. How many more minutes before she knew? How many steps across shale and seaweed? How to measure the distance between not knowing and knowing? The distance between the moments before you learn something and a lifetime of not being able to forget?

There was no mistaking that he was dead. No head that held a living brain could look so battered. Hector knew what to do when faced with a corpse. A point of honor. He knelt and touched his fingers to Mr. B-C's neck, beneath the soggy collar.

"No pulse," he said.

I laid a palm on the shoulder of Mr. B-C's shirt, where the sun had dried the cloth to its normal beige color. "His shirt is warm," I said.

"His skin is not," said Hector. "Does he get trapped by the tide? Lose his footing? Bump his head? And then the sea, it catches him?"

I waved at Everett, a *please-come-quickly* sort of a wave. He waved back, not understanding. Arthur tossed away the stone he'd held and started toward us. Everett summoned the lagging Oscar and followed along.

"Do you suppose"—I'd best say it while we still had privacy—"that this is something other than what it looks like?"

"What do you think it looks like?" said Hector.

"It looks as if he stumbled, trying to outrun the tide," I said. "Exactly what Everett warned us against doing."

"But . . ." Hector looked around. "Why is he on the beach, far from one of the paths to the top?"

"Do you suppose," I whispered, "that we'll be so lucky as to have another murder?"

"Hallo!" called Arthur.

Hector stepped in front of the body. Was he protecting Arthur from the sight for one more minute?

"What have you got?" Arthur took antelope leaps and arrived in a skid of pebbles. "Oh, horrible," he said, making sense of what lay at our feet. He rubbed his own arms, perhaps suddenly chilled. "Everett! Hurry!" he called out. "It's the professor!" Then, in a whisper, "He's dead, isn't he?"

"Yes," said Hector.

Everett arrived. He knelt at once beside the body to check the pulse, as Hector had.

"Is he dead?" cried Oscar. "Oh my God, he's dead! It's, it's, he's . . . oh, that's awful!" He backed away, tripped over a rock and caught himself before falling. "What's he doing here?" He glanced at the face of the cliff towering above us on one side of the beach, and at the draining sea on the other. "It can't be! It can't!"

Everett took charge. "You'll be quickest, Arthur. You know the way." He glanced toward the steep, narrow path that led up from the beach to the church, high on the cliff. "Can you run to the village for a doctor?"

"Do you mean the police?" said Arthur. "My cousin Ronnie is a constable."

"I suppose the police would be more useful," said Everett. He stared out across the ledges. "Oh, poor Nina!"

"Shall I go now?" said Arthur.

"At once," said Everett. "There is the matter of the tide. He must be moved before it comes back in." Arthur beetled away over the stones to fetch the police.

"I'll help Arthur," said Oscar, licking dry lips. "I don't like being here."

"Right. Off you go, then," said Everett.

Arthur's long legs had already taken him far beyond catching. Oscar started after him, but then paused beside a boulder, leaned over and was sick.

"Poor chap," said Everett. We pretended not to watch as Oscar wiped his mouth with a shirttail and glanced our way. Instead of pursuing Arthur, he abruptly turned and headed to the other end of the beach and the path that led up to Camp Crewe.

Everett took in a deep breath. "I must go and tell Nina."

"We'll stay with him," I said. "Won't we, Hector?"

"Certainement," said Hector. "Many times we meet the dead bodies."

"Three times," I said, "to be exact."

"That's three more than I've met," said Everett.

We assured him that we would keep company with the corpse.

"James would be horrified," said Everett, "that I'm leaving you with a—"

"James will understand," I said. Everett bowed his head in thanks and began the walk toward his unwelcome task. He cut across the wet, uneven seabed at an angle, hopping over the cracks between the ledges, skirting the rock pools. Nina stood still as he approached. After many minutes, he reached her and put his hands on her shoulders. He leaned in so close that the brims of their hats bumped, dislodging hers. Everett leapt to catch it and put it back on her head. He then must have delivered the news, for they both turned to where he was pointing, the deathbed that we guarded.

Nina's small figure swayed, and Everett's arm held her up. They were, for a moment, one bulky form as the new widow leaned briefly against her friend.

Hector and I were quiet for a long while, contemplating Mr. B-C. *It would not be such a dreadful place to die*, I thought, *with clouds blowing over and the distant tumble of waves.* If we humans really had souls, was his fluttering nearby, like one of the curious seagulls hovering above our heads? Or was that soul on its way to an afterlife? Perhaps the gulls were only waiting for us to straighten our strange bundled blanket and bring out a picnic.

"Madame Nina, she is coming now," said Hector.

"Very slowly," I said. Everett was still holding her arm, pausing as she occasionally stumbled. "Not so sure-footed as usual."

A shout behind us, and here was Arthur bounding along the beach. He'd summoned help in good time! Three policemen followed, not so agile as Arthur, who arrived in another spray of pebbles.

"The taller one, that's my cousin Ronnie. Police Constable Guff."

Clearly the lowest-ranking man among them, P.C. Guff swung a large pack down from his back with a grateful grunt. The doctor was delivering Mrs. Brewster's baby, Arthur explained, but the coroner was coming shortly. "The body being dead and all."

A sergeant was apparently the most senior officer that Lyme Regis had to offer. This one was tall and very handsome, even I could see that. Two eyes, a nose and a mouth, as most men possessed, but mysteriously arranged in a way that made him look like a historic portrait or an actor in the theater. The serious eyes were brown, the fine nose straight, the mouth barely visible.

"What a splendid mustache," murmured Hector. In this case, accompanied by broad shoulders and shiny boots.

"I am Sergeant Harley. These are my constables, Sackett and Guff."

"P.C. Guff is my cousin," said Arthur, "on account of being married to my cousin Bess."

"You've mentioned that," said Sergeant Harley. "Thank you."

P.C. Guff began to assemble a stretcher from parts he drew out of the pack. P.C. Sackett leaned over for a closer look at the corpse, and then glanced out at the water.

"The waves must've rolled him a few times," he said. "He might be landed here, but he went in near Church Cliff, I reckon. The drift brung him along this far."

"Sackett likes to fish on his day off," said Sergeant Harley. "Thinks he knows everything about the sea. Are you children alone here?"

We pointed to Everett and Nina, who now were nearly to the beach.

"Your parents?" asked the sergeant. Perhaps he needed spectacles. Everett was the age of a brother, and Nina not much older than that.

"No, no," said Hector. "Madame is the wife of the . . ." He looked down at the corpse.

Sergeant Harley heard only that we were attending a dead body without our parents present.

"You'd best step away," he said. "This is no place for young eyes. Constable Guff, take them elsewhere."

"Taking is not necessary," said Hector. "We will go. We wish to assure the widow of our—"

"Can't we watch for a bit?" said Arthur.

"Guff." The sergeant's voice said plenty more than one word. *Remove the boy with the eager smile. We've got a corpse here and the fellow's wife is a mere minute away.* "Guff, take your cousin and have your wife wrap some sandwiches. And if you see Mr. Pallid, tell him to hurry!" Arthur and P.C. Guff obediently headed off, up the path to town. The body must urgently be examined and then moved to make way for the tide. Hector and I reluctantly backed up two steps.

"Who found the body?" the sergeant thought to ask.

"We did." Hector and I pointed at each other.

Sergeant Harley's brown eyes crinkled ever so slightly at the edges. "Pretty plucky, eh?"

We nodded.

"I'll want to speak with you later. But, later. You see?" He nodded toward Nina, who had wrenched herself from Everett's protective arm and now ran clumsily over the stones toward us.

Hector clasped my arm and we hurried along the beach, heading to the cliffs beneath St. Michael's church, instead of in the direction of camp—or anywhere near Nina.

"By going this way," said Hector, "we must again pass the body on our return."

"Clever!"

We stomped along for a few yards and then Hector stopped short.

"Police Constable Sackett, he says . . ." He waved a hand toward the sea. "It makes sense, yes? The 'drift'?"

"It sounds right," I said. "The tide and the current would move him, the way it does when you're bathing."

Hector shuddered. He had never bathed in the sea, and never intended to.

"When *I'm* bathing," I corrected myself. "Let's think. P.C. Sackett said he likely went in near Church Cliff. But what was he doing there?"

"Does he walk home from the pub along the beach?" said Hector.

"He walks home *drunk* along the beach?" I said.

"He walks home so drunk along the beach that he falls down—*oof!*—in a stupor?"

"Falls down—*oof*—in a stupor," I echoed, "and the tide rolls in to drown him?" Hector shuddered again, and this time so did I. Imagine going to sleep and waking up in a dark, angry sea!

We were nearly as far as we could go. The base of Church Cliff, jutting distinctly into the sea, rose straight from the water with no beach even now at low tide.

"Why would he come along here in the dark?" I said. "It's the wrong direction, if he meant to end up in camp."

"There is no moon," said Hector. "Does he get confused?"

"It *was* pretty dark," I said. "Remember when Oscar arrived at the bonfire? But the professor would know the water should be on his right . . . You can't really get lost at the seashore! Wait! What's that?" My eye had snagged on something dangling above our heads on the face of the cliff. "There. Caught on a bramble?"

"The yellow hat," said Hector.

"How did it get all the way up there?" I said.

"Too high for even the biggest wave," said Hector.

Stones crunched behind us.

"What have you found this time?" said Everett. We'd been too absorbed in our scrutiny of the scene to notice him coming along. "Well spotted!" he said. "If you two ever decide to look for fossils instead of bodies, you'll do a super job. Eyes like hawks." He tipped his head back to examine the rock face. "Was it so dashed windy last night that the hat blew way up there?"

Hector and I looked at each other. We looked at the hat. We looked to where Mr. Blenningham-Crewe lay ignobly on a bumpy bed of stone. A fourth man had joined the police and knelt closely over the corpse. Nina paced between boulders and kept her face averted from her husband's body. Two beach umbrellas now sheltered the professor, as if he were sunbathing and getting too pink in the noon heat.

"I came to say that Mr. Pallid has arrived," said Everett. "He's the coroner. Sergeant Harley suggests that I take Nina back to camp. You both need to come too. The tide will soon be in to cover the beach." He looked again at the hat halfway up the cliff face . . . or was it halfway down?

"We'll report this find to the sergeant," said Everett.

I waited until he was noisily tramping on pebbles a few yards ahead.

"I suppose the coroner will know whether or not he drowned," I said to Hector. "But doesn't this stranded hat suggest that he might have fallen?"

CHAPTER 11

A SECOND CLUE

GETTING NINA BACK TO CAMP was like guiding a blind dog to its bed. She knew the direction in which she was meant to be going but kept veering off the path or stopping in her tracks as if realizing all over again that her husband was dead.

"How did this happen?" she said, seven or eight times. "What was he doing there?"

Everett patiently repeated the answers: *The police will tell us. We'll have to wait for more information. It certainly is baffling.*

As we neared the camp, Miss Spinns hurried toward us on the path, sunbonnet pulled low over her eyes and blue coat flapping. She carried a thermos in her hands and a bulky collecting sack over one shoulder.

"Can it be true?" she said. "The American boy told me—"

"I'm afraid it's true, Miss Spinns," Everett said gently.

"He rushed up the path, blurted, 'The professor is dead,' and raced away," said the old lady. "A drowning, was it?"

Nina ignored her, pushing past with a glazed expression. She went ahead to the work tent, propelled by habit.

"I'm taking tea to the policemen." Miss Spinns lifted the thermos to show us and hurried away.

"Good idea," said Everett. "I will do the same for Nina. Hot sweet tea. Will you two find Oscar? He had rather a shock, I think. We all have. Try to be a friend to the poor boy."

Hector and I found Oscar curled on his cot like a six-year-old with a tummy ache. He sat up quickly and came out into the sunshine.

"I'm all right now," said Oscar. "I . . . well . . . It was pretty nasty, wasn't it?"

We agreed that it was pretty nasty. Hector retrieved a blanket from their tent to spread out on a patch of grass. Everett went by, bearing two mugs.

"His face was horrible," said Oscar. "Did he go la-la and jump into the ocean?"

"In England we call it the sea," I said.

"I do not know this word, la-la," said Hector.

Oscar circled a finger beside his temple to show one's brain going loopy. "I never saw a dead person before," he admitted, "except for my mother's aunt. But she was lying peacefully in her coffin, wearing her favorite necklace, not—" He shuddered. "Did anyone say *when* he died?"

Hector and I looked at each other.

"No one mentioned *when*," I said. "The body needs to be examined by the coroner. Properly, in his examining room, not a quick peek on the beach. Oh, here's Arthur."

Arthur saw us waving and trotted over from the cliff path.

"Odd bird, Miss Spinns." He plunked himself down on a corner of the blanket. "I offered to carry the thermos, and she said, 'Certainly not, young man, do I look defective?'"

"What did we miss down there?" I said. "Has the tide turned?"

Arthur's face shone. Partly with a sheen of sweat, but partly, I saw, because he had a story to tell. Arthur's cousin's wife, Bessie, had made a smashing lunch of fish paste sandwiches and cheddar with pickle, but only Arthur and the constables ate anything. Sergeant Harley (who was *smashing*) and Mr. Pallid, the coroner (a bit *weedy*), had turned the body over. They'd knelt on the stones poking the dead man, lifting bits of his clothing and muttering to each other in voices too discreet to be overheard. The coroner left to make preparations at the morgue, and Sergeant Harley barked at Sackett to get over to Cobb harbor and bring around the fishing boat he was so proud of because *that's* how the body was to be moved! Sadly, this was when the sergeant noticed Arthur and sent him packing. P.C. Guff was to remain on guard duty while Sergeant Harley returned to the station to summon more assistance.

"If I'd been there, I could have offered to row," said Oscar. "I'll bet that podgy policeman can't row for beans."

Arthur objected to Oscar's boast. "I thought you lived in a desert," he said. "Isn't Texas a desert? How do you know how to row?"

"It's dry, yeah," said Oscar, "but we've got rivers! The Rio Grande is where I won a race last summer and I would have this year too, except we came to England."

Arthur looked utterly disbelieving. I quickly brought the corpse back into the conversation.

"I wish we could watch when they move the body," I said. "It was too dark the last time we saw a body moved, and we were upstairs behind a window."

"That's why I asked to help Miss Spinns with the thermos," said Arthur. "I wasn't being polite. I wanted a reason to go back."

"Since Arthur mentions sandwiches," said Hector, "I am most ravenous."

We all were ravenous, and we went to see if food would be served despite the exit of Howard Blenningham-Crewe from the universe.

"I knew people would be hungry," said Helen. Her eyes were pink-rimmed. From crying? "My dad's crousty, his last words to the deceased being angry ones. He'd take it all back in a minute." She gave us each a plate. "Eel pie and crab cakes."

Arthur was first to help himself from the covered dishes, despite having eaten Bessie Guff's picnic. I was not wildly fond of eels, and chose crab cakes with bread and butter. Hector had small helpings of everything, hoping there'd be one edible offering.

"Eels?" said Oscar. "Those black things like giant, evil caterpillars? What I'd like is a grilled Texan steak." He chose bread and butter, and Helen kindly cut him a wedge of cheddar cheese.

"What's that noise?" she said.

Mr. Cavalier Jones had arrived on his Runabout machine.

"What's he doing here?" said Oscar, sounding rather like his father.

The clamor drew Everett and Nina out of the work tent. The Spotted Pony's tail had been braided with a gold ribbon and she swished it proudly. Mr. Jones dismounted with his usual aplomb. He slapped his hat against one thigh, dislodging small puffs of dust. His lower lip was swollen from some small injury. One of the dangers of lifting large objects, I guessed.

"Hallo, one and all!" Mr. Jones greeted us as if from the circus ring. But we were a miserable audience, awash with calamity.

"Tell him, Everett." Nina backstepped a few paces, ready to retreat. "Did he have an appointment with—?"

"Mr. Jones," said Everett. "I am grieved to inform you that we've had a tragedy this morning." He quickly told the news.

Mr. Jones looked stricken. "Oh, my lady!" he said to Nina, bowing his head. "My heart breaks for you! I will leave you in peace." He turned to climb back on the Runabout but paused to look at Everett. "We are mere minutes' away," he said. "Please send word if I can be of assistance . . ."

"Thank you, sir, for understanding," said Everett.

Mr. Jones looked at Nina most sympathetically. "What of your mission, madam? It will now be forgotten?"

"We are going ahead." Nina spoke in a rush. "We will recover the fossil this weekend, during Sunday's spring tide."

"Nina," said Everett. "Need we decide now?"

Miss Spinns came along the footpath, thermos swinging in one hand. Clouds were gathering over the sea, promising rain.

"I see in you a passion for science that I applaud most ardently," said Cavalier Jones.

Everett sighed.

"The circus moves to Seaton on Sunday," said Mr. Jones. "However! If at all possible, I would be thrilled to witness this unique moment in the history of our wondrous earth! A great creature dies and lies at rest for many thousands of years, gently rocked in the arms of the sea. It is no less than our duty to honor the resurrection!"

I slipped my notebook out of its pocket and scribbled in haste, *gently rocked in the arms of the sea.* Would it be cheating to use that in a poem some day?

"Howard would wish us to proceed," said Nina, and disappeared through the flap of the work tent.

"It may be more complicated than wishing," said Everett. "And you Young Scientists should be prepared for a quiet day or two, as we adapt our priorities. But if Nina says we're going ahead, no argument will change her mind . . . unless she remembers that her husband needs a funeral." The drizzle began, as light as mist. Mr. Jones returned his hat to his head and lifted a hand in farewell.

"Young man," said Miss Spinns, her crackly voice louder than usual. "Mr. Jones? I have a pressing errand in the village. I wonder if you would be so kind as to—"

Mr. Jones did not even blink, as if the delight of driving an old lady to town was the purpose for which he'd come to Camp Crewe. He assisted her in boarding the Runabout, cautioned her to secure her hat and away they bounced.

"That's quite a sight," said Everett.

"And the first time Miss Spinns has ever accepted a ride," said Helen. "She walked even during that crashing downpour last week. What errand is so urgent?"

"Maybe she's smitten with our friend the ringmaster?" said Everett. We all had a chuckle at that, but soon squelched our merriment. Mr. B-C was dead and always would be.

"Let's go for a walk," I said, tipping my head west so Hector would understand. "This rain won't last." Everett had told the sergeant about our discovery on the slope of Church Cliff but none of the others knew. Our guess was that the professor had fallen into the sea from a great height. Likely from the churchyard or nearby.

"To the cemetery?" Hector said. "Would anyone care to join us?"

Helen vigorously shook her head no. "I'll be helping my father make supper. And I don't fancy walking over there, now or anytime soon." She flushed pink. "What if . . . what if his ghost is lurking?"

"I won't go either," said Oscar. "My father will come for me. Soon, I think. Our arrangement was unclear."

"Your father was here shortly after dawn," said Helen. "We'd hardly got the kettle on."

Oscar stared at her. "Dawn? *This* morning?"

"It did seem a bit odd," said Helen. "He went to your tent to make certain you'd shown up here. He'd been

112

expecting you to stay with him last night in the fancy hotel." She tipped her head, prodding for an answer. "Only you didn't."

Oscar blushed the color of strawberry jam. "Did he . . . say anything else?"

"He asked my dad for a beefsteak to put on his black eye," said Helen, "but we haven't got beefsteaks to give away around here, so I made him a packet of ice chips instead."

"*Black eye*?" Oscar jolted upright. "Where did he get a black eye?"

"Not likely I'd ask!" said Helen, laughing. "It were nasty, though. I will say that."

"Oi!" called Spud from inside the kitchen. "These potatoes won't peel themselves!"

"Come on." Helen tapped Oscar's arm. "You help us prepare for tea. We're behind because of all the upset." Then she leaned in to whisper, "Me own dad weren't too sharp this morning either, thanks to a few tipples at The Crow's Nest."

"But how did my father get a black eye?" said Oscar. "He didn't have one last night before he went to The Crow's Nest."

"He's staying an extra day," Helen said. "Needs time to recover. If it were me, I'd be on my bed with the shades down."

"If he does show up," I said, "tell him he can't take you away until we're back. Hector, if we hurry now, we might see the boat carrying Mr. B-C."

"Smashing idea," said Arthur. He felt he'd been cheated earlier, being booted off the beach.

Hector collected his binoculars and the three of us set out. The drizzle had subsided and a nice breeze riffled the grasses along the path. The ledges were slowly being swallowed by shallow swirls. A while from now the beach would be swamped with the incoming tide. Any sign of disturbance or evidence near the corpse would be swirled away. We paused to take turns with the binoculars, and *could* see the rowboat, with poor tubby Sackett hauling on the oars as Oscar had predicted. The professor's body had been wrapped in white sheets and laid out on the stretcher that P.C. Guff had assembled. The stretcher nearly filled the boat, with Mr. B-C's feet nudging the constable's knees. The men had propped him in place so he wouldn't roll with the motion of the sea. Through the binoculars we tried to identify the odd assortment of objects holding him. A tackle box. A mackintosh raincoat. The beach umbrellas. A blanket.

"I hope he feels honored to be transported by boat," I said, "since he liked history." Hadn't the Vikings buried their dead in boats, believing the custom would allow for safe passage to the afterlife? Constable Sackett was rounding the bump of Church Cliff and about to disappear from sight. Sergeant Harley and P.C. Guff had packed up and were climbing the path at the west end of the beach, heading to meet the body in Cobb harbor, we guessed.

"How will they get him to the coroner's office?" I said. "He can't be carried through town over their shoulders like a sack of laundry."

"The coroner uses a hearse," said Arthur. "He shares it with the undertaker. For funerals it has black bunting and the horses wear plumes, but when a body is moved, they leave it plain."

In the churchyard, we passed the grave that Mary Anning shared with her brother and three infants. A bouquet of weeds and wildflowers lay in the grass above her resting place.

"Visitors leave flowers here all the time," Arthur said. "Or sometimes fossils. She's the most famous person ever born in Lyme Regis. Except possibly for Captain Thomas Coram, who was a captain, after all. He started the Foundling Hospital in London, and saved thousands of foundling children from dying. I suppose that's easily as important as saving the bones of a few prehistoric monsters. He's not buried here, though, and Mary Anning is."

"What would you choose to have on your headstone?" I asked, looking at the few plain words under *Anning*.

"Here lies Arthur John Haystead," said Arthur. "England's greatest prime minister."

We laughed.

"Hector Perot, 1890 to 1995," said Hector. "One of a kind."

"A hundred and five years old?" I said. "Grannie Jane is sixty-seven and she is already antique!"

"What about you?" asked Arthur.

"Aggie Morton, poetess?" I said.

"Aggie Morton, mystery queen," said Hector, "if Mr. Fibbley is still alive to write your obituary."

We wandered through the cemetery and closer to the cliff's edge, but not *too* close because the sound of the sea was a steady reminder of the peril waiting below. Was it possible that a person might get disoriented in the dark and topple right off the cliff? Thinking back, the moon had shown itself rarely last night, during the bonfire. The clouds had been dark, in an even darker sky.

"Look there," I pointed. Something white and wrinkled was caught in the brambles growing beside the narrow path at the edge of the cliff. "Is that a collecting sack?"

Arthur bounded over and gently tugged the cloth free of prickers. "That's what it is, all right." He showed us the embroidered initials in the lower corner.

Hector poked the bulges and we heard clinking.

"Huh," said Arthur. "These are half-pint pub glasses."

He pulled out one and then another bevel-edged glass with a short stem, the second with a chipped rim. I held them while he reached inside the bag to bring out a flask. A plain pewter hip flask with a monogram etched into its side: H.B.C.

CHAPTER 12

AN UNCOMFORTABLE SUGGESTION

"It's his," I said. "Full or empty?"

Arthur shook it and we heard a slight slosh. He unscrewed the cap and held it under my nose.

A quick, potent whiff. "I'd say Scotch whisky," I said, "but I am not an expert."

He put the cap back on.

"Should we not leave this where we find it?" said Hector.

My heart sagged and so did Arthur's grin. We shouldn't have touched it, in case the police—

"The police!" I said. "They'll likely be in the camp by now. We should give the sack to them. It's too late to put it back where it was. They don't like people to tamper."

"Carrying evidence half a mile is tampering," said Hector.

I laughed, outwitted by Hector's logic yet again. "Ugh," I said. "Why are you always right?"

"Evidence of what?" said Arthur.

"This we do not know," said Hector.

"You can't think he jumped?" said Arthur. "From Church Cliff? On *purpose*?"

"We do not say this," said Hector.

"We can't know anything yet," I said. "But don't you think it's a bit peculiar that we found his flask at the top, his hat halfway down and his body several hundred feet to the east?"

Arthur looked back and forth between us. "We should give the sack to the police."

He was right. Mr. B-C's death was looking more like murder every minute.

"It's drizzling again," I said. "Let's go back. Oscar might be leaving soon."

Hector peered over stalks of rosemary that clung to the edge of the cliff. "In some places we have plants or bushes, elsewhere nothing. The police perhaps can match the place of the hat with a spot along this path where an *exit* is indicated?"

The sky spat rain all the way back. Arthur tucked the collecting sack under his shirt and held it tightly while we ran so that the glasses didn't knock together. When we came into camp, Sergeant Harley was speaking to Nina and Everett at one of the tables under the kitchen canopy.

"Must we hand over the bag straightaway?" said Hector.

"Let's go the long way around," I said. "We might be able to listen for a bit before we interrupt."

Arthur grinned. "I say! You two are playing Sherlock Holmes! So, if we go to the backhouse tap to wash our hands, and then sneak along beside the kitchen where they can't see us but we—"

"An excellent plan." Hector lifted his eyebrows at me to say, *Mon Dieu, but Arthur is a bit slow sometimes.*

The back wall of the cook tent had been rolled up to allow a breeze to pass through. It also allowed the crew to spot anyone wandering past. I didn't see Helen, but Spud looked up from stirring something that sizzled in a pan. He grunted and went back to stirring. Oscar sat on a low stool with a paring knife in one hand and a potato in the other. Between his feet was a basin full of peelings.

"Hey, hello!" he said. "You're back!"

All three of us put fingers to lips and said, "*Ssh!*"

Oscar's brain cells were a little livelier than Arthur's. He put a finger to his own lips, nodded and kept peeling. By the time we'd got into a useful position, the sergeant was speaking solemnly to Nina. I ducked down to peer through the underpinnings of the service trolley so I could watch as well as listen.

"I'm very sorry, ma'am, but in a case like this, we have to consider the possibility that it was not an accident. Any death involving a cliff must be considered suspicious."

Everett began to shake his head quickly, back and forth. "No," he said.

Nina's eyes narrowed. "When you say 'not an accident,' are you referring to a *suicide*? I am a scientist, Sergeant. I prefer to label things accurately."

The sergeant coughed and tapped one shiny boot against the other. "It's not a thing anyone wants to speak about, ma'am."

"It's a *dreadful* thing," said Nina. "Sad for the family, and tragic for the victim. But that is not what happened here. Howard was as committed to being alive as anyone I've ever met."

Everett's head was now bobbing up and down in agreement. "Yes, yes, absolutely yes."

"That may be," said Sergeant Harley, "but duty compels me to look for a letter, or some other indicator of an intention to end his life. Evidence of an imbalanced mind, maybe."

"No!" said Nina and Everett together.

The sergeant's gaze went back and forth between them. "You object to my looking?"

"Oh, you may look as much as you wish," said Nina. "You will find nothing. We said no because *imbalanced* is not a word that could be applied to my husband."

I nudged Hector and pointed at Arthur's lumpy chest. "Now?"

Hector nodded and Arthur said, "Right-o!"

We'd meant to make a casual entrance, but three of us popping out at the same time drew some attention.

The sergeant lurched to his feet, alarm jumping in his eyes.

"Oh, hello," said Everett. "Children, you know Sergeant Harley. No cause for fright." He pretended he was talking to us, but it was the sergeant who needed calming.

"We found something on our walk to the churchyard," I said. "Two things, really, that we think you ought to know about."

Sergeant Harley sighed and looked at Everett. "Must we play this game of including children?"

I suspected that Nina was no more eager than the sergeant to hear our news, but she could not resist provoking him.

"What is it, Aggie?" she said. "What have you got there?"

I put a hand on Arthur's arm, to prevent him showing the collecting sack just yet.

"Perhaps you do not know, madame," said Hector. "This morning we find the yellow hat of monsieur le professeur."

"His hat," she said.

"It was along the beach some hundred yards or so from where the body was found," said Sergeant Harley.

"From where my *husband* was found, Sergeant." Nina's words were clipped. "And the hat was where, exactly?"

"There's a reason I haven't mentioned it, ma'am," said the sergeant. "We're still looking into—"

"I want to know everything," said Nina. The sergeant sighed.

"We observe the hat resting on the cliff face below the churchyard," said Hector. "This gives us the idea that Monsieur B-C, he does not drown but instead falls from above."

"Hold up a moment," said the sergeant. "Why are we letting a *boy* tell stories about what happened?"

"Blast and dammit, let him speak," snapped Nina. Sergeant Harley glared, and Hector kept talking.

"We go for a walk to see the grave of Miss Mary Anning. Near the edge of the cliff we are surprised to see another item that belongs to your husband." He stepped to one side, allowing Arthur to reveal our discovery.

"Bring it here, Arthur, please." Everett reached out a hand to receive it. "Where did you say you found this?"

"Caught in a prickly bush. At the edge of Church Cliff."

Everett offered the sack to Nina, but Sergeant Harley's hand shot out to snatch it. "There might be a letter inside, or some other sort of evidence," he said. "Best if I look first, if you don't mind."

"I *do* rather mind, Sergeant." Nina reached for it, catching a corner between her fingers.

The sergeant stood from the bench and roughly jerked the bag from Nina's grasp. We heard a *cra-a-ack*, and Arthur cried out. He'd done all he could to keep the contents safe and now the policeman had damaged them!

"You might have told me it was fragile!" said Sergeant Harley. He marched to his bicycle and tucked the sack in the basket attached to the handlebars without even looking inside. He flung a leg over the seat and pedaled away.

"Care to tell us what he took with him?" Everett said. "Was there a letter?"

"No letter," I said, "but Mr. B-C's flask is in there." Nina winced. "I'm sorry. That's how we knew the sack was his."

"Helen?" called Everett.

Helen appeared after a moment. "Sir?"

"Might it be possible to have some tea?"

"I don't need tea, Everett, thank you." Nina pulled herself up. "We're too far behind as it is. Today is nearly over. Tomorrow is Friday already."

"Nina," said Everett. "Your husband died last night."

She closed her eyes for several seconds before asking, "Has Miss Spinns come back yet? We have a number of letters to write. Though I suppose they should be in my own hand. Howard's mother and sister. The university. The museum. They will all need to know." Everett put an arm around her shoulders.

"Did I hear correctly?" said Nina. "The git of a sergeant said there'd be a delay before we could have the body for a funeral?"

"Yes," said Everett. "That is something to tell his mother." He led Nina gently into the work tent.

"How can she be working while her husband is . . . ?" said Arthur. "She can't be thinking straight."

Helen appeared with a tray holding several mugs of tea. "Where'd they go?"

"We'll drink it," said Arthur. "Here, let me help."

Oscar followed Helen with a plate of ginger biscuits, and soon we had a little party. We toasted Mr. B-C and clinked our mugs and tried to think of a nice thing or two he'd said or done in the few days we'd known him. Spud finished making the corned beef hash and gave us bowls full and then second portions because Everett and Nina did not come out of the work tent. We pitched in to help with the washing up, because it had been a long, peculiar day for all of us, including Helen.

"My Grannie Jane is coming tomorrow," I said. "She is a guest at the Royal Lion Hotel on Broad Street. Hector and I are going to stay with her overnight."

"That's our hotel," said Oscar. "Where my dad is. We were meant to be leaving, but who knows? He hasn't got his fossil but apparently he has a black eye."

Spud came out to say goodnight to his daughter. "No pub tonight," he said. "The walk to town is twenty minutes and I'll be asleep in twenty-three."

"Me too," said Helen. "I'm done in. This has been the longest day I've ever known." She gave us a wave and went off to bed. I walked the boys to their tent and then Hector walked me halfway back to mine.

"What did you think of the sergeant grabbing the bag from Nina?" I said. "It seemed a bit rude, but if there *had* been a letter, perhaps he was saving her from distress?"

Hector considered. "A letter is possibly not so upsetting to a new widow as what we *do* find. By chance, the sergeant saves madame from seeing."

"Precisely what I've been thinking," I said. "Why was he carrying *two* glasses inside his sack?"

CHAPTER 13

AN UNEXPECTED ANNOUNCEMENT

THE ADVANTAGE OF A FLASK was that a cup was not needed. A person merely tipped it to his lips and drank. Two cups unquestionably meant two people.

But *which* two people? The professor and . . . who else?

The balding professor, afraid of losing the affection of his lovely young wife, invited her to a romantic tryst with a view of the sea . . .

The regretful professor, wishing to patch up the quarrel with the cook, suggested a night of joviality with the sunset as a backdrop . . .

The selfish professor, craving a resolution with the American millionaire, ignored his wife's objections and requested a tête-à-tête to settle the matter . . .

The remorseful professor, eager to placate the scorned photographer, begged for a chance to repair ill will . . .

The aging professor, tired of his young wife's demands, arranged to meet the cook's daughter to share a flask of whiskey in the privacy of the graveyard . . .

The conniving professor, considering a ploy to sabotage his wife's correspondence, planned an encounter with the sly secretary, far from prying ears . . .

The muddled professor, uncertain how to proceed, agreed to meet the flamboyant ringmaster, to discuss his absurd idea for celebrating the ichthyosaur . . .

My brain cells faltered eventually and allowed me to sleep—but the questions hummed again in the morning when Sergeant Harley made another appearance. As I helped Helen clear the breakfast dishes into the washing-up bin, we heard the squeak of an approaching bicycle. The sergeant hopped off and engaged an iron prop to keep the bicycle standing upright.

"He is the handsomest man I ever laid eyes on," Helen whispered, "but nothing so nice as my Ned." She sent Arthur to alert Everett and Nina that the morning had begun with a manly but unwelcome visitor.

"They'll be along," Arthur said when he came back, "but Miss Spinns hasn't shown up for work. Nina wonders if she'd made an excuse to one of us?"

"She rode away on the Runabout," I said. "That's the last we saw of her."

"Is she brokenhearted?" said Hector. "About Monsieur—"

"About the Mister?" Helen shook her head.

"That seems unlikely," I agreed.

"Children?" said the sergeant. "You two, who found the body."

I said, "Yes, sir?" And Hector stepped forward with his little bow.

Sergeant Harley's brow lifted. "Did you touch or disturb him in any manner?"

"I ascertain that he has no pulse," said Hector. He put two fingers against his own neck to show how he'd done that.

"*Ascertain*, eh? Not just foreign but smarty-pants foreign."

Hector sighed. I wished to kick the man.

"Did you drop anything on him?" said the sergeant. "On his chest?"

Hector and I exchanged a look to ask, *What is he talking about?*

"Why would we drop things on a dead man?" I said.

"His chest is not available, monsieur. He is . . . we say in French, à plat ventre!"

"Facedown," I said.

"And the hat," said the sergeant, "that you felt necessary to mention to the widow?"

"It seemed important," I said. "No one else wears a yellow hat."

"Nor should they," said Hector.

Sergeant Harley laughed, and looked at us more closely. "A poor fashion choice, to be sure," he said. "Did you witness anyone else touch the body?"

"Everett checked for a pulse after Hector did," I said. "And he was still dead. We knew from the squishy-looking eye."

The sergeant blinked. "That was some eye," he agreed. "I'll speak with the widow now." He took his leave abruptly.

Arthur and Hector set up their checkerboard for another game. Arthur was determined to win a match before the end of the week, poor boy. I considered the characters in the unfolding drama. So far, Nina had not shown herself to be the sort of widow Mummy had been—and occasionally still was. No smelling salts or black-edged handkerchiefs. No copious weeping or taking to her bed. Her cot. My imagination tried to summon a vision of Nina Blenningham-Crewe in a mourning dress and veil, but landed on bare toes peeking from beneath the hem. She had returned to work scarcely more than an hour after seeing her husband's body sprawled on the shore. And Everett had returned with her.

Mr. B-C's death meant that he still had a job. It would be careless to ignore this point.

The handsome photographer pushed a lock of dark hair from his brow and watched the scientist with ardent anticipation. Her pale ears peeked through auburn curls, making the breath catch in his chest. Could she forgive him? One moment of temper on the top of Church Cliff . . . The echo of an agonized scream as the victim fell . . . Had this destroyed his dream of happiness? Or had it secured his employment—as well as a place in the heart of his beloved?

How could I think such a thing?! James said Everett was his great chum! Could he also be a murdering scoundrel? Was he so besotted with Nina that he'd been driven to madness?

Or perhaps . . . the widow herself had planned the catastrophe? Was that the reason for her dry-eyed calm? Her determination to keep working despite this abrupt change of fortune? And not a tragic change for the worse, as everyone assumed. She was rid of the man who had belittled her and diminished her rightful place in the world of paleontology. Had she arranged for her own freedom?

"Ha!" cried Hector. Arthur stared at the board in dismay. Hector had engineered a leapfrog move that eliminated four of Arthur's checkers in one go.

Luckily, we were distracted by the approach of another bicycle.

"Hallo, Ronnie!" called Arthur.

"That's P.C. Guff to you, lad," said P.C. Guff, climbing off his bicycle. Arthur grinned, but his cousin's face remained grave. "Where's the sergeant?" he said. "I've got a preliminary report from the coroner." He held up an envelope.

Arthur nipped over to the work tent and poked his head in. Out came Sergeant Harley, followed by Everett and Nina. P.C. Guff, waiting under the kitchen canopy, presented the envelope with both hands. The sergeant withdrew a single page and skimmed the typed words. His eyes widened and he let out a grunt, as if something might be hurting him.

"Mrs. Blenningham-Crewe," he said, after a moment. "The news from Mr. Pallid is . . . perhaps not unexpected after all. Your husband did not drown. He appears to have fallen from a great height."

Nina gasped. Everett said, "No!" From inside the cook tent, we heard Helen's cry of alarm. Hector squeezed my arm. We'd guessed correctly!

The sergeant took a deep breath before continuing. "Because of the location of the hat"—he glanced at Hector and me—"and the subsequent discovery of the bag . . . we surmise that he fell from Church Cliff. The tidal drift then carried him dozens of yards to where his body was found."

"Sackett guessed right," said P.C. Guff. The sergeant glared at him. Everett nudged Nina to sit on a bench, and urged her to take a sip of lemonade. Her face, and even her lips, had paled.

"The evidence insists," Sergeant Harley shook the paper, "that we investigate the steps leading to the man's demise."

"Demise," said Nina, scarcely above a whisper. "My husband is dead."

"Uh, yes," said Sergeant Harley. "That he is."

"I do not believe he died by his own hand," said Nina. "You will excuse me." She did not wait for permission but hurried to the work tent with her hands covering her mouth. Everett, naturally, followed. The sergeant flapped the coroner's letter and fiddled with his mustache. He did not seem to know what he should do next. A beeping horn made us all turn to see Mr. Osteda behind the wheel of his hired motorcar.

"A Vauxhall 6HP!" said Sergeant Harley.

"No better initials than *H* and *P*," said Hector.

Oscar gave a half-hearted wave. "That eye!" he murmured.

"Ouch!" I said. "Helen did not exaggerate!"

Sergeant Harley gazed at the motorcar with a look of longing. But his admiration lasted only a moment before he straightened up and studied the driver's face instead.

"Good morning," said Mr. Osteda, climbing down. His eyes—or, rather, the one that could open—met Sergeant Harley's and skittered away.

"What happened to you?" Oscar said.

Mr. Osteda did not answer, because Everett emerged from the work tent, pulling the door flap taut behind him.

"I am here to collect my son," said Mr. Osteda, "but I hear that you have suffered a terrible loss. I wish to express my condolences to Mrs. Blenningham-Crewe before we depart."

"Nina is . . . not seeing anyone at the moment," said Everett.

Mr. Osteda nodded with solemnity. "We can return in half an hour on our way out of town." He patted Oscar's shoulder. "Hard to believe this unhappy occurrence, after my encounter with Mr. Blenningham-Crewe last night. We had a wonderful meeting." Pat, pat, pat on Oscar's shoulder. "Absolutely wonderful! We patched up our misunderstanding and settled on agreeable terms . . ."

Whose stare was wider, Oscar's or Everett's?

"Can you explain—" Sergeant Harley tried to interrupt, but Mr. Osteda had offered an envelope to Everett.

"You'll need time to consider the logistics," he said, "but I believe . . . this bank draft will speed your decision?"

"Dad! No!" said Oscar.

Everett stepped back with his palms raised. "Any

agreement you might have had with the professor is not necessarily binding with his wife," he said.

"Take a look at the amount on that slip of paper," said Mr. Osteda, laying the envelope on the table, "and we'll see if that changes your mind. Meanwhile, Oscar, where's your suitcase?"

A glum Oscar pointed to where it sat beside the tea trolley.

"Come on, then," said his father. "Let's go." But then he snapped his fingers, as if remembering something.

"Girl." He was speaking to me.

"Sir?" I said.

Oscar blushed furiously. "Her name is Aggie, Dad. Jeez!"

"Of course. Aggie." Mr. Osteda's smile was wide beneath his bristly mustache. "I met your grandmother earlier, in the lobby of our hotel," he said. "You are staying with her tonight, you and the French boy?"

I glanced at Hector, who mouthed the word *Belgian*.

"I assured her that I'd be happy to deliver you when we stop back there to collect my luggage. And then I nearly forgot! How would it have looked if I'd shown up without you, eh?" He laughed.

"Mr. Osteda?" Sergeant Harley had been rereading his letter. "Did you say you were hoping to go somewhere?"

"We're traveling on to Southampton for a few nights before we sail back to America," said Mr. Osteda, not seeing Oscar's grimace. "I need to make arrangements to have the magnificent fossil transported . . ." He looked pointedly at Everett, who glanced toward the work tent.

"Leaving will not be possible," said Sergeant Harley. "We are conducting an inquiry into the death of Professor Blenningham-Crewe. I must ask that you remain in Lyme Regis until we have all the answers we need."

"That's out of the question!" said Mr. Osteda. "We are booked on the RMS *Saxonia*, in the Princess suite."

"You arrived as I was going through the preliminary coroner's report." Sergeant Harley raised the paper. "I didn't see notice earlier that there is more information on the reverse side. The wife needs to be present to hear the rest of it."

"You've already told us that he fell from a great height," said Everett. "Surely his poor widow can be spared further details?" But no, the sergeant insisted that Nina must hear the full account. Reluctantly, Everett went to fetch her.

"Thank you for joining us, Mrs. Blenningham-Crewe," the sergeant said. "We are faced with a grave situation." He cleared his throat. "During our examination on the beach, the coroner noticed—as did I—a certain unusual aspect of the deceased's remains. Mr. Pallid is quite clear in his report. There is firm evidence that our victim had some help going over the cliff."

CHAPTER 14

A Circle of Suspects

Hector and I locked eyes.

There is firm evidence that our victim had some help going over the cliff.

Murder, after all. Goosebumps prickled up my arms. What evidence might that be? I looked around the circle of faces staring at Sergeant Harley. The widow. The photographer. The millionaire and his son. The cook and his daughter. Missing only the lady secretary. Had someone here in Camp Crewe assisted the fall?

"This redirects our inquiries," said the sergeant. "No one is leaving town just now, and certainly not sailing to America."

"You can't think that I—" Mr. Osteda began.

"I am a scientist, Sergeant Harley," said Nina. "I'd like to know what evidence you think you have."

"It's all here!" The sergeant waved the letter from the coroner. "It does not suit the investigation to make public the particulars." Did I detect a note of excitement in the policeman's voice? Or was that because excitement was buzzing in me like bees in a strawberry patch?

"I am not the public," said Nina. "I am the widow."

"Of a murdered man," said Sergeant Harley.

Pay attention! I told myself. Here were the suspects at the moment of a heinous plan gone wrong! I looked from one to the next in a rapid examination. Nina's expression was utterly blank, as if she were willing herself not to reveal a wisp of emotion. Helen's father stood at the door of the cook tent, tapping a large wooden spoon against his thigh. Helen's face was as white as yesterday's ashes. Arthur watched the sergeant, his fingers mimicking the way the officer idly polished the brass buttons on his jacket. Everett's hands clenched into fists and then unclenched. Clenched and unclenched. Oscar's father had the look of someone bonked on the head with a bottle, stunned and furious at the same time. Hector's eyes, and Oscar's, were darting from face to face, as mine were, making their own assessments.

My grandmother came suddenly to mind. She was admirably astute about such matters. If only she were here to consider the company and offer her opinion! She had advised Hector and me each time in the past when we'd been faced with a corpse. A neighbor we all disliked lying prone under the piano. A body bleeding on the library carpet. A gentleman slumped on a bench in the garden, quite dead. Hector and I could look forward to telling her all about our most recent discovery when we met her later at the hotel.

"I hope you're up for this, Sergeant," said Mr. Osteda, "though you've given no reason, so far, to inspire confidence. My son and I will be sailing to America in four days' time, so you'd better get rolling. Ever solved a murder before now?"

Sergeant Harley narrowed his eyes. "No time like the present, Mr. Ostid," he said.

"Osteda," said Mr. Osteda.

"Funny how foreign names never come out right," said the sergeant. "I'll ask you a few questions right now, to kick things off. The rest of you can make yourselves scarce."

He meant us, the children. Nina and Everett were already halfway to the work tent, Helen and her father inside the kitchen.

"Pack your bags," Mr. Osteda told Hector and me. "The Royal Lion shuttle will leave in five minutes."

We heard the sergeant's lazy voice as we moved away. "What can you tell me about that eye of yours, Mr. Oscada?"

As much as we wished to hear the answer, Hector and I collected our overnight kits—already packed in the tents—and sat on a patch of grass with the other boys. We could watch but not hear Oscar's father being questioned by Sergeant Harley.

"This will leave him in the foulest temper," said Oscar. "As if failing to buy the fossil wasn't bad enough."

"But he said he'd fixed things with Mr. B-C," said Arthur.

"I heard what he *said*," muttered Oscar.

"His eye looks miserably sore," I said.

Oscar threw himself down on his back with a heaving sigh. Hector asked the English name of a particular weed with a yellow flower, but neither Arthur nor I knew the answer. Arthur said that his cousin Phyllis worked in a flower shop in Bournemouth. She could tell us, if she were here. Oscar did not speak or sit up until we heard his father calling his name. I felt a bit of a pang as we left Arthur. Would he be alone with a killer on the loose? Or . . . was it *we* who had accepted a ride in a motorcar with a killer at the wheel? A chill crept up my arms as Mr. Osteda pulled on his driving gloves and flexed his fingers. Might those same hands have tussled with the professor at the edge of Church Cliff?

Stepping out of the drizzle into the cozy lobby of the hotel felt like arriving in the drawing room of a favorite aunt.

Oscar's father strode to the desk. He had checked out this morning, but now requested to be given back his suite. The clerk was very sorry, but the suite was no longer available. They could provide a fine room on the first floor, if that would do? No! That would *not* do, not at all! Mr. Osteda launched into a tirade about being a captive at the whim of Sergeant Harley.

I had just wished myself to be invisible when I spotted Grannie Jane waving from a sofa across the room. It was her great pleasure to sit in hotel lobbies, for the purpose of eavesdropping. I felt such a rush of love for her in that moment that I scarcely said goodbye to Oscar, nor to his irritable father. Poor Oscar had the face of a rodent dropped into the cage of a green anaconda from Trinidad.

"I'll come find you," he said. "Please let me."

"Of course," I said, succumbing to the quivering-mouse look.

Grannie Jane was as happy to see us as we were to see her. She put aside her knitting (royal blue, now that we'd welcomed Baby Jimmy into the family), and hugged us both.

She then asked a difficult question. "Which will you have first? A bubble bath, or a cup of cocoa?"

July 11, 1903
Royal Lion Hotel, Lyme Regis

My dear Marjorie,

I hope you and little Jimmy are faring well
this afternoon, and that your mother's presence
has allowed you some rest. I have arrived
safely in Lyme Regis and am nicely situated
at the Royal Lion. I wish to ask that James
not come to fetch me on Sunday as planned,
for my visit at Owl Park, but to await further notice.

You will forgive the last-minute nature of
this request when you hear that our Agatha
and young Hector stumbled across a dead body
at the base of a cliff yesterday morning,
resulting in some palaver. We shall write soon
with details, as they unfold. Agatha will attach
a postscript below.

Fondly,

your loving grandmother

Dear Darling Baby Jimmy,

This is your Auntie Aggie writing your first-ever letter!
We went to see a circus, which I will describe for you
minute-by-minute. I liked the Spotted Pony best, and
I think you would too.

Please tell your mama and grandmother—

(Goodness! My Mummy is the same person as your
Grannie Cora!)

—that Hector and I are fine and being helpful and not
in danger in the least. Tell your papa that his friend
Everett is smashing.

Your loving aunt,

Aggie

CHAPTER 15

A LOVELY RESPITE

UNTIL THIS EPISODE of tent-dwelling, I had been required to have a bath twice a week. A chore, because of waist-length hair. Stepping into the bathtub in Grannie Jane's hotel room, however, was a moment of exquisite delight. Hector had offered me the first turn and I had selfishly accepted. *Ahhh.* Hot water, bergamot bath oil, de-sanded hair!

When we both were washed and dressed again in clean, if slightly wrinkled, clothing, Grannie suggested that our next activity might require some refreshment.

"Yes, please!" we said.

"I expect some insight," she said, "into the particulars of the situation in which you are embroiled."

A Detection Consultation!

Our table in the Royal Lion restaurant was serenaded by a hum of fans overhead, the gentle clink of teacups and ice rattling in tall glasses of lemonade. A pot of Hector's favorite chocolat was delivered to the table, along with a plate of deviled egg and watercress sandwiches with neatly trimmed edges.

Hector sighed with joy. "The accommodations," he said, "are magnifique." Given a choice, Hector would never sleep on a cot in a tent again.

"It seems to me," said my grandmother, "that the death of the leading paleontologist is a good reason to end this experiment of the League of Young Scientists." Her sharp blue eyes went back and forth between us. "I have suggested to James that he may need to step in."

"We appreciate your concern, madame," began Hector, "but—"

"He was not really the *leading* paleontologist," I said. "Nina is far cleverer and more hardworking, wouldn't you say, Hector?"

"You are intentionally missing my point, Agatha." Grannie stirred her tea with vigor.

Hector reached for another sandwich, his third. "As happy as I will be to never again eat a bowl of stew cooked by Monsieur Spud, I see two logical reasons for us to endure a little more. Non, pardon! I see *three* reasons." He dabbed a fleck of chopped egg from his lip.

"Reason one, perhaps not of tremendous importance, but a reason nonetheless: Arthur's parents are with his ailing grandfather in Cornwall. He must remain in camp until they return next week. How can we abandon him?"

I nodded eagerly. Grannie tilted her head, waiting.

"Reason two is that the great ichthyosaur is to be recovered from its grave two days from now, on Sunday. The rehearsal—as you know, because you will be with us to witness—takes place tomorrow. The tide is at the lowest point midmorning."

"The fossil has a nickname," I told Grannie Jane. "Izzy. Because *ichthyosaur* is a bit of a mouthful in regular conversation. You won't believe how old it is, Grannie! And how big! Three of these tables end to end might give you the idea."

"As big as that?"

"It is most illuminating," said Hector.

"And Nina is relying on us, the Young Scientists League!" I said. "We're to be specially trained tomorrow in how to pad and protect the fragile bits of the fossil so that it can be transported safely."

"Many hands are required for this operation," said Hector. "The wrapping must occur at great speed."

"You see, Grannie? We mustn't let them down. And, it's positively educational!"

"And when, I wonder," said my grandmother, "will

the topic of a catastrophic fall from a great height enter the conversation?"

Hector had the cheek to smile at her. "The Morbid Preoccupation of your granddaughter, it cannot be ignored, madame. This is my third reason. We go for a walk. We discover a corpse. Naturellement, we wish to know how such a calamity occurs."

Despite his dearest wish to sleep with a feather pillow under his cheek, Hector had presented a persuasive argument in favor of prolonged discomfort! Grannie Jane lifted the lid of the teapot to see whether there was enough for another cup.

"Correct me if I have miscalculated, Agatha, but I believe this is the fourth such unexpected discovery you have made this year?"

"You know perfectly well, Grannie Jane!"

"May I suggest that we do our best to avoid further corpse-stumbling after this week?"

"It's not as though we go out *hunting* for bodies."

"This is precisely the purpose of the Young Scientists League," murmured Hector. "A fossil is the skeleton of a body, yes?" I kicked him gently under the table. He gave me the look of someone receiving unfair punishment.

"I am unfamiliar on this occasion," said Grannie Jane, "with the players in the drama. Will you be so kind as to fill me in?"

"Oh, thank you!" I cried. Her words were as firm an endorsement of our sleuthing as she would ever utter. "And thank *you*, Hector. Your sacrifice is acknowledged and appreciated."

His cheeks reddened. If there'd been another egg-and-cress, he would have eaten it. As it was, we began our first official Detection Consultation about the grave matter of the body on the beach.

I plunged right in, explaining to Grannie everything I could think of relating to the cast of oddly matched characters at Camp Crewe. The professor was our victim, sharp and pleasant in turns, except in the presence of his wife with whom he was dependably grouchy. His wife did all the work except the cooking, because that was Spud. And not the drawing or photographs, because that was Everett. And not the letter writing, because that—

Hector waved his hands in the air to stop me. "Do you have with you the notebook, Aggie? You are telling the tale in a most disorderly manner."

"Thank you, Hector," said Grannie Jane. "I am quite bemused already. Please make one of your lists, Agatha. Each person must have a name and a reason for disliking the man who died."

"Everyone dislikes him," said Hector. "We must examine each motive methodically, and in order."

I opened my notebook and took the pencil from behind

my ear. "Where do you wish to start, Mr. Logical?" Hector grinned as I divided my page into three columns, with the headings <u>Suspect</u>, <u>Motive</u> and <u>Opportunity</u>.

"We already know the means," I said, "as he died falling over the cliff."

Hector nodded his approval of my sudden ability to organize.

"Madame Nina is the wife of the professor," he told Grannie. "Her motive is wishing not to be squashed like a wasp."

"Really she is a bee," I said, "doing all the work to make the honey, while he sat about like the queen, pretending to be the clever one." I put Nina under <u>Suspects</u>.

"Also," said Hector, "there is Monsieur Spud, who is the cook-of-not-much-talent." Grannie made a noise that might have been a snort if she were not such a refined lady.

"Spud and Mr. B-C had a terrible row on Wednesday," I told her. "Mr. B-C offended Spud's daughter."

"Vraiment, it is Spud who is offended," said Hector. "The professor, he is too familiar with Helen."

"I share a tent with Helen," I said. "She's our minder, though we don't need minding. She also helps her father with the cooking. She's very nice and jolly, and not like a servant in a big house. Camp Crewe is not like anywhere else, is it, Hector?"

"The rules of social manners do not apply," Hector agreed. "The employers, the staff and the servants, they *mingle*. Even children are permitted an opinion."

"Heavens!" said Grannie Jane, only partly teasing. "Whatever next?" She signaled to the waiter. "Shall we have a slice of cake?"

"But Mr. B-C overstepped with Helen," I said, "and Spud was furious."

"A protective father," said Grannie Jane, "always has a motive."

I wrote *protecting his daughter* in the <u>Motive</u> column. I shut my eyes for a fleeting moment, wishing I had Papa here to protect *me*. How suddenly such thoughts arrived, like a paper cut, and then stung for longer than expected.

I felt Grannie's hand cover mine and blinked away the threat of tears.

"What about the other workers?" she said, gently distracting me. "The friend of James, Mr. Tobie? And the secretary?"

"Mr. Tobie is almost as nice as James," I said. "Arthur says he's smashing, and I agree. We call him Everett, because of what Hector said. Manners are looser on a dig."

"Yes, we like him," said Hector, "but—"

I sighed. "But his motive is even stronger than Nina's."

"Oh?" said Grannie.

"It may be that Nina *is* his motive," said Hector.

"Ah," said Grannie.

"Also, the professor argued with him an hour after hollering at Spud," I said. "In the afternoon of the night he died. Mr. B-C told Everett he was to pack up and leave by the next morning."

"And the reason?" said Grannie Jane.

"Everett was speaking up for Nina because she wanted a say in what happens to the ichthyosaur. Mr. B-C said, 'She's *my* wife, not yours,' and then, as quick as a bee-sting, Everett said, 'Will that be true forever?'"

"Goodness," said Grannie. "What sort of murky, scum-covered pond have you landed in? Everyone behaves so badly! Did James not anticipate your exposure to low and extravagant displays?"

"I think he imagined that we'd be sitting on our little stools, peacefully examining bones and writing tidy labels."

"Alas," said Hector, "there is much discord."

"And a *murder*!" I did not even try to hide my satisfaction. "No 'alas' about that!"

Grannie winced. Had I been a shade too bloodthirsty?

"Also, there are the two quarrymen," said Hector, hurrying to repair my misstep. "They are peculiar and taci-turn but not, I think, sinister. And the secretary."

"Miss Spinns does not seem like a killer to me," I said. "Not that we've become in any way acquainted. But she is more the variety of victim who gets knocked off for knowing somebody else's secret."

"Always she is ducking her head," said Hector, "and slipping sideways into the tent, or huddling in a corner with her typewriter."

The waiter appeared with three plates. We paused for a moment to taste and sigh with pleasure.

After a few bites of a dense and flavorful lemon cake, I said, "There is another big battle we haven't even mentioned."

"You're making me dizzy," said Grannie Jane.

"We haven't told you about the Americans, Oscar Osteda and his father."

"Or Cavalier Jones and his Cavalcade of Curiosities," said Hector. "Mr. Jones and Mr. Osteda each wish to possess the ichthyosaur for his own purposes."

"Everyone you've encountered is a person of suspicion?" said Grannie.

Hector and I nodded together. "Probably."

We explained about our afternoon at the circus, and the tremendous strength of Cavalier Jones, Hector's ride on the Spotted Pony, and the exhibit of Rare Sights. We told about the scheme suggested by Mr. Jones to carry the ichthyosaur from town to town in a caravan, and how B-C had said he'd die of mortification if the world of science heard that he'd allowed one of his fossils to join the circus.

"To die of mortification," said Grannie Jane, "would not cause the bruising of a cliff fall."

"Nina reminded him that it wasn't *his* fossil," I said. "*She*'d found it and *she* was arranging its recovery, and how could he say the circus was a worse place than a terrace overlooking the dusty hills of Texas?"

"Texas?" said Grannie. "Really, Agatha, this is sounding more far-fetched with every sentence. You now have villains arriving from Texas?"

At that moment, a grinning Oscar appeared beside our table, his father close behind.

"Gracious," murmured Grannie Jane, after a glance at Mr. Osteda. She had good reason for alarm. The dark slash of his sealed eye surrounded by violet swelling looked particularly villainous in the flickering light of the restaurant. Introductions were conducted, and my grandmother made an admirable effort to pretend there was nothing unusual about the man's face.

"May we join you?" said Mr. Osteda. "Oscar seems to like these kids." He did not give Grannie the chance to invite or demur, but pulled up an extra chair and sat himself down. Oscar slid onto a seat next to Hector. "The boy doesn't have too many friends," said his father, "so it's nice to see him with new pals."

"Dad!" Oscar's cheeks flamed.

Grannie could not resist. The man had insulted his own son. "And you, sir? You show signs of being a well-loved man."

Mr. Osteda threw back his head and laughed. He touched his eyelid gingerly and signaled to the waiter.

"Will you join me in a glass of champagne, Mrs. Morton?"

"I think I will, Mr. Osteda. I'd like to hear the story of your injury. Did it occur on Wednesday evening, by any chance?"

Mr. Osteda smiled. "You are practically American in your frankness, Mrs. Morton. You want to know if I killed Mr. Blenningham-Crewe."

"*Ssh*, Dad!" Oscar glanced around the restaurant, but as we had no close neighbors, we needn't worry about eavesdroppers.

"What happened on Wednesday night was a damn shame," said Mr. Osteda. "There is no question about that. When a man loses his life due to violence, the rest of us shiver a little. It can happen to a person at any time, isn't that right, Mrs. Morton?"

"I am well aware of the fickle nature of life and death," said Grannie Jane quietly. She had often said that no mother wishes to outlive her son, as she had with my Papa. I thought for a moment about Mr. B-C's old mother, who would soon receive a letter containing the most terrible news of her life.

"I went for a drink at the pub along from the hotel," said Mr. Osteda. "I'd gone the night before as well, and it's a friendly place. Oscar stayed in our room, where I assumed he'd read his book and gone to bed. I was wrong about that. I was wrong about plenty that night."

I looked at Oscar. He stared at the dregs of cocoa in his cup, not lifting his eyes or offering an explanation. Oscar had turned up at Camp Crewe as our bonfire was burning low and said that he was bored. Had there been other cause to venture out alone on a moonless night?

"I walked into The Crow's Nest," said Oscar's father, "and the first person I saw was Mr. Blenningham-Crewe. We'd parted with heated words a few hours earlier and now here he was, sitting at a table in the middle of the pub. No way to avoid him—and he wasn't keen to see me, despite having invited me there earlier. But, I thought to myself, we're civilized men. I wanted that great stone beast, and here was one last chance to win my prize."

He shifted his chair with a scraping noise and took a gulp of champagne. "This is what I know about the professor's last night on earth . . ."

CHAPTER 16

A FIRSTHAND ACCOUNT

GRANNIE SIPPED from her glass. Bubbles sparkled, catching light. Mr. Osteda was telling the story to her, not to the children at the table. But we were listening with wide-open ears.

"I'd chatted the night before with Kenny, the barkeep, so I waved a hello. Three or four men sat on stools at the bar, but I didn't see who they were until later. I asked Blenningham-Crewe if I might join him. He nodded, without pleasure. He kept looking over my shoulder as if he was expecting someone else." Mr. Osteda again lightly touched his swollen eye and glanced at his son. Oscar was folding his napkin into the shape of a canoe.

"The barmaid at The Crow's Nest is Kenny's sister, the lovely Yvonne," Mr. Osteda went on. "She brought me a pint and another whiskey for Mr. Blenningham-Crewe. Yvonne's a chatty one, all smiles and nudges, even if she must be forty. The professor cheered up after a minute or two. Yvonne filled his flask and put up with his invitation for her to drink it with him. I was waiting for her to go away before he got much tipsier. I wanted to remind him that we'd had an agreement." Mr. Osteda shook his head several times, with a defeated sigh.

"I've been lying on my bed for a day and a night, thinking over all the pieces of what happened on Wednesday. At the time, I was fixed on my own purpose, and didn't notice that I was not the only man in the pub who was mad as hell at the professor."

"I'd like to know more," said my grandmother smoothly, "about who you encountered that evening."

Thank you, Grannie Jane! It was useful to have a nosy grown-up on the team. People answered her questions as they never would with a twelve-year-old.

"Well, in struts Mr. Cavalier Jones," said Mr. Osteda. "Everyone in the place gives a cheer, because they've all seen the show. Another fellow from the circus is with him, one of the musicians."

One of the musicians? Could that be Helen's beau, Ned?

"Did he have ginger hair, by any chance?" I said. Grannie and Hector, as if tugged by the same string, raised their eyebrows at me.

Mr. Osteda said, "That's the one." And then, "Hopping about like a court jester he was, with Cavalier Jones the visiting royalty."

"Dad," said Oscar. "You loved the circus as much as we did."

"That was before Jones tried to steal the ichthyosaur out from under my nose," said Mr. Osteda. "Mr. Jones turns out to be the man the professor is waiting for. In a puddle of a town like this one, Mr. Jones is a celebrity. He struts round the room, clapping men on the back, and then sits down at our table, all charm and good cheer, with the trumpet boy hovering behind him." Mr. Osteda filled his own glass from the bottle and offered more to Grannie Jane.

"No, thank you," she said. "Please go on with your story."

"The lovely Yvonne brings Mr. Jones a pint," said Mr. Osteda. "'*Courtesy of the house!*' she says, as if he's Zeus down from Mount Olympus on his day off. I was ticked, I'll tell you. He stands up, raises his glass and proposes a toast. 'To the glorious future and the even more glorious past,' he says. 'To the oldest creature ever known joining Cavalier's Cavalcade!'"

"Uh-oh," said Oscar. His father grimaced and nodded a couple of times.

"That's right," he said. "I couldn't just sit there, could I? I sailed all the way from America, only to be double-crossed by a circus showman and an oily professor who can't make up his mind without his wife telling him what to do? Not a chance! I am Alonso Osteda!"

"So, you—" Oscar began.

"So, I jump to my feet and—" He stopped to regard his audience, an elderly woman and three children. Possibly the next part would offend our delicate sensibilities?

"You hit the professor?" said Oscar.

"No," said his father, quieter now. "I *tried* to hit the professor, but Mr. Jones stepped between us. My fist connected with *his* face instead of the intended target. His musical sidekick squeaked like a mouse."

This explained the small injury on the strongman's lip! A gift from Alonso Osteda.

"I will have another splash of champagne, after all," said Grannie Jane, offering her glass. Mr. Osteda replenished her drink.

"I'd like to know more," I said, mimicking Grannie Jane's interviewing style, "about your own grievous injury?"

"I was quickly escorted to the door," he admitted. "Kenny called on the men sitting at the bar and I found myself surrounded. One of them was your cook from out there at the camp."

"You mean Spud?" I said.

"That's him. Not too friendly with the professor either, from what I heard later. He had a couple of surly-looking pals, one of them a foreigner with a furry beard."

That sounded like the quarrymen, Mr. Jarvis and Mr. Volkov!

"The sort you wouldn't want to meet in a back alley," added Oscar's father.

"I don't suppose there is any sort of man I'd wish to meet in a back alley," said Grannie Jane. She cast one of her Withering Looks in the direction of Mr. Osteda, but he failed to wither.

"Tell me," Hector said. "An American in England, he also is a foreigner?"

Mr. Osteda laughed his hearty laugh. "Clever boy!" he said. "You caught me on that one!"

"Surely you don't mean to leave the story dangling, Mr. Osteda?" said my grandmother. "You were being accompanied out of The Crow's Nest?"

"That's where my memory gets slippery," he said. "Too much happened too quickly, if you know what I mean. The cook and his buddies were flanking me, nudging me out to the street. I realized they were hoping for a brawl. Your Spud was egging me on, saying, 'Try it again!' Blenningham-Crewe comes out and Mr. Jones is with him, along with the kid from the circus band."

Helen's Ned was another witness!

"I may have said something unpleasant," said Mr. Osteda. "I may even have"—he made a motion with his right arm— "done something my boy would not be proud of."

"Who got you in the eye, Dad? Sounds like you were surrounded."

"Five men? Six? All against me. Even Yvonne was there for some of it. The cook and those other two switched from guarding me to keeping the professor upright. He was as drunk as a lord on Christmas Eve, kept asking Yvonne if she'd marry him, never mind that he had a wife already. That left Mr. Jones."

Mr. Osteda opened and closed his fist, wiggling the fingers. "I took a swing but . . ." His fingers gently tapped the swollen purple eyelid. "I got this shiner from the Strongest Man in the World."

"No wonder it looks so bad!" Oscar sounded impressed.

"What happens next?" said Hector.

"I fell down," said Mr. Osteda. "That's the sorry truth. I saw stars, I cried for my mother, I thought my head would burst."

"But who went with the professor?" said Oscar. "Cavalier Jones and his circus pal? Or one of the other guys?"

"I missed a few beats, I admit," said his father. "I've been trying to remember, but it's a fuzzy, dark fog. One minute I was on the cobblestones with my face on fire. The next minute I was at the hotel desk with that young trumpet player holding me up, asking for the key to my room."

How did Ned end up assisting Mr. Osteda? And what about Mr. B-C? Mr. B-C was *dead*. Mr. Osteda had been a pretty fair witness up until now. Was he about to falter? Or could he name the killer?

"Excuse me," I said, "but do you have a *guess* as to what happened while your head was spinning?"

"I wish I could pin the blame on Cavalier Jones, but I confess that seems unlikely. My theory is that the cook and those friends of his lured the professor to the edge of the cliff and gave him a little nudge. Or maybe it was those two fierce-looking rogues on their own."

"But why?" said Grannie Jane.

"Aha!" Mr. Osteda raised a wagging finger. "You have asked the eternal question. And I have the eternal answer . . ." We waited. He rubbed his fingers against his thumb. "Money!" he said. "They were *paid* to kill him!"

"Who would pay for such a service?" said Grannie Jane.

"The little lady herself," said Mr. Osteda, leaning back in his chair with a smirk. "Missus. Blenningham. Crewe."

My grandmother sipped her champagne and looked at Mr. Osteda.

"Is there a reason for your certainty, sir?" she asked. "Or is the accusation merely wishful thinking?"

"Mrs. Morton!" he cried. "You have exposed my prejudice!" Another throaty chuckle. "There is no evidence, if that's what you're looking for. My guess is based on the instincts of a mistrustful man who moves among dubious men."

"Have you told the police of your suspicion, sir?"

"The police are not interested in what I have to say. These village Brits take one look at a brown face and assume they've got a criminal."

Hector and my grandmother again lifted their eyebrows simultaneously, silently saying what we all were thinking. With such an eye as his, he *did* look like a criminal.

Not a jolly night for anyone! The only person who'd been pleasant during the evening was Yvonne, the barmaid. But six men—Alonso Osteda, Cavalier Jones, Helen's beloved Ned, Spud the cook, and the two quarrymen, Jarvis and Volkov—had seen the professor leave The Crow's Nest. He'd been drunk, and was disliked by all. Had one of them walked him to his death?

"Monsieur Osteda," said Hector. "There is a matter I am not understanding."

"And what's that?"

"You report to Mr. Everett Tobie that you patch up the quarrel with Mr. Blenningham-Crewe on Wednesday night. You say that you make an arrangement to take the ichthyosaur and you decide on a price, yes?"

Mr. Osteda's amiable demeanor darkened as if Hector had pulled a string. Oscar, beside me, went still.

"What of it?" said Mr. Osteda.

"When does this patching up occur?" said Hector. "Before or after you are receiving a punch in the eye?"

163

Mr. Osteda began to laugh. "Never," he said. "There was no patching up! I told your Mr. Everett Tobie that on the off chance that he'd believe it and let me have the fossil. Any good businessman would do what I did. That's how the world works!"

He had confessed, in front of his son, to being a barefaced liar! How much else of his story was also a lie? Did he, in fact, remember every moment in sharp detail? Was it *he* who had accompanied Mr. B-C to the edge of the cliff?

CHAPTER 17

A LURID PHOTOGRAPH

THE STORY OSCAR'S FATHER told us remained vivid on Saturday morning, when there came a knock on the hotel room door. Hector read Sherlock Holmes at the little table, though we had yet to order breakfast. I was tying my laces and Grannie Jane was in the bath. A quiet *tap-tap* at the door compelled me to peer over Hector's shoulder into the corridor. Oscar held up a newspaper for us to see the front page. A photograph of the professor's dead body was displayed above a commanding headline:

THE SEASIDE CORPSE!!
Esteemed Fossil-Hunting Professor
BEACHED LIKE A WHALE.

"God's breath!" I said, as Hector muttered, "Mon Dieu!"

"I was pretty sure you'd want to see," said Oscar. "I know your grandmother is visiting Camp Crewe this morning, and I wanted to show you before—"

"Let me get my shoes," I said. "You can't come in, because—"

I stopped. How improper to say that my grandmother was in the bath! Hector stepped outside and quietly closed the door. I finished doing up the buttons on my dress, and pulled on my shoes and stockings more quickly than I ever had.

"We'll be in the corridor with Oscar," I called to Grannie Jane. "You may surprise us with the breakfast order." I had a moment's pang, thinking how lovely it would be to stay another night in the hotel, to have another bath and breakfast on a tray . . . but that was not to be. We had a murder to attend to! If Hector could face mosquitoes and nettles, I most certainly could do without a bergamot bubble bath.

The boys were kneeling on the carpet, Hector's eyes scanning the newspaper story. I made him spread it out on the floor so we both could see at the same time.

A human body has been found a few dozen yards from the location of a giant fossilized sea dragon, near Lyme Regis, in Dorset. Is there a connection between the two? The dead man has been identified as Mr. Howard Blenningham–Crewe, eminent professor at the University of Edinburgh. He and his wife, Mrs. Nina Blenningham–Crewe (an emerging expert on marine reptiles), were preparing to recover a fossilized ichthyosaur Sunday next, from a site near the low–water mark east of Church Cliff. This remarkable specimen, dead for over a million years, appears to be intact and close to nine feet long.

The body of Mr. Blenningham–Crewe showed signs of having been immersed in the sea for several hours at least. Because of this prolonged dunking, the coroner conducted a cursory waterfront analysis but could not, at press time, be precise as to the hour of death, beyond "likely to have been late Wednesday evening." This estimate was based on the tidal drift. Why would he have been on the beach alone at night? Why was he not reported as missing? The body was removed by boat to Cobb harbor and taken to

167

the coroner's examining rooms to undergo closer scrutiny. Though it was first assumed to be an incident of accidental drowning, new information indicates a murder most foul.

The professor, known for both his temper and his charm, leaves behind his widow. The couple had no children. He is also survived by his widowed mother, Mrs. Audrey Blenningham-Crewe, and a spinster sister, Adele, both of Tunbridge Wells. The names of the children who discovered the body will be familiar to readers in Torquay. Miss Aggie Morton and Master Hector Perot, both twelve years old, are no strangers to the world of mortality, having attended crime scenes on numerous occasions. They came to Lyme Regis to participate in a fossil-finding expedition under the mentorship of the deceased.

The investigation is led by Sergeant Richard Harley, with dubious progress. No arrest seems to be imminent and activity at Camp Crewe remains uninterrupted. The victim's wife insists that the long-awaited recovery of the impressive ichthyosaur will proceed as planned on Sunday, claiming that "he would have wished it so."

Hector's finger pointed to the byline: "Reprinted with permission from the *Torquay Voice*, by Augustus C. Fibbley." My eyes had already jumped to the name and my blood simmered.

"We didn't pay enough attention to that first piece two days ago," I said. "We should have known, when Everett said to hide the newspaper from Nina, that the reporter most resembling a snake must have written it."

"But why does he come to Lyme Regis *before* there is a murder?" said Hector.

"The ichthyosaur is a pretty big story," I said. "He probably has spies all over the country telling him when something might be newsworthy."

"He takes a particular interest when a woman does something that is not usual for a woman to do," said Hector. "A woman who does what is considered to be a man's job."

"Right," I said. Since Augustus Fibbley was just such a woman. But I was terribly aware of Oscar listening and did not pursue that thought for now. "Well, he got lucky this time. A murder fell straight into his hands."

"You know this guy?" said Oscar, sounding very American. "The reporter?"

"We do," I said. "He's from our town. Or he lives there now, anyway."

"How does he learn so much without coming to the camp?" said Hector.

"And how did he take a photograph of a corpse under police watch?" I was practically sputtering. "Nothing stops that weaselly, conniving—"

"Why don't you like him?" said Oscar. "He asks better questions than the police."

"He's very good at asking questions," I agreed.

Oscar's interest confirmed that we must be careful. Mr. Gus Fibbley *was* a conniving weasel, but also clever and charming—and ruthless in his pursuit of a story. And the secret he carried—that he was not a mister at all—was one that Hector and I had pledged with honor to never tell.

Hector neatly folded the newspaper and offered it to Oscar.

"Wait," I said. "Let me look again." Under the light of a window at the end of the hallway, I examined every grain of the photograph. How had it come to be taken? Mr. B-C was not facedown as we had seen him, but lying on his back. His head was turned away from the camera— luckily for the reader! His body had been tidily laid out, arms and legs aligned, as if already on the coroner's table. I noted the toes of a policeman's boots on the far side of the body and a bucket that held seawater, perhaps to sluice away any mess? Tea mugs from the cook tent rested on the pebbles, and the shadow of a beach umbrella cut across the edge of a folded blanket beside the professor's head.

My neck and shoulders prickled with cold as I passed the newspaper to Hector.

"Mugs," I said.

Hector peered carefully at the picture, as I had done. The truth clobbered me as soundly as the thwack of a cricket bat. There had been an imposter at Camp Crewe. Hector and I were dupes! Again!

"Ooh la la," said Hector.

"I knew you two would like this," said Oscar. "With all your sleuthing shenanigans." He had no idea why we were suddenly speechless. Down the passage a door opened. Grannie Jane—fully dressed, thank goodness—looked toward the stairs and then in our direction.

"There you are. Good morning, Oscar. Will you be joining us for breakfast?"

"No, thank you, ma'am, I stopped by to—"

A maid came up the stairs, bearing a tray laden with a teapot, a pot of chocolat and several other dishes covered with silver lids. A newspaper, facedown for the moment, was tucked under a napkin, like a firecracker with a lit fuse. What if seeing this grisly photograph changed Grannie's mind about us remaining at Camp Crewe? Hector held the door as the maid maneuvered her way inside, while Oscar spoke hurriedly to my grandmother.

"Mrs. Morton, forgive my boldness, but as you are going out to the camp this morning, I wonder if I could come too? They're doing the rehearsal for the big recovery effort, and since I might have to miss the real thing . . . What do you think? Can I come with you?"

"*May* you come with us? Is that what you intended to ask, young man?"

Oscar looked confused, not recognizing the grammar lesson being offered, but he nodded. "Yes, ma'am, that's what I'm asking."

"Come back ready at eight forty-five precisely," said Grannie. "I understand the event we are witnessing depends upon the low tide at ten-twenty. I have arranged for a trap and there is room for one more. You will, naturally, inform your father that you are in my care."

I had been tempted to slide the newspaper under the bed, but she would simply ring for another. Grannie did not let a day go by without reading the news. She sat as I took a deep breath and poured her tea. I put the paper to one side to postpone the inevitable clamor. Hector's eyes rested on it, while eating his shirred egg and buttered toast fingers. His brain cells must have been creating the same frantic friction that mine were. We could not consult with Grannie listening because the secret we held between us like a smoldering chunk of coal belonged to Mr. Gus Fibbley, and was not ours to share.

172

Grannie finished her kipper. She reached for the newspaper to read with her second cup of tea.

"May we please be excused, Grannie?" We tidied the breakfast plates onto the tray. "We need to pack our things."

"Yes, pet." And then we knew she was looking at the photograph of the professor's corpse because of the quick inhalation and the extended *hmmm*. "Your old friend Mr. Augustus Fibbley is up to his tricks again," she said.

We stood behind her and made convincing noises of surprise.

"The professor was on his belly when we found him," I said. "This is not an accurate picture of the scene of the crime."

"A nice turn of phrase, Agatha," said Grannie Jane. "But I wonder . . . Is *the scene of the crime*, as you put it, at the bottom of the cliff? Or at the top?"

"The crime itself must have been at the top," I said. "If he was pushed. But where exactly did he die? Halfway down, when he hit his head or broke his neck? Or later . . . gently rocked in the arms of the sea?"

"Is the reporter with you at the encampment?" said Grannie Jane.

"Mr. Fibbley?" said Hector. "He is not present."

"I have not seen him at all," I assured her, with utter candor.

"In that case," said my grandmother, "he is resorting to his typical style of journalism, one that depends on rumors."

A knock at the door announced that Oscar was early. Hector and I had not yet been alone for a single minute to discuss the secret revealed in the photograph. No chance to whisper the name of the person we now knew to be responsible for taking it.

Miss Spinns.

Miss Spinns had carried tea mugs and a thermos to refresh the poor constable guarding a dead body on the beach. And tucked into the lumpy bag slung over her shoulder, there must have been a camera—the essential tool of a ruthless reporter.

The old lady was another disguise of the cunning Mr. Fibbley—and Mr. Fibbley himself was also a disguise, of a young woman we had never encountered.

I had one question.

How could we have been *so dim*?

CHAPTER 18

A VIEW FROM ABOVE

GRANNIE'S LEGS WERE WOBBLY climbing down from the trap. That last bit of track from the town road to Camp Crewe was perilous. Through hard wooden seats, swerving to go around boulders, we'd felt every bump.

Arthur hallooed and waved before the trap had even stopped. He must have been terribly bored without us, being the sort of boy who liked company. His brain cell friction when alone was likely as active as a snail on grass. Everett emerged from the work tent with a wide smile of greeting. We all were abuzz in anticipation of watching the practice run of retrieving the ichthyosaur. Everett's shirt-sleeves were rolled up and he was hatless—not the usual appearance of a gentleman in Grannie's circle, but his gracious manners soon won her heart.

"We're a bit out of sorts, I'm afraid," said Everett. "From the loss of Mr. Blenningham-Crewe, most certainly, but a photograph of the death scene is in the newspaper this morning."

"Dear, dear," clucked Grannie Jane, quite as if she hadn't read the story with greedy fascination.

"Luckily, Nina doesn't care for the news," said Everett. "She lives in the world of long-ago history. So far, I've been able to keep the horrible picture out of sight."

"How grim," I said.

"Not for the eyes of the widow," agreed Hector.

"Arthur, be a good lad," said Everett. "Fetch a camp chair for Mrs. Morton. Oh, and I've forgotten the stopwatch!"

"I must have my binoculars!" said Hector. They scurried in different directions as Nina came out from her tent and the quarrymen arrived from the shop yard. The pockets of Nina's waistcoat bulged, as did the tool belts at the men's waists. Mr. Volkov and Mr. Jarvis commandeered their specially constructed fossil barrow, a platform nearly as big as a church door, edged with a low rim to prevent anything sliding off. The iron wheels had been salvaged from an ice wagon. The time it took to be pushed out to the fossil site and back to dry land—full of stones that weighed as much as the ichthyosaur—was part of the calculation for the precision operation the next day.

Grannie Jane tipped her head to Nina in gracious greeting, as if the encounter were occurring in a parlor rather than a windy meadow at the top of a cliff.

"My sincere condolences," said my grandmother. "A husband and a colleague in one blow. Your loss is great indeed."

"It is woefully unfair," said Nina.

Grannie patted her arm. "A sudden death *is* unfair, when there is no chance to say goodbye."

Nina bit her lip. "Please excuse our distraction, Mrs. Morton," she said. "Timing is critical to our success. Every half minute counts. Low water is at twenty past ten this morning, meaning that we must be on-site at five minutes before the hour." She and the quarrymen set out along the path. Nina was not barefoot today, but wore boots! Surely not designed for a woman's foot but for a farm boy.

"I'm here, I'm here!" Everett waved the leather case that held the stopwatch. Grannie took Hector's arm for steadiness on the rough path. Arthur hoisted the folding chair to one shoulder and began to whistle twittery birdcalls.

"Constables have been posted at the top of both paths," Everett murmured to me, not wanting to distress my grandmother. "That newspaper article this morning has stirred up the ghoulish interest of people in town. Nina thinks we'll soon have muckraking reporters from elsewhere."

I made a noise of sympathy.

"Who might have taken such a photograph?" said Everett. "Do you have the sense that Helen is untrustworthy in this respect?"

"Not Helen," I said. This was a most uncomfortable conversation, as I knew the certain culprit!

Everett scarcely paused for my reply. "I suppose anyone might have sneaked to the beach from town, but the journalist had details of our plans. Was it Spud, do you think? Still angry at B-C? But how would he take pictures?"

"He never leaves the cook tent," I said. And was busy making tea, I did not add, for the real guilty party—Miss Spinns—to use as a decoy in accomplishing her plan! Duping Arthur's foolish cousin, P.C. Guff, into allowing her to snap a photograph cannot have been difficult. I wavered, confronting a dilemma. Should I tell the truth to Everett? But what if Nina was a murderess? And he her willing assistant? It seemed a dubious notion to consider, while sunlight and fresh sea air bathed our faces. Even if they'd killed Mr. B-C—which I did not yet have hard evidence to suggest—they were surely no danger to anyone else? Though one never knew with murderers. I'd sadly had occasion to learn that a cornered villain might strike again. Let Nina extract her ichthyosaur, I decided, and be arrested afterward. I'd keep mum for now, in the doubtful case that

Everett was a conspirator. And still, I squirmed at my duplicity in knowing something that he so wished to know.

"I think," he announced, "that this is the best spot from which to witness our rehearsal. I must rush along to catch up with Nina and the others."

We overlooked one end of Back Beach, its long curve broken partway along by the tumbled mass of the landslip. The sea slid out across the ledges as if someone had tilted a saucer to let the water run off. Away in the distance, at the other end of the beach, was Church Cliff, where Mr. B-C had fallen.

Arthur unfolded and latched together the canvas seat for Grannie Jane. She retied her hat more securely, and scolded the salty breeze for its persistence. Oscar objected to staying up here on the cliff while the action occurred so far below. Hector fussed about the itchiness of grass on his legs, one inch being exposed between the cuff of his short trousers and socks pulled up to the knees.

"Can you see Nina and the men, Grannie Jane?" We helped her focus Hector's binoculars to watch the small group make their way toward where the black marker stones slowly emerged from the ebbing waves. The fossil site appeared to be a craggy boulder from this distance.

"Up close, Grannie, wait till you see. The head is as big as our heads put together, with a great long snout like a dolphin, and so many teeth!"

"More than one hundred," said Hector, who had tried to count.

"The better to eat you with," said Grannie Jane.

Oscar settled himself amid the weeds and dirt on the ground near Grannie Jane's camp stool. He did not share Hector's qualms about getting his trousers dirty. He'd brought a tin of biscuits from Spud, and opened it now to pass around.

"Thank you, young man," said Grannie Jane. "I am partial to brown sugar shortbread."

I surveyed the scene, from the miniature adventurers crossing the ledges, to the nearby constable removing his helmet every few minutes to wipe his brow, to the small group of people from town gathering on the adjacent clifftop. They were not here to watch the fossil recovery— for that would happen tomorrow. They'd come precisely because they were forbidden access to the murder site on their own beach. But wait! What was that flash of blue? I nudged Hector to request his binoculars. Grannie Jane relinquished them. I fiddled with the rings around the lenses and brought the townspeople into focus.

"Can you see along the cliff edge there?" I handed the binoculars to Hector. "In the cluster of villagers . . . is that Miss Spinns? Wearing her blue coat?"

"Looks like a kingfisher from this far off," said Arthur, shielding his eyes from the sun.

Hector polished the lenses before pressing the viewing end to his eyes.

"It is she," he said. "She also is using binoculars." Indeed, we saw a slight flash as the sun caught the glass of her set. Was she spying on us?

"Crazy old bat," said Arthur.

But Hector and I knew that she was far from crazy. Whatever her scheme, it was minutely plotted.

Our lookout spot provided an excellent view of the Camp Crewe team, but the rehearsal was a disaster. I forgot about Miss Spinns within moments of spotting her. My gaze was pinned instead on Nina and the men crossing the ledges steps behind the receding water.

"Something's not right," I said. "They're moving too slowly."

"There is trouble with the barrow," said Hector. "You see?" He passed his binoculars back to Grannie Jane. "The wheels, they catch on the bumpy stones."

"Not a good sign," said Arthur. "It's not even carrying anything yet."

Grannie Jane readjusted the focus on the binoculars' lenses. "I had the impression they intended their pace to be urgent," she said.

"They should be quicker than this, Mrs. Morton," said Oscar, "to outwit the Atlantic Ocean."

Mr. Jarvis and Mr. Volkov took turns trying to steer the

barrow, lagging several yards behind Nina and Everett. Nina had two spades resting on her shoulders, while Everett carried what was called a mattock, something like a pickax but with a two-sided head.

"Deadly looking," said Grannie Jane.

"One side is for digging and prying up," said Arthur, "and the other bit is for chopping. A mattock is mostly to pull out tree stumps, but if the blades are sharp, they can cut through layers of shale."

"They carry the tools today to know how much the weight affects the timing," said Hector.

"Every half minute counts," I said. "As Nina says."

Mr. Jarvis, as if he were a horse, dragged the barrow laboriously behind him. The Russian, on his turn, gathered some momentum by trotting while he pushed, letting the barrow wheels bounce and skid where they might. It was this that caused the accident. We on the clifftop gasped in unison as one of the front wheels snapped. The barrow tipped to one side, so that poor Mr. Volkov rammed into it and staggered from the impact. Everett sprinted back to help. Nina paused mere seconds before hurrying on, now walking backward and calling out as she went.

"A determined woman," said Grannie Jane.

The barrow was abandoned and the men caught up. There appeared to be a lively group debate, with waving arms, while they all kept moving forward to make up time after the delay. When they reached the ichthyosaur's grave, there still was water to splash through, but only for a few minutes. Hector had the binoculars again, and gave us a running commentary: Everett pulled his stopwatch out of its case and pressed the button. He made a note in his book. He glanced at the sun and positioned himself to take a photograph. Nina and the quarrymen knelt and poked with their tools. They did not dig but seemed to be testing the ground, preparing themselves for what must come tomorrow.

"It is not so entertaining, is it?" I said. "We're too far away and they're clumped around the fossil like ants on a sugar cube."

"Not quite as energetic as a horse race," agreed Grannie Jane. She stood with a little difficulty from the flimsy camp stool. When she'd rearranged her skirt and fixed her hat, her eyes narrowed to examine me. "The trap is waiting," she said. "But I am wrestling with my conscience, Agatha."

"Why is that?"

"I am loath to leave you children here," she said. "I find myself imagining the scene in which I explain to your agitated mothers my unforgivable lapse in allowing you to sleep in the vicinity of a murder."

"The murder happened nowhere near the camp!" I said. "It was all the way over there." I pointed at the distant spires of St. Michael's, shimmering faintly in the midday sun. "You mustn't worry, Grannie, you really mustn't. Look around. Does it feel dangerous to you? We're safe, we have each other."

Grannie cradled my cheek in her hand. "Do not make me regret the decision of leaving you behind," she said. "No reckless adventuring or villain baiting, do you understand?"

"Yes, darling Grannie."

"Look out for each other."

When the patient driver had assisted Grannie Jane in mounting the trap and we'd waved them off, the rest of us sat under the welcome shade of the kitchen canopy, chewing our way through rubbery mackerel. We ate slowly. Was it worse than cow's tongue? Very possibly.

Nina and Everett had returned to camp, with Mr. Jarvis and Mr. Volkov dragging their failed fossil barrow. The mood was storm-cloud miserable. Helen came out with a platter of ham sandwiches and discreetly removed the fish debris.

"Dad's got good days and bad days," she whispered.

"Do let us know when a good one comes along," said Everett. The sandwiches were gone in a flash, but for crumbs.

Nina stood, so we all could hear, and began to speak.

"We've had a bad week." She took off her hat and pushed sweaty hair back from her forehead. "We've . . . lost Howard . . ." She paused to breathe in deeply. "We've

184

angered a potential buyer, whether we want to sell or not. We've got policemen and reporters popping up at odd moments, and now, our barrow is broken!" She took a long drink of water. "But spring tide is tomorrow. You all know that our responsibility to excavate this extraordinary treasure must take precedence over our grief, for a few more days at least. Howard would have wanted us to do this much, no matter where Izzy ends up."

"How do we make that happen, ma'am?" said Mr. Jarvis. He wasn't being rude, but he was a man used to practical solutions—and one of those was not in sight.

Mr. Volkov shifted in his seat and lifted his calloused hands, to remind us that he'd only got two. Even Everett's shoulders sagged, fingers turning his tea mug this way and that.

Nina's weary smile went around the table. "We're going to be resourceful," she said. She pounded one fist into the other palm like the rallying beat of a drum. "We're going to *think*." A long minute went by, and then another. The glum silence stretched.

"Excuse me, Madame Nina," said Hector. He cleared his throat and stood up. I would rather eat another serving of mackerel than address a table full of staring grown-ups. But Hector? He just spoke.

"Please excuse that I mention your husband's departure, but that is what inspires the idea that comes to me."

"Go on," said Nina.

"Yesterday the boat of Constable Sackett carries the professor from the beach to the harbor. Can this method not also be used to carry the ichthyosaur?"

One, two, three seconds more of silence, and then Everett began to clap.

"Smashing idea!" said Arthur.

We all joined Everett's applause. Within moments, our spirits were dancing anew. The quarrymen wore grins of relief. Even Spud popped his head out of the cook tent with a crooked smile—and reminded Helen there were carrots to be scrubbed. Everett assigned Mr. Jarvis, with Arthur as assistant, to find P.C. Sackett in town and to hire his boat for the next day.

"We can salvage the upper part of the barrow, don't you think?" said Everett. "Craft a board to lift Izzy from the ledge into the boat?"

"She'll come out in pieces," said Mr. Volkov.

"Get started on cutting the barrow bed into four smaller planks," said Mr. Jarvis. He had a bicycle, and Arthur sat on the handlebars. Inspired by the lady cyclists at the circus, he held his long legs wide of the wheel and away they went.

Miss Spinns chose that moment to appear, blue coat folded over her arm. The walk must have been warm. When she understood the reason for our jollity, she joined right in. Only Hector and I knew that she was a rotten, double-dealing opportunist, undeserving of the right to celebrate. And wasn't it bold of her to appear in camp, when her sly use of a camera could momentarily be exposed!

"You seem to have a mix-up on your calendar," said Everett. "You missed Friday and yet here you are on Saturday."

Miss Spinns managed a brittle chuckle. "I was unwell yesterday. I apologize," she said. "I did not know how to inform you. Alas, I seem to have left behind my fountain pen. Perhaps Miss Morton will be so kind as to assist in finding it? It must have rolled under a table in the work tent."

She trapped me as easily as that. How could I refuse to help an old lady find her pen? Obediently, I stood to follow.

"Hector too," I said.

"Hector too," she agreed, in her creaky old-lady voice. "Four young eyes are better than two for seeing into dark corners."

CHAPTER 19

A DUPLICITOUS REPORTER

"This isn't safe," I whispered as soon as we were inside the work tent.

"Madame Nina or Everett may enter at any moment." Hector glanced fearfully at the door flap.

"What do you want, *Mr. Fibbley*?" I said. "I'm so mad I could spit."

Miss Spinns straightened her curved elderly spine to the youthful posture of . . . of who? Who was she, really? She grinned, removed those thick spectacles and looked forty years younger.

"What took you so long?" she said.

"Tell me the minute Jarvis and Arthur get back with news about the boat, will you?" Nina's voice came from just outside. "I'm going to send a note to Mr. Wemberly at the museum that we—"

Miss Spinns jammed her glasses back on, and hunched into her old-lady disguise. She snapped open her handbag and snatched out a royal blue fountain pen.

"Such sharp eyes!" she cried. "Thank you, children!"

Nina came in.

"The pen, it is found!" said Hector.

With Miss Spinns in front, we awkwardly bundled ourselves past Nina and out through the door flap. Everett was crossing the field with Mr. Volkov toward the shop yard. Oscar had cadged an empty jar from Spud and lay on his tummy collecting beetles.

"Where can we go?" said Miss Spinns. "It is urgent that we speak."

"Aggie's tent?" said Hector.

"Why mine?"

"Better that she be found there than in the tent of the boys," said Hector.

Miss Spinns patted her face with a lace-edged hand-kerchief, slipped off her shoes and ducked into the girls' tent. I glanced around to see that we were not being observed. Except that we were. By Oscar.

"Will you please hum when no one is nearby?" Hector said. "You must appear to be idle, not on guard.

If someone appears, you speak. Yes? Say hello out loud."

Oscar nodded. Hector put his shoes tidily beside those of Miss Spinns and went inside. I hurriedly unlaced and kicked mine off too.

Oscar looked at me and lifted his eyebrows. "What does *she* want?" he whispered. "She could be the killer!"

She was the one person I knew for certain was not the killer. But I couldn't say that, because then I would have to explain why.

"I don't think she killed him," I said, "but she might possess information we can use to figure out who did. She saw lots of the B-Cs' goings-on, remember?"

"Scream if you need me," he said.

I sat on Helen's cot with Hector and let Miss Spinns have mine.

"We must be quick," the old woman whispered. "I'm about to get nicked for that photograph on the beach."

"We wish for you to tell us—" said Hector.

"What I want is—" said Miss Spinns at the same time. She and I had each pulled out our notebooks, ready to record essential points.

"Shall we take turns?" said Hector. "You may begin."

"Thank you, young man," said Miss Spinns, in her Miss Spinns voice. "So polite."

Too polite on occasion, I could not help but think.

"You don't deserve a single answer from us," I hissed. "You are the most deceitful, conniving trickster I ever met."

"Where precisely did you spot the hat retrieved by the police?" The reporter's voice this time.

"It is snagged on a prickle bush, on the face of the cliff below St. Michael's church," said Hector. Perhaps he was more polite than I, but he was only telling her what the police already knew.

"It could have been blown there by the wind!" said our guest. "What made you think otherwise? Was there any scrap of evidence that the professor had been up top?"

The second it took for Hector and me to glance at one another was long enough for her to know the answer.

"Aha!" she said. "There *is* something—"

Dash it! Despite my particular determination not to cooperate, we'd already put a nugget in her open palm. Well, *humph*.

"I believe it's our turn to ask a question," I said. Oscar was quietly humming outside. What should I ask? What did she know that we could learn from no one else?

"What are you doing at Camp Crewe?" I said.

Miss Spinns and Hector both looked surprised. I wasn't asking about the murder, but about why this old lady—who was not really an old lady—had been here before the murder had occurred.

"I answered an advertisement in the *Torquay Voice*," said Miss Spinns, shrugging like a casual young man.

"The newspaper where you work?" said Hector.

"Yes," she said. "A secretary was required to assist at the site of a paleontological survey. She must be able to type and must not be bothered by having a female employer. That was intriguing enough for me. Worth a few days of investigation. Then Nina made the discovery of a lifetime. I had a scoop to set the world of science alight! The murder, to be crass, was butter on bacon."

"So, you came along in disguise," I said.

"Well, yes," said Miss Spinns. "A woman must always have an escape route ready."

"And you watched them up close for weeks," I said. "You wrote their letters. You read their letters. You faded into a corner of the work tent and—"

She nodded. "And eavesdropped on every word they said."

"Did you see anything that makes you believe she killed him?" I said. "Because what I don't understand is, why would she do it like that? Why would she push him off a cliff?"

192

Miss Spinns' fingers slid up and began to scratch behind one ear. I suddenly realized that her flat gray hair in its tight chignon must be a wig. A hot and uncomfortable wig.

"I don't know yet," said Miss Spinns, "but I truly hope that she is not the killer. Clever women—especially when it comes to skeletons—are too rare! If Nina killed her husband, she has tainted the cause for hundreds of others! People will think, *Ha! Women can't be scientists! Women can't be* trusted. *They are unreliable, hysterical murderers* . . . More than anything I want her to be innocent."

"But it is not what we want that matters," said Hector. "Innocent or guilty is merely what we must determine."

"Hello," we heard Oscar say, quite suddenly.

"Hallo, Oscar!" Arthur's voice rang right outside the tent. "Jarvis rode me both ways on his handlebars. I'll wager he hasn't washed in a month!"

"That's nice," said Oscar, clearly not too interested.

"P.C. Sackett agreed to row the boat for us tomorrow," Arthur said. "Jarvis told him Everett would pay five pounds!"

Miss Spinns turned to a fresh page in her notebook and wrote that down.

"Waste of money," said Oscar. "He's too podgy to tie his own bootlaces. How can he row a heavy boat?"

"Well, he owns it, doesn't he? And he rowed the dead body, didn't he?" said Arthur.

"Like a podgy old man." I could almost hear Oscar's eyes rolling.

"What are you doing?" said Arthur.

"Counting the legs on this spider," said Oscar.

"Probably eight," said Arthur.

"Eight?" said Oscar. "You don't say."

"The police are here again," said Arthur. "Sergeant Harley and my cousin Ronnie. Looking for Miss Spinns. Ronnie won't speak to me because of being on duty. He's over in the shop yard, grilling the quarrymen. Have you seen her?"

"What would I want to see her for?" said Oscar.

"Clever boy," whispered Miss Spinns. She grinned at me and I grinned back. It was one of Mr. Fibbley's favorite tricks—to evade a question by asking another question. But then I remembered she didn't deserve a smile, and I scowled instead.

"Do you think she killed him?" said Arthur. "Are they here to arrest her?"

"I don't think she killed him," said Oscar, "but she might have a clue or something—from being with B-C so much, you know?"

They were quiet a moment. We could hear the thwack of a hammer from the shop yard, where Mr. Jarvis and

Mr. Volkov were adapting the broken barrow into something suitable for boat transport. If P.C. Guff was trying to ask them questions, those hammer thuds meant that he was being ignored.

"If Ronnie Guff were my cousin," Oscar said, "I'd plague him till he told me about the coroner's report. Don't you want to know what they found on B-C's body that makes them think it's murder?"

"I suppose," said Arthur.

"It's the key to the whole mystery!" said Oscar.

"You think?"

"And you're the only one who can find out," said Oscar.

"I suppose it can't hurt to ask him," said Arthur.

"Worst thing that can happen, he tells you to piss off," said Oscar.

"Right," we heard Arthur say. "I'll give it a try." Footsteps swished through grass and Oscar began to hum again.

"Hold on!" Arthur's voice called out. "Who's in the girls' tent?"

"Is someone in there?" Oscar sounded surprised.

We'd been so quiet! What had given us away?

"Extra shoes," said Arthur.

Dash it! We'd taken them off without thinking. Miss Spinns too. They sat outside like a circus banner advertising hot popped corn. Three pairs! Even Arthur could count.

A moment later, the flap parted and Arthur's head poked through.

"I say, didn't you hear me outside?" said Arthur. "Sergeant Harley is here. He wants to speak with you, Miss Spinns."

She sighed an old-lady sigh. Hector and I traded a look of barely disguised exasperation.

"Please to tell him that you do not find us," said Hector. I gaped. He expected *Arthur* to lie to the police? "Or perhaps you walk in a different direction from the one that leads directly to the sergeant?" Hector said. "For a few minutes more?"

"I do need to find my cousin," said Arthur. "P.C. Guff." He began backing out of the tent. "With my family connection, I may be the one person who can persuade him to talk."

"Excellent," I said. "Off you go."

We counted to ten and listened to Oscar hum.

Miss Spinns leaned closer and whispered, in a rush of words, "Miss Spinns is about to lose all access to Camp Crewe. But you two will be here, with your bright little eyes and your sharp little ears and your keen little brain cells. When we've worked together in the past, I got my story and you solved the mystery. So, can we do it again? You tell me if—"

"You want us to pass along our deductions?" I said. "That's not working together. That's us working for you!"

"You know I always—"

"Oscar?" We froze at Everett's voice. "What are you doing?"

"Examining spiders," said Oscar. Hector shuddered.

"If you see Aggie, please let her know I'm looking for her. And the sergeant is here for Miss Spinns."

"If I see them, I'll tell them," Oscar added.

"Right-o," said Everett.

A minute went by. Oscar began to hum again. I poked my head through the gap in the tent flap.

"Has he gone?"

"Yes. And the sergeant is inside the work tent right this moment, so maybe get the old lady out now."

I lifted the flap and beckoned to Miss Spinns. Hector followed, blinking in the bright light.

"Go to the backhouse," I suggested to Miss Spinns, "as if you've been washing your hands." Shoes back on, she scuttled away, elderly again. A few moments later, Sergeant Harley and Everett emerged from the work tent.

"Aggie!" called Everett.

"Hullo!" I waved. "Have you seen this bug in Oscar's jar?" Grannie Jane would have been suspicious in an instant, but Everett did not know me well enough to discern such false enthusiasm.

"Have *you* seen—oh!" Everett stopped. Miss Spinns ambled up the path from the backhouse, patting her hands on her skirt, as we all knew there was no towel beside the makeshift basin.

Then Arthur arrived from the shop yard, looking slightly sweaty and very pleased with himself. He pulled up short at the sight of the men, his cousin a few steps behind. Arthur bugged his eyes wide at us, wiggling his hands in a signal known only to him. I ignored him for the moment, wishing to hear what the sergeant wanted with Miss Spinns.

"There you are, Constable Guff," said Sergeant Harley. He indicated Miss Spinns, and asked in a stern voice, "Is this the person you encountered on Thursday morning on the beach near the deceased?"

"Yes, sir," said Constable Guff. "That's her. She tricked me, she did. She told me—"

Sergeant Harley put up a hand. "Thank you, Constable." I'd have stopped him too, if I were the sergeant. What foolish policeman allows a secretary to take pictures of a dead body?

"Miss Spinns?" Nina's quiet voice penetrated the kerfuffle of men. She stood in the entrance of the work tent, hands plunged into the front pockets of her waistcoat.

Miss Spinns drew herself up. This must be the encounter she dreaded more than any other.

"Were you not happy here?" said Nina. "You appeared to be fascinated with our work."

"I was," said Miss Spinns. "I still am. But I—"

"How dare you!" Everett's vexation swirled like a cloud of gnats. "You have broken our trust!" He towered over Miss Spinns' small form. "Was this your plan all along? To spy on us and sell nuggets to greedy journalists? What a bit of luck to suddenly have a murder along with a major fossil discovery!" Everett's shoulders trembled with indignation. "Or *was* it luck? Where were *you* on Wednesday evening, I wonder?"

"Everett!" said Nina. "Don't be silly. Look at her."

"Looks can be deceiving," he said. "As we all have learned by now."

"Mr. Tobie," said Sergeant Harley. "Leave the questions to us. Miss Spinns, if you'll come this way." He nodded at P.C. Guff.

"Hold on." Everett pushed his way closer. "I'd like to know if there are other grim photographs waiting to pop up. This man was your employer's husband!"

Miss Spinns blushed and studied the canvas wall of the work tent.

"Where is your camera, miss?" said Sergeant Harley.

Miss Spinns glanced sideways at Everett. "I had the film developed at the chemist in town," she admitted in a low voice. "Your own photographs, of the ichthyosaur and the ammonites, they're in an envelope under the cushion on my stool."

"You used *my* camera? *My* camera took that terrible

picture?" Everett batted clenched fists against his thighs. It seemed entirely possible that he might knock the old lady to the ground. "You *stole* my camera!"

"I *borrowed* your camera," she said. "It is back in its case. Not stolen."

"Sergeant! She stole my Brownie camera!"

"Constable?" said Sergeant Harley. "Accompany her to the station. I will ride ahead and meet you there."

Miss Spinns turned abruptly and marched up the track to the town road at her usual energetic pace. P.C. Guff bumbled after her. He picked up his bicycle and pushed it with vigor to catch her up as the sergeant rode easily past.

"Arthur," said Everett. "Be a good lad and watch that they reach the main road. She is perfectly capable of escaping and darting off across the fields. If that happens, please come back to warn us." Arthur saluted and raced away.

"You're giving her too much credit," said Nina.

"I could wring her neck," Everett said. "May that be the last we see of her."

No chance of a neck-wringing, I was certain. Miss Spinns would not be seen again. But Hector and I knew that Mr. Gus Fibbley could never be got rid of so easily as that.

CHAPTER 20

A SIGN OF MALEVOLENCE

As ARTHUR FOLLOWED P.C. Guff and Miss Spinns, I followed Arthur, with Oscar and Hector on my heels. The prisoner seemed quite submissive and even whistled a few bars of "Under the Bamboo Tree." She kept well ahead of the constable, who stumbled behind with his bicycle. Only when P.C. Guff waved us off with a glare and a foot stomp did Arthur end his pursuit.

"Arthur!" I said. "Come on. Spill your news!" We sat in the shade of a hedge. "What did your cousin say about the coroner's report?"

"Ronnie wouldn't say anything to start," said Arthur, "but it came out after a bit, with me making it sound as if I knew most of it already."

"Good tactic," I said.

"So?" said Oscar. "What's the secret medical evidence?"

"Bruising." Arthur said it slowly.

"But naturally, there is bruising!" said Hector. "He falls from a great height!"

"This is different," said Arthur. "This is *un*natural bruising. Not from falling or being knocked about by waves."

"Well, go on!" Oscar said.

"He'd got two ovals, symmetrical ovals, here and here." Arthur pointed to his own upper chest, over the heart on the left and at a similar spot on the right.

"Ooh la la," said Hector, climbing to his feet. He rubbed his head where the brain cells must have been causing great friction.

"What do bruises like that mean?" said Oscar.

"The report says that the impact occurred shortly before he died," said Arthur. "By human hands."

Hector urged the boys to stand with him. "Make the fierce threat," he said to Oscar. "You wish me harm."

Oscar growled and raised his arms wide, as if to attack like a bear.

Hector whooshed his hands forward and tapped Oscar on the chest with the heels of his palms. "But I am angry," said Hector, "and the push is most violent. Hard enough to make a mark."

"That's what Ronnie said." Arthur was nodding vigorously.

"Is it anger?" I said. "Or fear? Maybe *he*'s trying to kill *you*? And you're fighting for your life."

He had some help going over . . .

"We've got so many suspects," I said.

"What if we start with the most likely?" said Arthur. "The one with obvious evidence of having been in a fight. The one with a blackened eye."

Oscar glared at Arthur. "Are you saying that my father is a murderer?"

"Someone has to say it," said Arthur. "Since you won't admit it yourself."

Oscar took the stance of a boxer about to throw a punch, his fists clenched and jabbing. Arthur raised his own fists.

"Non!" cried Hector.

"Stop it!" I pushed between them. "Both of you, sit! No one say a word for a full minute." I silently counted. "Mr. Osteda was one of *six* men in The Crow's Nest on Wednesday night who was on bad terms with the professor. Any of them could have been with him in the cemetery. Arthur, sit down."

"I'm not sitting." Arthur's chin jutted out and his upper lip was sweaty. "And I'm not staying. You all think you're so clever, sleuthing and keeping secrets. Well, the professor is dead! Pushed over a cliff! And there's an American with a shiner right in front of our faces!" He spun around and marched across the field to the shop yard. We suddenly heard the hammering, as if it had become louder to welcome Arthur. Oscar glared after him, and then at the ground. He wasn't sitting either, so Hector and I stood again.

"I wouldn't have hit him," he muttered. "Just, you know, he insulted me."

"It would be hard to accuse a person's father of being a murderer," I said, "without it sounding like an insult."

"I know it looks bad," said Oscar. "My dad has already admitted he's a liar, and now someone is dead. We have only his word that the black eye came from Cavalier Jones, and not from Mr. B-C. Why would anyone believe that?"

"Do *you* believe that?" said Hector.

Oscar raised his eyes to look at Hector directly and gave a curt nod. "I do," he said. "I've had a lot of practice deciphering my father's truths and lies. I'd vouch for truth on that one."

"What about the other people in the pub?" I said. "When your father was telling his story last night, who seemed suspicious to you?"

Oscar looked at the ground again, rubbing his toe along the same patch of spiky grass.

"Yvonne?" he said, at last.

"*Yvonne?*" I said.

In the same breath, Hector said, "The barmaid?"

"It wasn't my father. I'd swear to that!" said Oscar. "It wasn't any of the men. The killer was a woman, that much I know." He looked about, as if for an escape route. "That's all I'm going to say, whether you like it or not." He spun around and began to run. *Run!*

"Wait!" I called.

"You wish to race after him and pin him to the ground?" said Hector.

"A *woman*?" I said. "Why does he think that?"

"A most intriguing declaration," said Hector.

"He must know something we don't know," I said.

"Indeed, he must. And what if he is right? Where does the logic take us?"

"Mr. B-C was a visitor in Lyme Regis," I said. "How many women did he even know? His wife. And Helen. We know it's not Miss Spinns."

"As Oscar says, there is also the third girl. Yvonne."

"He met her an hour before he died!" I protested.

"Do we know this?" said Hector. "Is it not possible that he visits Yvonne many times since Camp Crewe is established? We are latecomers, you and I. The others, they are living here already for three weeks."

"I suppose . . . but I still think the women at the camp are more likely," I said. "Shouldn't we look at them before getting distracted by a barmaid?"

"The young daughter of the cook and the unhappy wife," said Hector.

"Nina has the most obvious motive," I said.

The young paleontologist picked up the most recent issue of the Old Bones Scientific Journal, *and stared at the table of contents with a drumming heart. It held the article that had tested her brain and her faith and her science for several months of devoted writing. The title was there in boldface type—"Envisioning Prehistory: How evidence of ancient life confounds the Bible." She swallowed. Beneath those daring words was a grievous error. Hot, furious tears threatened to fall. Her husband had promised that her work would be published under her own name—or not at all—but there, in bold print, was* his *name instead! Behind her back, he had grandly assumed that it mattered more to have her theories shared with the world than to acknowledge whose theories they were. She wanted to slap him. She wanted to feel the burn of her palm against his cheek, the hard shield of his chest bone as she pounded him with her fists. How dare he?*

"Nina had plenty of reason to kill her husband," I said. "She didn't like him very much, to begin with."

"She disputes everything he wishes," agreed Hector.

"She likely had wishes of her own!"

The blustery professor had insulted her—along with everyone else—on the day he died. Each time he argued with someone, his wife had secretly rejoiced. Her plan was unfolding without a flaw. She had no trouble provoking him into a last outburst, overheard by those useful children, as well as the fussy old secretary. Carrying a collecting sack and her husband's flask, the gleeful wife engineered a secret exit from the camp and had a message delivered to her husband at the pub.

"Shall we make amends? Let's watch the sunset together. 9:15, St. Michael's churchyard."

And there, on the top of the steepest cliff, her revenge could finally unfold . . .

"What if her plan depended on the body disappearing into the sea," I said, "instead of washing up so inconveniently on the shore? She had only to give him a push and let the tide do its work."

Hector nodded slowly and added to the hypothesis. "He disappears. She circulates a rumor that he abandons her . . . She alone knows he is lying at the bottom of the sea with the fishes and the fossils."

I said, "Why does she kill him, though, instead of simply leaving?"

"Leaving a marriage is not so simple," said Hector.

"No," I said. "I expect it's full of anguish. For both parties."

"But not so full of anguish as prison," said Hector, "or being hanged."

"Hanged," I whispered.

The hangman—usually so coldhearted—could not help but blink away a tear upon seeing the killer's pale, freckled face. Her light copper tresses had been shorn the night before, so as not to impede the action of the rope.

"If the tide had done its part," I said, "she would have got away with it. She could pretend that the professor became a bitter recluse, while she struggled on to make her name in science."

"She continues her studies and her excavations," said Hector. "A brave, mistreated young wife, but now the author of her own work."

"What about opportunity?" I said. "Did she have time to do it?"

Hector closed his eyes. "First, the sun is setting," he said, "and we are having the bonfire. Nina, she summons Everett and is noisily much worried. *Why does her husband not come home?*"

"We hadn't seen her worry about him before that evening," I said, "or particularly care anything about him. He'd only gone to have a pint of ale at the pub, after all."

"Everett joins Nina to search," said Hector. "We see the torch lights flashing here and there."

"And then Oscar arrived," I said. "The first thing he asked was whether Nina had gone to town. Why do you suppose he was thinking about that?"

"She also is a woman," said Hector, "as Oscar imagines the killer to be. What does he know, I wonder?"

"We assume Nina went to bed after going with Everett to look for her husband," I said, "but what if she actually sneaked away to meet him in the graveyard and knock him off the cliff?"

Our Detection Consultation was interrupted by a holler from Arthur that we were to come for our lesson in practical fossil-retrieval skills. Oscar came too, when called, wearing a face that pretended his earlier exit had been nothing unusual.

Nina had arranged new supplies on a clear area atop one of the worktables to instruct us in the art of making something called a field jacket. This was a method of wrapping the fragile bits of a fossilized skeleton for protection during transportation. Usually, she explained, a thick layer of plaster was involved, to make a hard shell that could be chipped away later. But because Izzy would have to be moved so quickly, there'd be no time for plaster to set.

"Your small hands will be particularly useful," said Nina, "for slipping into the cracks and crevices." Her own deft fingers showed us how to swaddle the bones instead of using plaster, encasing each in springy tufts of lambswool bound with linen bandages. We practiced on starfish and bits of vertebrates and other things that had sticky-outy parts or odd shapes.

Oscar said he'd done it before the real way, with plaster, when he'd assisted his father on a dig in America. He even mixed up a small bowl of plaster, under Nina's watchful eye. Using a fist-sized ammonite, he showed us how to put the wool padding on first and then the plaster. He set that aside, though, and we began to time ourselves with the stopwatch to see how quickly we could make the woolly jackets. We improved our speed with each try, knowing that every second mattered in tomorrow's enterprise.

Everett came along and had us prepare collecting sacks to be ready for the morning. In each, we put several bundles of linen strips and a great quantity of lambswool squished down tightly. We also packed a penknife and two flasks of drinking water. Finally, Nina said that *we'd do* and sent us away, ravenous for our suppers.

Oscar sat at one end of the big table, and Arthur pointedly sat at the other to devour the shepherd's pie and boiled carrots. While Helen was delivering Nina's plate to the work tent, we heard the ominous creak of Sergeant Harley's bicycle. Mutters of *What now?* went around the table.

"We shouldn't really be complaining," said Everett. "One of these visits will bring news of a solution to the mystery."

"This is most optimistic," said Hector. "You have *met* the sergeant, yes?"

The sergeant refused an invitation to join us for pudding, sniffing with self-importance. "Is there somewhere private we can speak, Mr. Tobie?"

"Is this about Miss Spinns? I've just calmed down, after being so vexed with her earlier. Shall I get Nina?"

"You may not want Mrs. Blenningham-Crewe to listen in," said Sergeant Harley.

"She's busy, in any case," said Everett. "We're rather down to the wire on the recovery plans. There is no private place in a camp. Can we not chat here?"

"This is not a *chat*," said Sergeant Harley. "I have questions."

"Spit it out, man," Everett said.

"This is not a casual matter!" The sergeant's voice got louder. "It has come to my attention that you and the deceased were in hostile conflict on the day that he died. He terminated your employ and insisted that you be gone by morning. Is that correct?"

"Did Miss Spinns tell you that?" said Everett. "The woman who stole my camera and took a photograph of a—"

Nina came out of the work tent at that moment and padded over in her bare feet.

"I heard raised voices," she said. "Has something happened with Miss Spinns?"

"She has provided further information about an incident concerning Mr. Tobie and your husband," said Sergeant Harley.

Everett sighed. "What you need to know is that Mr. Blenningham-Crewe had a bit of a temper. He was in a foul mood that afternoon, brought on by—"

"Did he or did he not ask you to leave the premises?"

"Well, he did say something like that, but—"

"And here you still are, *on the premises*!" The sergeant smirked, as if he were telling a clever story. "While *he* is now *dead*!"

"I take exception to your linking those two—"

"And I take exception to your not having mentioned a violent argument with a murder victim on the afternoon of his demise!"

"It was not a *violent*—"

The sergeant interrupted. "You omitted telling the police a crucial fact. Is that because you're guilty? Or because you're a foreigner? Or both?"

Everett's mouth fell open in surprise. "What makes you think I am a foreigner?"

"You don't look English. Were you born in England?"

"Well, no, but my father—"

"That makes you foreign," said Sergeant Harley.

"Stop right there!" Without seeming to have moved, Nina now stood directly in front of the sergeant, bristling at the unfairness of his remarks. "Blast, blast, blast and dammit!" she spat. "Where he was born is entirely beside the point! You—"

Everett put out a hand to touch her shoulder. "Nina," he said.

Nina shook her head. Everett withdrew his hand, but not before Sergeant Harley made a point of staring at the hand of an unmarried man on the shoulder of a pretty young widow.

"Mr. Tobie, you are to accompany me to the station in town," said the sergeant.

"Wait! Sergeant Harley!" Nina took a deep breath, seemingly to prevent herself from a further display of rage. "You are making a mistake. Mr. Tobie is a valuable and trustworthy member of our team. The argument with Howard was nothing important."

"Your opinion is noted," said the sergeant. "But he's clearly not from around here, and we've got plenty more questions."

CHAPTER 21

A BRAWNY REPLACEMENT

"YOU . . . OFFICIOUS PINHEAD!" cried Nina. "You narrow-minded cretin! You strutting—" Her array of insults grew as the sergeant took Everett's arm and led him to where his bicycle was parked. He hooked a strap around Everett's belt and attached it to the crossbar.

Nina, following, finally took a breath and transformed herself into a cool-tempered scientist.

"We need him," she said to Sergeant Harley. "We have a critical project underway. You are obstructing a venture sponsored by the Natural History Museum in London. How long will this take?"

"We'll have him overnight, and maybe longer." The sergeant flashed that smirk again. "Depending on how good his answers are."

"Nina, listen to me carefully." Everett's words poured out in a calm, steady stream, like water from a hotel tap. "Are you listening? You know exactly what you're doing, don't forget that for one minute. I will be fine. You can worry about me on Monday. If I'm not back by then, Aggie, you will please write to Lord Greyson. I had nothing to do with B-C's death. You know that. I was with you, Nina! Looking for B-C! Or with the children, sitting at the campfire. This is batty old Spinns dodging my accusation of theft. Don't worry. Jarvis and Volkov are loyal and strong. Maybe Arthur has another cousin or two to help with the lift. You'll—"

Sergeant Harley shook Everett's arm. "That's enough, you."

"You're making a mistake," Nina repeated. "You are arresting the person least likely to hurt—"

"You're awfully sympathetic to the man suspected of murdering your husband," said Sergeant Harley. "Will we think about whether he had an accomplice, Mrs. Blenningham-Crewe?"

Nina threw up her hands in frustration. "Idiot," she muttered. "Weasel-faced ninny."

Everett, tethered to the bicycle, walked up the rutted track with his head held high. The sergeant swayed precariously on his bicycle as he tried to match his pace with Everett's stride. We watched in silence until they disappeared. Should I write to James this minute and beg him to rescue his friend? But it was Saturday evening, and no post would go out until Monday. Tomorrow was what mattered! Spring tide and the recovery operation! A chill settled over the camp, and not only because dusk was looming.

Eventually, Nina shook herself. "Well, Arthur?" she said. "*Have* you got a nicer, burlier cousin than P.C. Guff? We need someone brawny and strong."

"You need Cavalier Jones!" said Oscar. "The Strongest Man in the World."

"That is a brilliant idea," said Arthur, forgetting his anger at Oscar. "Cavalier Jones can lift a pony over his head!"

Nina had not been with us at the circus. She'd heard us talk of his famous feats, of course, but had she listened? She often paid little attention unless a conversation had some impact on her work. She hadn't needed the Strongest Man in the World until this minute.

"How do we find him?" she said.

"At the circus!" Our cries tumbled over each other. "The circus is still in town! Tonight's the last night! We know him! Especially Hector!"

Nina agreed that it was worth a try, that we should walk to the circus grounds to ask the man. Did we feel we were well enough acquainted for such a mission? We were! Most certainly we were!

We gathered sweaters and brought our torches for the return journey.

The walk was not long, perhaps twenty minutes. We ignored the road we'd taken with Mr. Osteda on the occasion of our circus outing and used instead a route devised by Arthur. The farmers wouldn't mind, he said. He led us to a path marked by fence posts, along the edges of several fields, through a shadowy copse of trees and across a meadow of clover and weeds. From there, we could see the circus flags and even hear the rousing music of the finale parade booming into the gathering twilight. It must have been quite frightening for rabbits and peahens to suddenly have trombones as neighbors!

Hordes of happy circus-goers drifted away as we arrived at the backstage area between the main tent and the Rare Sights exhibit. Band members were putting their instruments into sturdy black cases. The flute lady corralled the dancing dogs, who were not quite so well behaved when faced with their dinner bowls as they had been in the ring. I thought of my dog, Tony, gobbling down table scraps, and approved of the performers' true doggy natures.

Mr. Cavalier Jones removed his top hat and sent it sailing, with a flick of the wrist, directly into the hands of Ned, the trumpet player. They both laughed, as if this were a ritual they practiced after every show and this time had performed perfectly. I surreptitiously examined the cut on the ringmaster's lip, in case it declared evidence of a tussle with the murder victim. But it had healed and was barely visible beneath the twisty mustache.

"Hello, my young friends!" he cried. "To what do we owe this honor? Has Master Hector come to visit our Spotted Pony?" Then his face became solemn. "Is the poor widow in trouble?"

"Of a kind, monsieur," said Hector. "We have a matter of importance to place in your hands."

"I am intrigued," said the strongman.

We told him quickly about the failure of today's rehearsal effort. As planned on the walk over, we did not give the reason for the extra burden of Everett's absence, except that he was assisting the investigation into Mr. B-C's death.

Cavalier Jones clapped his hands. "You need a man of my talents!" He was as delighted as a robin in a birdbath. "Nothing will give me greater pleasure! Do I bring chains? Tools of any kind? The circus is well supplied with anything that might be needed. Except an elephant, alas. Someday, I mean to have an elephant."

We arranged the time for tomorrow—in accord with low tide at eight minutes after eleven in the morning—and set off back to camp in high spirits, our mission happily accomplished. When we came among the trees, night blurred the path and shadows deepened. Our little troupe drew together, and our steps slowed over roots and brambles we could not properly see. The beams of our torches lit mere polka dots on the forest floor.

Then, *sna-app!* We froze as one. Close behind us came a shuffle and then another snapping twig.

"Who's there?" I whispered.

Arthur crouched to pat the ground around us and came up with a barbed stick.

"I don't think we need a *weapon*," I said, not quite believing my own words. "It's a deer or—"

"Oi!" called Arthur. "Whoever's hiding behind that tree had better show himself!" He puffed himself up, pretending to be big and bold. He took a giant step forward. "ONE!" he called. "TWO!"

Oscar crept away from us and darted among the trees, closer to where we'd heard the sounds.

"An animal will have run by now," I said.

"THREE!" cried Arthur. Oscar curled his hands into claws and made a snarling sound. Out stepped a small rumpled man in a gray linen suit. He wore a battered cap and had a canvas rucksack slung across one shoulder. The glass of his gold-rimmed spectacles glinted in the torchlight.

He cleared his throat and glanced at Oscar, still in attack pose.

"Mr. Augustus Fibbley," I said. "Fancy meeting you here."

"Miss Morton," he said, in Mr. Fibbley's husky voice. "Master Perot." Gone was the creaky old-lady voice of Miss Spinns. Mr. Fibbley was the disguise he was most comfortable in, and the one we'd known the longest.

"You know this guy?" Oscar lowered his claws.

"He's a reporter," I said, "from the newspaper in Torquay, where Hector and I both live. Mr. Fibbley, this is Oscar Osteda and Arthur Haystead."

"Why do you follow us?" said Hector.

Arthur held his stick at the ready. "It's not nice to scare people."

"It was not my intention to frighten you," said Mr. Fibbley. "I was worried about four little ducklings out for a walk at this time of night."

"How long were you behind us?" I said.

"I happened to see your photographer arrive with a police-and-bicycle escort at the lockup in town," he said. "I wondered what the solution might be to finding yourselves one man down for tomorrow's operation. Following you was one path to the answer."

"Wait a minute," said Oscar. "Is this the guy who wrote that article with the picture of B-C on the beach?"

"That wasn't nice at all," said Arthur.

"So, you're in league with Miss Spinns?" said Oscar. "That photo got her into deep trouble. You know that?"

"We hide the newspaper from the widow to avoid

220

causing the distress," said Hector, "but it is most upsetting for everyone else."

"Very unpopular," said Arthur, "your friend, Miss Spinns."

"She's the reason for Mr. Tobie being in jail tonight," said Oscar.

This situation was becoming ever more precarious.

"Mr. Fibbley?" I said. "I think perhaps you should go away—"

"Yes," he said. "I think I'll head back to town." He hoisted the rucksack further up on his shoulder and touched his cap in farewell.

I finished my sentence. "And do not let us see you again."

CHAPTER 22

AN UNUSUAL COMPANY

I FELT THAT MY WORDS to Mr. Fibbley had been firm and clear. *Go away and do not let us see you again.*

And yet, come Sunday morning, I arrived for breakfast at our table under the kitchen canopy and found Mr. Fibbley seated at my usual place, raising a teacup to be refilled by a giggling and pink-cheeked Helen. Helen, who'd hardly smiled since the news of Mr. B-C's death. She had never refilled *my* teacup! We were expected to go to the trolley and serve ourselves. But here she was, offering to bring toast to the most duplicitous man I'd ever met!

"Well, here she is!" he cried upon seeing me. "The lovely granddaughter of my friend Mrs. Morton! You'll be surprised at my presence here, no doubt?"

"No doubt." I glared my most ferocious glare. Helen cast me a puzzled look. Why was I being so rude to this charming person? Hector appeared from the direction of the backhouse. His hair was damp and flat, the way he liked it. His face shone from having been splashed. He looked from me to Mr. Fibbley and back.

"You remember my grandmother's friend, Mr. Fibbley?" I said.

"Naturally, I remember." Hector glanced at Helen. "It is not so long ago that we see each other, and Monsieur Fibbley is a memorable person, after all."

Mr. Fibbley gave a short chuckle at Hector's great wit, but was prevented from whatever irritating comment he might have made by the arrival of Nina. She came from the shop yard, where she must have been finalizing plans with the quarrymen. She appeared to be making calculations inside her head, raising one finger at a time while her lips moved silently. She paid no attention to the stranger in our midst as she poured tea for herself at the trolley.

"Mrs. Blenningham-Crewe," said Mr. Fibbley. "Please allow me to extend my heartfelt condolences at your grievous loss."

Nina barely looked his way. He had not offered his name.

"As it happens," he said, "I am a writer on the subject of digging up what has thus far remained hidden. Your ichthyosaur is of the greatest interest."

Nina stirred sugar into her tea. "I don't know how you got in here, sir, but we are not speaking with journa—"

"I bring a letter from Mr. Tobie," he said.

Nina spun around, face brightening. "What news?"

"I'm afraid he is still in custody, ma'am. He was confined to a cell when I spoke to him. He was permitted to dictate a letter for me to deliver to you." Mr. Fibbley pulled out a folded paper and gave it to Nina. As it was not inside a sealed envelope, I knew that Mr. Fibbley had most certainly read it. Wait! Had he said *dictate*? Mr. Fibbley had most certainly *composed* it! Hector's eyes met mine. The lift of his eyebrow told that he was thinking the same thing. A confidence trick was being performed as we sat quietly watching.

Nina beckoned to the reporter, disguised today as a caring person. "Come with me," she said. "I'd like to hear more about how Mr. Tobie is faring."

Mr. Fibbley stood, picked up his fresh cup of tea and gave Helen a cheeky grin. "Thanks, duck," he said.

"Grrr," I whispered to Hector.

"I require exercise," he said. "Will I walk around the work tent?"

"Yes, try," I said, "but—" He did not wait for me to add, *Be careful.*

Mr. Jarvis and Mr. Volkov trundled past, carrying a stack of wooden stretchers topped with a couple of horse blankets. Each stretcher had handles at both ends and along the sides as well, so that two or more men could lift a load together.

"Oi, miss," called Mr. Jarvis to Helen. "Give us a few buns, will you?"

"You men! Always hungry." Helen obligingly wrapped four buns in a tea cloth and laid the packet on top of the stretchers beside two spades, a mattock and a coil of hefty rope.

"Good luck, gentlemen!" she said.

The other boys had arrived for breakfast by the time Hector returned. From a shake of his head, I understood that he'd heard nothing of Nina's conversation with Mr. Fibbley. We had a momentary celebration when Helen delivered a platter of pancakes, sprinkled with brown sugar.

"What do you think Everett is eating in jail?" said Arthur.

A single night in the icy cell had turned the prisoner's hair the color of snow. Sunken cheeks, bloodshot eyes, a forlorn heart . . .

"Gruel," I said. "Infested with weevils."

Gloom fell upon us. But then came the mechanical clattering of an approaching vehicle.

Hurrah! The Strongest Man in the World was here to save the day! He hitched the Spotted Pony to the fence beside the backhouse and unloaded a coiled chain from the Runabout.

Nina emerged from the work tent, followed by a cheerful Mr. Fibbley. What devious plot had he set in motion that made him smile like that? Aha! Everett's precious Brownie camera hung on a strap around his neck.

"Good morning, dear lady!" called Cavalier Jones.

"What's *he* doing here?" Oscar was staring not at Mr. Jones but at Mr. Fibbley. Last night this man had been in the forest, lurking in the undergrowth. And here he was now, looking like a cat who'd unlatched a birdcage.

"He brought a letter," I said, "from Everett at the jail-house."

"Your timing is perfect," said Nina to Mr. Jones. "We're setting out now." To Mr. Fibbley, she said, "I'll leave you here with the young people. They'll bring you along in good time to reach the site at low tide, which occurs this morning at eight minutes after eleven. I'm heading down to meet P.C. Sackett and his boat."

"Wonderful," said Mr. Fibbley, "and thank you for the opportunity to use Mr. Tobie's camera as he requested. It is an occasion worthy of—"

Nina had already turned away with Mr. Jones, and they strode toward the path to the beach.

I scowled at Mr. Fibbley with what I hoped he recognized as disgust. "Does Everett know that he gave you permission to use the camera?" I said.

Mr. Osteda's motorcar arrived to interrupt, with horn blaring and with my grandmother sitting grandly next to the driver.

"Oh good, you're here!" I hugged her. It had entirely slipped my mind that she was coming! Since yesterday's farewell, we had seen the last of Miss Spinns, witnessed Everett's unjust arrest, ventured through eerie twilit countryside to recruit the Strongest Man in the World and watched our main suspect calmly prepare herself for battle with a prehistoric monster. The excitement of a visit from Grannie Jane had been overshadowed.

"Thank you, Mr. Osteda, for playing chauffeur," I said.

His eye was less swollen today, the livid violet fading to mauve and yellow on his brown skin.

"My very great pleasure," he said, "and one more chance to remind the lady that I am ready and willing to give the ichthyosaur a good home."

"Goodness," said my grandmother, suddenly face-to-face with Mr. Fibbley. "This is most unexpected. You do have a way of simply appearing."

"It is my specialty, Mrs. Morton," said Mr. Fibbley.

Grannie introduced him to Oscar's father. "This young man has been quite useful at moments of crisis," she explained. "Though I cannot say his presence is a comfort, as it often accompanies disaster."

"Alas," said Mr. Fibbley, "a reporter thrives on the disasters of others."

Helen bustled out from the cook tent with a small hamper, which Mr. Osteda gallantly hoisted. The rest of us were spurred to gather our own supplies. In my specially stitched pocket, I had my notebook and two sharpened pencils. Not that I expected time to write while excavating an ancient fossil! We also carried our collecting sacks, bulging with jacket-making materials and two flasks of water. Eager Mr. Fibbley declared he could wait no longer and hurried ahead, with Arthur and Hector close on his heels. The rest of us brought the lunch, a parasol, and a folding chair for Grannie Jane's vigil. She would view the drama from the same spot on the cliff where we'd watched yesterday's disappointing dress rehearsal.

"Can you see Constable Sackett's boat, Mrs. Morton?" said Helen. From this high up, the boat appeared to be as small and insubstantial as a leaf.

"Poor fellow," said Grannie Jane. "He's pulling against an ebbing tide!"

"He needs my Oscar," said Mr. Osteda. "One of the best young rowers in Texas." Oscar flushed, but he glanced at me to be sure I'd heard. His boasting had been true after all!

Mr. Jarvis and Mr. Volkov were as far across the ledges as the tide permitted, hefting the burden of four stretchers loaded with digging tools and horse blankets. Mr. Jones carried the chain draped around his neck and shoulders like a scarf. Nina, by herself, strode toward the heap of rocks slowly becoming visible above the water.

"Hadn't we better get moving?" I said.

"We cannot be late on this occasion," Hector agreed.

"Come on, then," said Arthur. "If you're quite comfortable, Mrs. Morton?"

But Oscar's father had recognized Cavalier Jones from afar and made a noise like a cat expelling a hair ball. "Why is *he* one of the party?"

"He has volunteered to assist with the lift," said Oscar. "Maybe you should stay up here with Mrs. Morton? You'll be helping no one if you start a fight. Look what happened last time."

Mr. Osteda ignored his son. No chance he'd allow Cavalier Jones any closer to the ichthyosaur than he himself planned to be. So, it was Helen who stayed with Grannie Jane at the lookout on the cliff, while the rest of us scurried our way down to the beach. I turned to wave at my grandmother before we set out across the ledges, and she twirled her parasol in reply.

P.C. Sackett's lovely boat was painted green with red trim. Gold letters spelled out *Touch Wood* on the side. He had maneuvered it close to the right spot. The boat still had water to float on, but we could see the top of Nina's marker pile every time a wave drew back. The constable tossed an anchor overboard and rested the oars while he bobbed up and down. The tide soon would leave him beached, and his part in the drama could begin. The men deposited their loads on the bumpy seabed, waiting for Izzy to be exposed, when they would all move forward in a rush. Nina paced back and forth, still a few yards from where the boat rocked on little more than a foot of water. She looked like *a hungry lioness stalking her prey, a scholar filling her pen before an examination, a singer humming the warm-up bars before her solo.*

"The weather is on our side, Missus," said Mr. Jarvis. "Wind from the north, offshore, keeping the waves low." There were no waves at all, just now. The sea was calm, the sky hazy, the conditions perfect for the mad race to dig up a poor old sea monster.

Nina had entrusted Hector with Everett's stopwatch, with instructions to report every few minutes on the time ticking by. Izzy would be fully exposed at sixteen minutes before eleven o'clock. Lowest tide would occur at eight minutes past eleven. That turning point, halfway through, meant there'd be twenty-four minutes left before the water came tumbling back to interrupt our task. Task? An almighty, gargantuan labor of Hercules! If we could not have the demigod himself, please let Cavalier Jones perform as heroically! At the moment, the strongman was examining the *Touch Wood*, rocking it gently as if to test its capacity. Mr. Osteda's eyes flicked between him and the fossilized carcass at his feet.

"The time is nineteen minutes before eleven o'clock," said Hector. "Three minutes to the starting gun."

The quarrymen were already wading around the site in their wellies, jabbing in stakes at either end of Izzy's visible parts.

"Sand buildup is light today," said Nina. "We'll have that off in no time."

She inspected her motley crew of rescuers. All but two of the grown-ups were pulling on gloves. Mr. Osteda's hands were jammed in the pockets of his very white trousers. He had not moved one inch from his viewing spot. Mr. Fibbley scribbled in his notebook. Oscar and Arthur and I had less durable cotton versions of the heavy canvas work gloves worn by Nina and the men, but we too were awaiting the signal to begin with pounding hearts.

"Ready?" Nina said.

"Ready!" said Hector. "Take your marks!" He clicked the button. "Go!"

The fossil recovery was underway.

CHAPTER 23

AN URGENT MISSION

"ALL HANDS!" NINA FELL to her knees and began to dig. Seven more of us knelt to help. We scooped and scraped off wet silt and debris left behind by the sea during the night. The scent of seaweed and brine filled the air. When we'd uncovered what was visible of Izzy above the seabed, Nina signaled for us, the children, to scramble out of the way.

"First, the trench," she instructed Cavalier Jones. "Observe the quarrymen."

Nina picked up her tools. Every man now also held a large chisel and a hammer. Mr. Jones watched Mr. Jarvis and Mr. Volkov intently, prepared to mimic their moves. Mr. Jarvis issued clipped instructions, and the others followed orders without hesitation. A chorus of thunking and cracking began.

"Forty-one minutes remaining," Hector called out.

A perimeter was marked by cutting a trough through layers of shale. It looked like the moat around a model-sized castle, about as wide as a man's hand, and a foot deep. Constable Sackett climbed out of his boat, now resting at an angle on the seabed. He grunted as his feet hit the rocky ledge and paused to wipe his forehead with his jacket sleeve. When the trench was complete around Izzy's perimeter, Mr. Volkov and Mr. Jarvis seized their mattocks, equipped with both chopping and digging blades. The work began in earnest, cutting through years of shale layered like the pages of a book.

The fossil would need to come out in pieces, as they could never raise it all in one go. I could not see everything, with so many bent backs blocking the view, but it seemed the trick was to first shift each of the slabs sideways rather than upward. This wrenched apart the connection with the solid layer below, making the actual lift much easier. The quarrymen turned the handles of their tools—*Craa-aack!*—and then came a smattering of praise.

"That does it!"

"You've got her!"

"Well done, men!" Nina had stepped aside when the heavyweight cutting tools appeared but watched every move from a nearby crouch.

"Thirty-one minutes," said Hector.

Mr. Volkov dragged one of the stretchers to rest beside the trench at Izzy's top end. The ferocious skull was the main prize, and first to be extracted. The jawbone full of teeth was more than two feet long, with a gaping eye socket so big it might have held a pineapple.

Time for Mr. Cavalier Jones to take center stage. With an apology to Nina, he removed his shirt and stood before us in only his vest. I'd not ever been so close to—nor seen so much of—a grown man's skin, apart from my own Papa. I felt my eyes double in size. Hector was staring in equal astonishment. The Strongest Man in the World had truly tremendous arm muscles! He squatted low, arms reaching wide. He spread his gloved fingers, and slid them into a place hidden for more than a million years. Ever so slowly, he lifted the stone skull with its fearsome grimace.

"Hold there!" Mr. Fibbley snapped a photograph in the half-second hesitation before Mr. Volkov stooped to help guide the slab with the head onto the first stretcher. Cavalier Jones stood up and gave a radiant smile, shaking out his arms.

Whew! We exhaled, all of us together, in a gust of amazement. Mr. Fibbley took another photo.

"No time to celebrate," Nina told the men. "Three slabs to go."

I peeled off my gloves, slid the collecting sack from my

shoulder and plunged my fingers into the wool wadding. Our part in the enterprise was about to begin! At Nina's signal, Arthur, Oscar and I dropped beside the massive, astonishing head.

"We've reached the halfway point," Hector called out. "Twenty-four minutes left."

"This is the perfect task for you," I said, over my shoulder. "Bossy boots." He smiled in absolute agreement.

"But we could use your help!" Nina spoke firmly to Hector. Every one of those hideous teeth needed a jacket! In less than twenty-four minutes! Hector, reluctantly, got down on his knees and joined us in cramming cushions of lambswool around every knob. The system we'd practiced yesterday was swiftly put into motion. Hector and I stuffed wool between each tooth, filling the gaps. Arthur helped Oscar wrap and tuck the strips of linen that kept the wool in place.

Nina showed the men where next to cut. Mr. Fibbley leaned down to capture a picture of her, hand hovering above the majestic rib cage, the bones as tidy and taut as strings on a harp. Nina shook her head at the reporter. "Enough," she said. "We're working here."

"But . . . the beautiful flipper," said Mr. Fibbley. He snapped quickly in case she stopped him. The intricate pattern of small bones in the front paddle was as lovely as a Turkish mosaic. Again Mr. Jones crouched low and twisted the slab already loosened by the quarrymen. With their assistance (though truly, he did not appear to need it), he grasped the chunk of stone and levered it onto the second waiting stretcher. At once, Oscar and Arthur moved over to the rib cage with a heap of woolly padding and linen strips. Hector and I continued with the teeth.

"I'm clearing off," said Mr. Fibbley. "I'll get this film to the chemist and be there on the beach to greet the boat when it arrives. Good luck, everyone!"

"Time?" called Nina.

Hector paused in his wrapping to check the watch. "Nineteen and a half minutes," he said.

"I'll come with you, Mr. Fibbley." Mr. Osteda looked with dismay at the wet sand attached to his calfskin boots. "I anticipate a happy meeting with the creature on dry land."

"Goodbye, Dad." Oscar, absorbed in bandaging ribs, did not glance up.

Mr. Jones flexed his muscles and bent his knees to make the third and then the fourth extractions, shifting each to its own waiting stretcher. The skeleton was deeper into the shale on these slabs, not requiring so much padding as the skull had.

"Fourteen minutes," said Hector.

Mr. Jarvis and Mr. Volkov heaved together (what

Mr. Jones had lifted alone!) and moved the stretchers closer to the *Touch Wood*. Nina's fingers raced over our bindings and found no fault.

But now, the side of the rowboat, nearly as high as Hector was tall, became an imposing barrier. Mr. Jones did not hesitate in recruiting P.C. Sackett. Together, using the heavy chain, they engineered a winch to raise the loaded stretchers into the air. One after another, the slabs of rock-hard bones were laid along the bottom of the boat and covered with horse blankets.

Sackett, however, found that he could not climb up the side.

"What do you weigh?" said Mr. Jones. "Two hundred forty pound?" A keen eye for measuring weight! "The poor vessel will struggle to float as it is," he said, "let alone with you on top."

"I don't see as you've got a choice," said P.C. Sackett, insulted. "I goes with the boat."

"Let Oscar row," said Hector. "He wins the races, rowing."

Nina looked at Oscar, who was nodding furiously. "I can do it," he said.

"P.C. Sackett," said Nina. The constable's fingers twitched, as if he'd been tempted to salute her. "We've paid you five pounds for the use of your boat. We will double that for not holding things up now. Step aside

237

and let us get on." Her eyes darted to where the tide was eagerly rolling our way.

P.C. Sackett looked at his beloved *Touch Wood* and then at Oscar.

"You're asking me to let a young scamp take my boat, with a load what's terrible heavy, and row it agin the tide around Church Cliff, all by hisself? Not for ten pound nor five times ten."

Mr. Jones put a hand on the constable's shoulder. "Sir," he said. "If you've been to the Cavalier Jones Cavalcade, you'll know that people can perform the most marvelous—"

But P.C. Sackett was shaking his head. "Nuh-uh," he said. "We hasn't been yet to the circus, what with having five little ones and—"

This admission allowed Mr. Jones a new tactic. "Why then! Get yourselves over to Seaton this week, and I will be honored to provide your family with a private box, in gratitude for—" A whoosh of water rolled over the toes of his boots.

"Put the boy in the boat," said Nina.

Mr. Jones slipped his hands around Oscar's waist, lifted him over the side and dropped him directly on the seat. Oscar spun himself around to face the right direction, back toward the prow. His knees were bent up, but that was due to the skull beneath his feet. P.C. Sackett's eyes filled with tears. He put a hand on one of the oarlocks.

"If anything happens—" he said.

"If anything happens," Oscar interrupted, "if I'm swamped or we go down, I'll swim for shore. My father will buy you a new boat, even better than this one. The fossil is too heavy to float away! It will be safe until the next low tide. Meanwhile, the ocean is barely fluttering, see? I do know how to row. All I need is a bit of water." And he laughed.

"You'll be all right?" Nina said. "Until the sea lifts the boat?" She plonked her foot down like a baby in a puddle, making a noisy splash. No one seemed to mind their feet getting wet.

"I'm fine," said Oscar. "You go on ahead."

Mr. Jarvis and Mr. Volkov had shouldered their tools and were already striding across the ledges. They would meet Nina and the *Touch Wood*, to manage Izzy's transportation from the town beach to Camp Crewe. First, though, they needed to climb all the way up the cliff path, past the church and along the road, lugging those tools that would have added unnecessary weight in the boat.

"Let's move." Cavalier Jones clapped a large hand on Oscar's head to wish him luck, and nudged P.C. Sackett toward the beach. Hector and Arthur also waded ahead. After a few splashing steps, Arthur looked back.

"Come on, Aggie!" he hollered, and waved me on. Hector must have been unhappy with having wet shoes and stockings, because he didn't even turn around.

"I hate to leave you all alone," I said to Oscar. "Shall I come with you?"

"Nice of you to offer, Aggie. But there's a small chance something might go tipsy. I don't want to be worrying about you if I have to swim for it." He leaned over and peered at the rising water. Nearly knee-deep, but not yet helping the boat to float.

"Your father will be proud to see you at the oars," I said. It seemed impossible for anyone to row so far with such weight in the boat.

"I'd like that," he said quietly. "Now, go on! With any luck, I'll see you back in camp in about an hour. You'll be completely soaked if you don't hurry!"

As it was, my shoes and stockings and the hem of my skirt were awash. I sploshed a few paces, lifting my skirt high, remembering the journal in my pocket. I turned to make certain that Oscar and the *Touch Wood* were safely launched. But the boat sat unmoving on the seabed as the water crept up its sides. Oscar swung himself to-and-fro, trying to generate some motion—but no chance that a meager boy could rock the mighty ichthyosaur!

"Keep going!" he yelled at me. Heart thudding, I inched backward toward the shore, unwilling to abandon Oscar if he were about to be swamped. What if the boat was simply too burdened to float?

But then, with a great slurping whoosh, the *Touch Wood*

let go of the ledge and rose, bouncing almost, to the surface. Water sprayed as Oscar cheered. He positioned the oars and glanced over his shoulder to where he was headed. I clapped my hands and turned to push on toward the beach.

"Aggie!" Oscar's shout spun me around. The look on his face chilled me right through. "We forgot to bring up the anchor!"

The rowboat couldn't move. Oscar was penned in by pieces of a massive stone sea monster, unable to reach the cable holding the anchor. The water was nearly up to my waist. I could not wait to consider. The sodden notebook knocked against my thigh as I waded back to the boat. A cable pulled tautly from the prow, straining against the weight it was trying to hold.

"Why isn't the boat dragging it?" I said. "The boat is heavier than the anchor."

"It might be wedged in a crack," said Oscar.

I slid my fingers down the chain as far as I could reach, but knew I'd be taking a plunge.

"Can you move the boat," I said, "to let the tension slacken a bit?"

"I'll try," he said, "but I don't want to hit you."

I took in a full breath and pulled myself under, both hands holding the cable. The anchor *was* snagged between ledges. I surfaced to tell him, and to inhale. Oscar maneuvered with the oars, doing his best to lessen the tug on the chain. On the next plunge, I dislodged the anchor and stood up. The task was done in the space of one breath. I clasped the anchor by its neck, trying to keep my balance in the swelling sea. Oscar let the boat rock a little closer. He rested one oar and stretched out a hand to help topple the anchor into the boat. There.

He pulled away at once. I swam toward dry land, now farther away than ever.

CHAPTER 24

A Frightening Interlude

THE BOYS WERE WELL AHEAD OF ME, clambering over the ledges near the shore. Arthur would already have been safe on the beach had he not slowed down to wait for Hector. But even Hector was moving at an impressive pace—for Hector. I guessed that the fear of not knowing how to swim must be propelling him forward like wind under a sail. Each of them had a collecting sack slung over his shoulder, empty now but for the flasks of water. I set my sights on the two boys, my yearned-for destination. *The beam from a lighthouse on a stormy night. A flag raised in the smoky aftermath of battle. A simmering soup waiting at the end of a snowy day.*

I thought the tide might help to carry me in. But with the tide came a surprising lift and fall. Only minutes ago, it had not been enough to float a boat but now, spring tide! Higher and stronger than the usual one. I could not touch down, except occasionally. I swallowed a nasty salty gulp. I began to swim as hard as ever I had. The water buoyed me up, but then pulled back and left me breathless. My dress clung around my legs like a fisherman's net around an octopus. An octopus with two legs. Wearing waterlogged shoes. I despaired for my notebook.

Arthur and Hector had got to where the shore usually existed, but the pebbled beach was wetter with each inflow. Hector finally noticed that I was not right behind him. He took a few steps toward me before Arthur grabbed his arm, as I got another face full of seawater. My hat was tugged from my head and sailed away. Coughing, with stinging eyes, I kept going. The boys shouted and I swam harder still. Next time I could see, they were climbing up the rough slope of what Arthur called the landslip. With the sheer cliff rising behind it and the incoming water lapping at its base, this bumpy bluff offered refuge above the reach of high tide. Arthur must have known, from living in Lyme Regis, that it was wiser to seek elevated ground than to splash along the fast-disappearing ribbon of dry land. The sea would not pause to let frightened children slip by unharmed.

My foot knocked against something underwater. And then my other foot! I tried to stand and got washed off course, but the ledges were there. Frantically cycling my legs, I swiped a sharp ridge of stone that tore wide the bottom of my shoe. Between the tugging waves, my stupid skirt and the flapping leather sole, I could not kick with any power. I tried to find my laces to untie them, but it was impossible while being tossed about.

Hector and Arthur jumped and hollered when I finally found my footing. I pulled my skirt right up away from my legs and held it bundled at my middle. I lunged forward through shallower water, jump after jump after jump. The water tugged and tumbled, what would have made for fun wading on a usual day at the seaside. Until, at last, the pitted side of the landslip. The boys hauled me to safety, a slippery and miserable water rat. I wrung the sea from my skirt while Hector rubbed my arms. Arthur wrung my heavy braid, squeezing out a torrent of drips and a very small crab. From the height of this new vantage point—above the waves instead of *in* them— we saw Oscar and the *Touch Wood* move steadily over the gently rolling surface of the water.

"Flatter out there than close to shore." I was still catching my breath. Our perch on the landslip was nearly surrounded by rolling waves. Where we were sitting had been a disaster when Arthur's great-grandpa was a boy. Rocks and mud, cottages and even sheep had tumbled down the face of the cliff in a terrifying slide, landing in this tremendous heap of rubble. Today, it was our refuge. I looked at the cliff face above our backs, as high as two churches. We were safe, but until the spring tide subsided, we were also trapped.

Plunked down on the scrubby ground, Hector cajoled my wet shoelaces to loosen and my shoes to come off. I rolled down the clammy stockings, shivered, clapped my hands against my arms and spread my skirt across my lap. I took the notebook from my pocket and peeled apart the pages, fanning each one briefly. With the book spread flat, the penciled pages were nearly legible.

"Come on, sun, do your job!" I longed to be warm. I stood up again to jiggle and hop about. Moving helped a bit, so I kept at it a while longer. Arthur offered his cardigan, but I said no. We'd be stuck here for hours and might need a sweater later. Silly for it to get wet too.

"How long?" I said to Arthur. Each minute had seemed an hour since Cavalier Jones hoisted those tremendous stone blocks into P.C. Sackett's rowboat.

"Six hours and twelve minutes between highest and lowest tides," he said. "We're still ages from the high point. And then it will have to recede partway for us to cross the beach. We've got hours and hours to go."

I slumped onto my back and summoned warm thoughts. The eiderdown quilt on my bed at home. Tony snuggling and snuffling on my lap. The crackling fire in the nursery at Owl Park. The steam room at the Wellspring Hotel in Harrogate.

Yooo-hooo, we heard. I looked about for an injured bird. "What is that peculiar hooting?"

"Your grand-mère," said Hector.

My heart turned over in my chest. Grannie Jane and Helen, way up on the cliff to the east, waved their arms like children at a passing train. Oh, Grannie! She must have seen me caught by the sea and been frantic! To the point of making most unladylike noises to catch my attention! But now she raised her parasol and twirled it, as calmly as could be. I blew her a fistful of kisses, and wrung out my skirt another time.

"I'd take off my underslip," I said, "except that Grannie Jane is watching." Arthur blushed the color of a sunburn.

"Oscar is rowing still," Hector said, "as if someone winds him up with a key."

"Turns out his boast was true," I said. "Lucky for Nina."

"He may be regretting that boast by now," said Arthur. "I'll wager the sea is harder than a river."

"The sea plus a ton of ichthyosaur," I said. We watched the dot of a rowboat for a long, long time, until finally it disappeared around the curve of Church Cliff.

"The grown-ups dispersed pretty quickly," I said. "No one noticed that we hadn't kept up."

"They all went to meet Oscar," said Arthur, "and Izzy, of course. P.C. Sackett must be having a heart attack, waiting to see his boat come safely ashore."

"Mr. Fibbley is hot on the trail of the fossil story," I said. "Passing time until the killer is found."

Hector made a little cough to put me on guard. As if I would blab in front of Arthur about Mr. Fibbley also being Miss Spinns!

"I know that cough is a code of some kind," said Arthur.

I rolled my eyes at Hector.

"And I'm not blind either," said Arthur. "Just not the sharpest knife in the drawer, is what my father says."

"Does he really say that? How awful," I said. Even if it was true.

"While you're playing detective," said Arthur, "who do *you* think killed Mr. B-C?"

"Oscar thinks the killer is a 'she,'" said Hector, "but he does not say why."

"Pah!" said Arthur. "Oscar would say anything to distract people from blaming his father."

"He may not have all the facts," I said, "but I don't think he's a liar."

"Not like his father," said Hector.

"Well, I don't trust him," said Arthur. "Sneaking about after dark, saying Helen was going later to visit her mum. Nine o'clock at night? Mrs. Malone goes to bed much earlier than that!"

"How do you know when she goes to bed?" I said.

"Everyone knows," said Arthur. "She's up and baking

248

by half four in the morning. All the bread we eat at camp is made by her—before she starts the laundering."

"Goodness." Certainly a baker must rise before the sun. I trusted Arthur on this point. So, why did this news send a prickle across my shoulders?

I flapped my notebook at Grannie Jane to show that we were still safe. She twirled her parasol and Helen waved again. A series of hand motions followed, but it was only when their figures disappeared that I understood they were departing. I trusted that the signaling had promised their return.

"Is it lunchtime?" I said.

"Well past," said Arthur.

A curious herring gull landed a few feet away and hopped closer, beady eye swiveling.

"He hears you say lunch," said Hector.

"Sorry, Gully. We have no sandwiches to share," I said.

"Don't mention food," said Arthur. "We've missed lunch *and* we'll miss tea stuck here."

"Seven silly seagulls," I said, "sat upon the shore. Eating seven sandwiches till they could eat no more."

"Jolly good!" cried Arthur.

"You try thinking one up," I said. But Arthur was a hopeless poet. He tried to rhyme *amazing* with *raisin*.

"Seven soggy sandwiches," Hector said, "sink into the sea. Silver sharks eat sandwiches instead of eating me."

I'd finally stopped trembling. My arms and legs stopped tingling. A salty residue was beginning to itch my skin. Had Oscar made a hero's landing at the Gun Cliff jetty, where they were expecting him? Maybe someone would think to bring the rowboat back to rescue us! That was optimistic, I supposed. Oscar mightn't realize we were trapped. They all likely assumed us safe and sound at Camp Crewe.

We'd be here for ages yet.

I rolled onto my tummy and closed my eyes, letting the sun dry the back of me. *Ahh*, finally warm, and almost comfortable. Even the rough ground did not stop me drifting off for a while.

The lonely professor looked out at the glittering twilit sea. Was he so unlikable that he could not name one true friend? Would anyone care if he did not return to camp this evening? But where else could he go? How had he lost the love and respect of everyone around him? He determined that tomorrow he would be more patient, possibly even kind! Everett could keep his position. Spud would keep cooking inedible food, and he'd allow those pesty children to . . .

How long did I nap? How much longer would we be here? The landslip was still surrounded but I could see a distinct waterline *above* where the waves were hitting now. Grannie Jane and Helen had not returned to their perch on the cliff. Watching children lie about on a rock, I supposed, was not compelling enough to keep them rooted to their seats. The boys must have dozed as well, but now they became noisy again and got up to explore the terrain. They poked at stones in the hopes they were actually skulls—as if we hadn't done enough fossil-finding for one day. Arthur told Hector not to step in a slurry. These were mudholes that looked hard and firm on top, but were ghastly sinking mud below and would suck off your shoe when you tried to pull out. One of nature's nasty secrets.

Renewed hooting came from the top of the cliff. Grannie and Helen were back!

"Hallooooo!" I called, blowing kisses. Had Grannie Jane perhaps needed a rest? Had Helen somehow made her comfortable in our stuffy tent? She'd be tuckered out with no afternoon siesta. I tried to picture my grandmother lying on my cot in her corset, but such a sight was impossible to summon.

My brain cells whirred back to Helen's mother's bedtime. The point that had bothered me earlier came clear . . . What if it were not *Oscar* who had told a fib, but *Helen*? What if she'd told Oscar she was going to see her mother when really she'd had somewhere else to be? She'd not come back to camp until quite a bit later than Oscar had. The bonfire was well over and we'd all been in our tents. Had Helen sneaked off to meet Ned? Or had she witnessed something she was afraid to tell about? Had she seen her own *father* in a place where he shouldn't have been? Was Helen protecting *her* father, a key to the mystery, rather than Oscar protecting *his*?

Or . . . was there a more complicated explanation? Spud had an alibi, vouched for by more than one person. For whom else might Helen lie to protect? Did *Ned* have a reason to attack the professor? They'd never met! And Ned was tending to Oscar's injured father at the hotel for much of the evening. I blinked. I was circling the obvious answer, like a puffin ignoring the fish in its beak.

My eyes flew to where Helen stood at the top of the cliff, a mere push away from my grandmother. Why was Oscar so sure that the killer was female? Could Helen be the "she" that he meant?

A noise pierced my thoughts, like the cry of a seagull but longer.

Agonized rather than greedy.

I had never heard Hector scream before.

CHAPTER 25

A POISONOUS ENCOUNTER

"It bites!" he shrieked. "It bites!"

I saw movement in the scrub at Hector's feet, a telltale slither, black zigzags on silvery-gray scales. For a moment, I assumed that he'd seen the snake and succumbed to panic.

"Adder!" Arthur scooped up a stone and threw it.

But Hector crouched to grab his ankle and fell to one side with a sob of pain. Arthur and I sank to the ground next to him, my blood sizzling in alarm. Hector had been bitten by a venomous snake!

"Let's have a look, old boy," said Arthur, with unexpected gentleness. His father must have used those very words at a moment when Arthur had been injured. It took some coaxing for Hector to let go of his ankle and lie back. His straw hat was useless as a pillow, so Arthur tore off his cardigan and rolled it under Hector's head.

"You mustn't move," said Arthur. "Rule number one with adder bites. No jiggling."

Hector froze. The whimper died on his lips and he did not make another sound, even when Arthur peeled down his sock to reveal an ankle already puffy and pink.

"Only one real puncture," said Arthur. "That's good! The other fang must have got caught in the sock."

"F-fang?" Hector whispered. This was the very worst thing that could happen to him. Even looking at a picture of a snake in a book he found to be loathsome. *Revolting* and *reptile* were the same word in his vocabulary.

Arthur took Hector's sock all the way off and handed it to me. "Can you douse this in seawater?" he said. "We should clean the puncture as quickly as possible."

"Pity my skirt has dried out," I said.

"We need more than a dribble anyway," said Arthur. I scrambled down as near as I could get to the waves splashing against the base of the slip. One dunk to soak Hector's sock and back I climbed. Hector's face was paler and sweatier than I'd ever seen it, his ankle even redder now. The wound was tiny but vivid scarlet. Arthur dabbed at the spot and then wrapped the sock all the way around, tucking in the ends to make a secure compress.

"You're meant to keep the bite below the heart," said Arthur. "Slows down the venom."

"V-v-venom," Hector repeated, with a slight tremor.

"Lie with your head farther up the slope for now." Arthur's calm, and his skill as a nurse, was admirable.

"Should you be sucking out the poison?" I whispered.

"My dad says not," said Arthur. "He says if you don't know how, you shouldn't try. You'll end up poisoning yourself."

"What do we do now?" I said.

"The main task," said Arthur, "is to keep the ankle still. The best thing would be to wrap it and make a splint, so that the venom in the blood can't—" Arthur raised his voice, as if a snakebite caused deafness. "Just don't move, old chap!"

"I feel sick," said Hector.

"Wrap it how?" I said.

"If we had bandages," said Arthur. "But we used all the linen strips on the fossil."

"Do you have the penknife?" I said.

"Well, yes, but—"

I snatched it from him and jabbed the knifepoint through the linen of my skirt. One slice was enough, about three inches above the hem. I tore the fabric the rest of the way around and soon had a length of perfectly good bandage—and a somewhat shorter skirt. For a splint we used my notebook, nearly dry by now. Its cover was soft leather and bent easily enough. Arthur swiftly and carefully bound the book as a brace around the ankle . . . while Hector moaned. I dribbled water from the flask over his lips, making him splutter.

"Hard luck we haven't got B-C's flask," said Arthur. "My dad would say whiskey is the best antidote for an adder bite." His grin was not entirely happy. "Of course, he'd say whiskey is the antidote for everything else too."

"No whiskey," said Hector. "Already my head is . . ." He made a stirring motion with his hand.

"You're dizzy?" I said. "Is that normal?" I whispered to Arthur.

He nodded and leaned in close. "Pray he doesn't faint," he said. "We've got to get him back to camp. As soon as we possibly can." We turned to look at the water. Surely it was lower than before? The waves weren't crashing anymore, but only swelling up and back.

"How deep do you suppose it is, where we'd be climbing into it?" I said.

Arthur inched his way down the slope to make a closer inspection. "About up to my thigh," he called. "My legs are longer than yours."

"That's not so bad," I said. "I've already been as wet as a person could be." I'd hold my skirt up around my waist so it couldn't tangle around my legs this time.

"We *could* wade," said Arthur, coming back, "except . . ." He nodded toward Hector, who lay utterly still with his eyes closed. "Except that he can't walk, and I'd hate to drop him into the sea."

My gaze went from Arthur's earnest face to the swirling water, to the top of the cliff where Grannie Jane and Helen had reappeared to stand vigil. They must have been wondering why Hector was lying down. I waved again. Helen waved back a bit frantically, and Grannie spun her parasol. Hector groaned. Arthur held Hector's hat as a sunshade, slowly fanning the pale face. We counted to one thousand, Arthur and I taking turns every other hundred. Hector tried to join us in French, but he got only to *trois cent seize* before fading. His lips were parched and cracked.

"Is there any water left in the flask?" I said.

Arthur dribbled the last mouthful between Hector's lips.

"This is about to get dire," I said.

"I'll look at the water again." Arthur made his way back down the slope.

"Hector?" I whispered. "Are you still here? I know it must hurt horribly."

He nodded, eyes shut, but with a single tear leaking out on each side. I brushed them away with my fingertips, though by now I trusted Arthur not to be a ninny about a boy crying when bitten by a snake.

"I think we can get started," said Arthur, coming back. "This first bit will be tricky. It's awfully steep. We'll have to hold him across our laps and edge down on our bottoms. Do you think we can do that?"

We had no choice. I crammed my shoes and stockings into the collecting sack with the empty water flasks. Arthur and I sat side by side and slowly nudged our legs under Hector, ignoring his moaning for now. His face was as white as bone. Arthur held Hector's head and I was in charge of the feet. The leg above the ankle wrapping was quite red by now, and swollen. I repeatedly bumped it, despite my care. I must have apologized twenty times in the many minutes it took us to shimmy down to the water's edge.

"I'll carry him piggyback," said Arthur. "Can you keep his foot steady at the same time?"

Steady Hector's foot, carry the collecting sack out of the way and hold up my skirt to prevent it tangling around my legs. Arthur would be looking ahead and Hector was practically unconscious, so I needn't worry about my knickers showing. Also, it was a dire emergency. Grannie must understand that. Once started, we got through the water pretty smoothly, though the person with a poisonous snakebite may have felt differently. Hector did his best not to whimper, but with an ankle so horribly puffy and the vivid pink of a geranium, I'd have been howling.

"Hellooooo!" Helen was halfway down the cliff path, waving with both hands! "Agg-eeee! What's happened?" she hollered. The waves turned over, with a great scraping of pebbles every time.

"Adder!" called Arthur, but the effort of carrying a boy on his back choked his voice.

"Don't waste your breath," I said. "She'll know soon enough. How's your back?"

"Truthfully? I would never have guessed someone so small could be so heavy," said Arthur.

"It's his brain," I said. "It weighs twice what yours or mine does."

Hector, who might have been delirious, began to giggle.

"Don't laugh!" cried Arthur. "I'll drop you!"

Helen had got to the beach and was trying to splash toward us across the wet and slippery stones. Her hair floated about her head like sunshine, pins lost to the wind. Cheeks flushed pink, blue eyes frantic with worry, she looked nothing like a murderess. And yet, did she carry the weight of guilt, even heavier than the one Arthur bore on his back?

CHAPTER 26

A SIGNATURE IN QUESTION

MORE SURPRISING THAN HELEN being here was the man who lumbered behind her. Thickset and dressed in his cook's striped trousers and white jacket, Spud was unexpectedly agile as he navigated the steep path.

"Adder," said Arthur again, grunting a little.

Spud took Hector into his arms and set off straight back up the hill. One of his hands braced Hector's ankle in its make-do splint. Arthur staggered slightly, leaning into Helen's friendly embrace.

"You did it!" I said. "You saved his life, Arthur."

"I can't believe how strong you are!" Helen teased, poking his arm where the muscle must be—though it looked nothing like that of Mr. Cavalier Jones!

"Where's your dad taking him?" said Arthur.

"To a doctor, I hope?" I said.

"Your Grannie wanted us to summon a doctor when we saw he must be hurt. We didn't know if he'd broken something or twisted his ankle or—" She paused. "I didn't think of an adder. Poor lad. That hurts something terrible. Goodness, Aggie, what's happened to your dress?"

"It's around Hector's leg," I said. "Did someone go to fetch a doctor from town?"

"Well, it's Sunday," said Helen. "And my dad were a medic in the army, so he's as good as."

But Hector needed help right away! "They didn't have snakes in the army," I said.

"They did in Africa," said Helen. "The Brits were fighting in Zululand when Dad was young. They had snakes and scorpions and spiders the size of pancakes."

Once back in camp, I raced to change my torn, damp dress and underthings, and then raced to hug my grand-mother as tightly as I ever had. She gave us the news that the fossil team had not yet returned.

"But shouldn't they have been here ages ago?" I said. "Do we know if Oscar got all the way? Please don't tell me that the boat tipped over!"

"The boat did not tip over," said Grannie. "Constable Guff was sent along to report on a series of mishaps. Spring tide made unloading difficult, and the vehicle they'd arranged for was not sturdy enough, which meant waiting for suitable transport. Goodness, Aggie, I didn't listen. I was rather more concerned with you and Hector. Are you hungry, pet?"

Helen would find us something to eat while I checked on Hector. His cot had been hastily moved, Grannie said, because the boys' quarters were too crowded for Spud to fit into. The work tent was a temporary solution, where Spud now tended to the wound.

"You did right, washing it with salt water," he said. "And you hobbled together an excellent splint with what you'd got. Clever as can be. Too bad about your dress, Miss Morton. I'm reusing the strips now, see? Along with a couple of napkins." He'd rewrapped the ankle and the leg right up to the knee, firmly but not so tight as to squeeze or confine.

"Is there a medicine for snakebites?" I said, reclaiming my notebook.

"Now, I've heard," said Spud, rocking back on his heels for a moment, "that in India they treat a cobra bite with venom from the cobra itself—but there's nothing like that here in England. Salt water and good luck, that's what we've got to be thankful for."

"You were a hero today, young man," Grannie Jane told a blushing Arthur. "I should now like to move the boy to a hospital—or to the comfort of my hotel, at the very least."

Spud looked up. "He can't be moved another inch, ma'am. Can't have his limbs shook any further. Not today, anyway."

This news disheartened Grannie. That we must stay put at Camp Crewe was the opposite of her wishes. But Spud was adamant. Hector must remain where he was.

"Should I not have carried him?" said Arthur. "It seemed urgent to get him here."

"We did our best to prevent jiggling," I said, "but—"

"You did just fine," said Spud. "Better than fine." He patted Hector's shoulder, making Hector startle and his eyes pop open. "Ssh." Another pat. "You'll live."

He waved us out of the tent so he could finish his nursing duties. Hector would live! Tears filled my eyes and a lump closed my throat. Helen waited outside in the fading sunshine, with packets of quickly assembled cheddar and chive sandwiches. Arthur ate four in under a minute. I'd thought I was famished but now could not swallow. With my worry about Hector subsiding, the matter of Helen pricked like a pin left in a seam. Did she know about what happened on Wednesday night? And if so, why hadn't she told us already?

"The sergeant's shown up." Helen tipped her head at the approaching officer. "As if we needed more bad news."

Where had he come from? When he spotted my grandmother, he squared his shoulders. She was the only adult among us, so it was she whom he addressed, though he had not met her.

"I am Sergeant Harley," he said. "I wish to consult with Mrs. Blenningham-Crewe."

"She is not yet returned from this morning's scientific endeavor, Sergeant," said Grannie. "May I be of assistance? I am Mrs. Morton. Agatha's grandmother."

"When will she be here?" he asked. "No one else will do."

"Has something happened with Everett?" I said. "Grannie, this is Sergeant Harley, who put Everett in jail."

"With very little reason, as I understand the matter." Grannie lifted a superior eyebrow. I vowed to tell Hector that the sergeant flinched.

Spud came out of the work tent.

"Dad?" said Helen. "What news? We're going mad!"

"He'll live," said Spud, again. It *was* all that mattered, after all. Then he caught sight of the policeman. "What now?"

"He won't tell us," I said.

"Bah," said Spud with a disgusted shake of his head.

"May I sit with Hector?" I said.

"He'll like that," said the cook. Arthur perked up, but Spud waved him back. "One at a time, mind. And don't expect much. He'll be low for days."

Inside, I knelt next to Hector's cot. "Hello," I said, clasping his pale, limp hand. The leg wrapping was now enhanced by long wooden spoons strapped to both sides for stability. "Where did you get such nice fat pillows?"

Hector's eyes fluttered open, and he gave me a half smile. "Helen brings to me from the bed of the professor."

His voice was a thin whisper.

"You're lying on a dead man's pillows?"

"He is not dead at the time of using them."

"Spud says you won't be dead either." I squeezed his hand. "Not for one hundred and five years."

"Ninety-three years," said Hector, so I knew his brain was working. "You and Arthur save me," he added. "Thank you."

"Arthur was an excellent man in a crisis," I said. "He did exactly what was needed." I had torn strips from my skirt and managed not to be sick. "I've had a thought about the murder," I said. "It's a wretched thought, but what do you think—"

Hector closed his eyes. Was he too sick to listen? I wanted to tell him about Helen. But he was clammy and dozy and—

Clattering wheels and shouting voices from outside, and was that the loud purr of a motorcar?

"It's Nina and the others!" I hopped to my feet. "They're back with Izzy!"

Hector struggled to sit up. "Will you assist me to—"

"No! Hector, you mustn't move, not for hours and

hours. Not for all night. Spud was very strict on that point because, you know, leaking venom and so on. Even Grannie agrees."

He made a noise of frustration and fell back. I gave him no time for further complaint.

"I promise to tell you everything."

The motorcar was Mr. Osteda's red Vauxhall, with a farm wagon hitched to its back end using the iron chain from the circus. But some miracle had occurred while we'd been trapped on the landslip! Oscar's father, behind the wheel of his fancy car, had the Strongest Man in the World next to him in the front seat. They looked to be entirely friendly! Even Mr. Osteda's black eye seemed jaunty rather than menacing.

Nina and Oscar stood on the bed of the farm wagon, grinning widely enough to split open their cheeks. Mr. Jarvis and Mr. Volkov were already assembling a sturdy ramp, to make moving Izzy a little easier. Woolen horse blankets covered the lumps of stone, as if hiding a dead body from prying eyes. Arthur climbed up to join Oscar and jump about with him as if they'd won a tournament. I had a moment's qualm on Hector's behalf, for both these boys had performed heroic deeds today, rowing a fossil-laden boat and rescuing a wounded comrade. Poor Hector had succeeded only in getting himself envenomed and put to bed!

Oscar hopped down from the wagon to let the men do their work.

"Arthur says Hector was bitten by a snake! Is he—?"

"Spud says he'll live. He'll be wild to hear about your boat ride."

"You're all right?" said Oscar. "You made it to shore!"

I laughed. "And you? You're all right? You made it to shore!"

"The boat got pretty banged up inside," said Oscar. "A ton of stone will do that. But my father agreed to pay for all repairs." He grinned. "It may have helped that your reporter friend was taking photographs of me with the constable's arm over my shoulder. Dad could hardly ignore the owner of the boat while a reporter was carefully spelling out *Sackett*."

Spud and Helen appeared with a tray of cups, offering fizzy lemonade to a thirsty, happy party. We drank a jubilant toast to Nina and her team. Mr. Jarvis and Mr. Volkov took their leave—but not before nudging each other and turning to us.

"Please tell Master Hector our wishes for swift healing," said Mr. Jarvis.

"We pray for him," said Mr. Volkov. He and his friend bowed deeply, in tribute to Hector's habit, and then backed away with solemn nods. We did not expect to see these men again, as the next day was to be a holiday for them.

That's when Sergeant Harley decided to end the fun.

"Attention!" He raised a hand, looking grim. "Mrs. Blenningham-Crewe?"

Nina's smile slipped a little. "Sergeant? Do you have news of Everett?"

"You are required," said the sergeant, "to verify a document."

"Now?" said Nina. Our merriment faded quickly.

"That pest of a reporter came to the station yesterday, demanding an interview with our prisoner. I permitted them to speak for five minutes. I do not believe in coddling killers."

"Everett Tobie killed no one," said Nina. The light in her eyes shifted from sunny to thunderous.

"That is for the police to decide," said Sergeant Harley. "The same reporter turned up again today, this time delivering a letter addressed to me that he claimed was from your secretary." He pulled an envelope from the pocket of his jacket and held it up in front of Nina's face. "Before I tell you what she says—or take any action that might result—I wish you to confirm that the handwriting on the envelope matches that of a Miss Sylvia Spinns."

Nina hesitated. How could she make a declaration without knowing the contents of the letter? What if Miss Spinns had accused Everett yet again?

"Excuse me," I said, rather boldly, as no one had

addressed me. "Where did the reporter encounter Miss Spinns?" Other than in the mirror, I did not say.

"I understood that she came to his lodging house," said Sergeant Harley. "She put the letter straight into his hands. If she'd delivered it to the police, she might have excited our interest—and did not wish to do so." The sergeant plucked at the collar of his jacket, looking overheated.

"But why would Miss Spinns look for *him* in particular?" said Nina. "Does that not seem odd? Why did she not come to me, knowing how concerned I would be for Mr. Tobie's well-being?"

"Perhaps she knew the reporter had visited with the prisoner?" said Sergeant Harley. "And that she could depend on him to assist in righting a wrong?"

Aha! He had accidentally told us that the letter would be in Everett's favor! Nina smiled faintly at the sergeant's blunder.

"Arthur," she said. "Will you fetch our record book from Miss Spinns' desk? Blue cover." He was back before another word was spoken. "Thank you. Please give it to the sergeant."

The sergeant lay the envelope on one of the pages of the open record book. Nina was not tall enough to look over his shoulder, but peered around it instead.

"I have heard," said Grannie Jane, "that in the study of handwriting, one is meant to look for differences rather than similarities."

"A name and address is a small sample," said Nina, "but I see no divergence in the formation of the letters. The hand appears to be the same."

"I agree," said Sergeant Harley. Reluctantly, it seemed. "You may read Miss Spinns' declaration and study the script further." He handed the envelope to Nina and the record book to Arthur to return.

Nina drew out the page and read aloud.

July 12, 1903

To Sergeant Richard Harley,

I write to suggest that I may have misspoken—or, more likely, have been misunderstood—in such a way that justice was diverted in the offices of the Lyme Regis constabulary.

Mr. Everett Tobie had a small disagreement with Mr. Blenningham-Crewe on Wednesday last, before the tragedy occurred. I may have inadvertently exaggerated the impact of that argument in such a way that the police interpreted my words as meaning that Mr. Tobie had possibly been involved in the professor's death. This was an error. To the best of my knowledge, Mr. Tobie was present at Camp Crewe throughout the evening.

*I hereby apologize to Mr. Tobie for the distress and
disturbance done to him.*

Sincerely,

Miss Sylvia Spinns

CHAPTER 27

AN IMPENDING DEPARTURE

THE ASSEMBLED LISTENERS met this reading with boos and hissing. Nina's trembling fingers handed the letter back to Sergeant Harley. I was secretly impressed at how, once again, Mr. Fibbley had used a lot of words to confess nothing at all—and yet to change the direction of the investigation.

"That lying old bat ruined Everett's chance to be part of our historic morning," said Nina. "And you"—her finger jabbed the air toward the policeman's chest—"you ape-brained fool, took her word for no good reason. This will teach you never to trust old women! They've spent a lifetime learning the art of deception for the sole purpose of doing what they wish without men getting in their way."

Grannie Jane made a noise that might have been a stifled laugh.

"Bring Everett back at once!" Nina demanded. "I shall file a complaint! You are a piddling fool with the wits of a tortoise! You are—"

"Mrs. Blenningham-Crewe?" Mr. Osteda touched her elbow. "Will you allow me to collect Mr. Tobie in my motorcar? I would be honored."

"Would you?" Nina bestowed a dazzling smile upon the American that he had surely not seen before. "I couldn't bear for him to spend another night under the watch of this driveling nailhead."

"You're not thinking of escaping, Mr. Ossted, are you?" Sergeant Harley puffed himself up again to forbid the Ostedas from leaving town. He also wished to forbid the circus from moving on to their next stop in Seaton, eight miles away. Mr. Jones inquired whether the hundreds of ticket holders might come to be entertained at the Lyme Regis constabulary instead? The sergeant changed his order and allowed that the circus could perform in Seaton, but travel no farther.

Mr. Osteda bowed to my grandmother. "Mrs. Morton? Are you perhaps ready for some repose? I can deliver you to the hotel on my way to pick up Mr. Tobie."

Grannie Jane hesitated. Not a common occurrence. "Agatha?" she said. "A word."

Obediently, but with a plummeting heart, I sat with her at a table beneath the kitchen canopy. We still were under the gaze of all those eyes, but hopefully out of earshot.

"I know what you're going to say, Grannie. You want us to leave too. But Spud said Hector shouldn't be moved just yet, and I won't go anywhere without—"

She put a hand on mine, to halt the flow.

"Naturally you wish to stay near Hector," she said. "But I am not content that a boy with an adder bite should lie about in a grubby tent waiting for an infection to descend."

Ugh, when she put it like that . . .

And she wasn't finished.

"We have an obligation to Hector's family to keep his limbs intact while he's in our care."

I nodded. His mother—so far away—would indeed be dismayed when she heard the news!

"Have you told Mummy," I said, "about the adder?"

"The adder struck three hours ago," said Grannie Jane. "I have not, as yet, had the opportunity to tell anyone. Mr. Osteda will drive me into town, where I will use a telephone at the hotel. I'll ask James to come in the morning, as early as he is able. Preferably with a doctor."

James! And a doctor for Hector! Those were both good! But leaving camp tomorrow morning when we did not yet know who killed Mr. Blenningham-Crewe? It was dashed unfair to be whisked away before the murderer was caught!

"We will inform the Reverend Teasdale in Torquay that we are keeping his lodger for somewhat longer, and Hector can recover under our watch in the comfort of Owl Park. In the meantime, I shall be precise with Helen that I expect her to care for you—and Hector in particular—with great attention this evening. Do you understand?"

Helen. What to do about Helen?

This should have been the moment when I shared my worries with Grannie Jane. She had trusted our sleuthing in the past. She had even assisted from time to time. But if I were to suggest that jolly, helpful Helen was very possibly a killer . . . Grannie would strenuously object to leaving us here. She would carry Hector away on her own back. No. Quite simply, no. Our few remaining hours must be spent solving the puzzle.

The fossil-rescuers had lost their air of celebration. Oscar's father assisted my grandmother into his motorcar. He'd given Oscar permission to stay in camp for another night. Cavalier Jones and Mr. Osteda heartily shook hands and clapped one another's shoulders before the strongman took his leave.

"Farewell, my lady!" cried Mr. Jones to Nina. "This day is the dawn of a new era!"

"Well, Oscar?" I said, as we waved goodbye. "What happened? Archrivals have become the best of friends in an afternoon!"

"I'm as mystified as you are," said Oscar. "It's a business arrangement of some kind, but my father says I must wait to hear more."

"Sounds fishy to me," said Arthur. "They're probably going to rob the museum."

"Come on," I said. "Hector is all alone, and he'll be wild to hear about Oscar's boat ride and all the rest of it."

Arthur ducked into the tent first. I held Oscar back.

"I need to ask," I said. "We've been trying to map what happened on Wednesday night, and—"

Oscar stiffened.

"And, Arthur mentioned a fib. We traced it back to—"

"I am *not* a liar," said Oscar.

"Wait! Please listen," I whispered. "Something Helen told you about where she was going—"

"Are you coming to see Hector or not?" Arthur poked his head through the tent flap.

"Um, yes," I said. "In a moment."

But Oscar leapt to follow Arthur inside, as if to shed my company—and my questions—as quickly as he could. What made him itch like a woolly jumper against bare skin?

Hector was livelier than he had been earlier. "Please to tell me everything," he said.

"There's not much to say," said Oscar. "When I saw the anchor was still down, and Aggie had to dive for it, I wanted to puke."

The odd moment outside the tent might never have happened. Oscar poured his energy into cheering up Hector. "I probably should have jumped in myself," he said, "but what if I couldn't get back into the boat? She was my best chance—and luckily, she's a really good swimmer."

I was blushing—but what for? Why did we blush when someone noticed something we knew already? I *was* a good swimmer. Thank goodness.

"Aggie dove," Oscar said. "She brought up the anchor and went splashing toward shore. I headed toward the open channel, kind of terrified, I admit. The ocean was much harder than the Rio Grande."

"I knew it," said Arthur.

"Or maybe it's that I never had such a heavy boat. I finally hauled myself around the bluff of Church Cliff . . . and then saw how much farther I still had to go . . . That was a bad moment." He shook his head. "But you can't give up when you're in the ocean, can you? And I had the most tremendous idea. *I am the only boy in the* entire world *rowing a boat with a prehistoric sea monster sitting next to me.* That gave me the spit to keep going."

"You are perhaps more like your father than you realize," said Hector.

"Always wanting to be the *only one*," said Arthur.

Oscar looked as if he might deny such an accusation, but then shrugged with a short laugh. "I'd like to think there's a difference between him wanting to own what no one else has and me wanting to do what no one else can . . . but I guess it's close to the same, isn't it?"

"It is human nature," said Hector. "The wish to be outstanding in some particular."

Arthur was quiet. Did he wonder where he might stand among the outstanding? He'd done one thing today I would remember forever.

"Like treating an adder bite," I said, "when no one else can."

"You think that counts?" said Arthur.

"Yes, mon ami," said Hector. "It counts very high."

"And rowing a boat," I said, "when no one else can."

Oscar's eyes met mine and darted away.

"And knowing the truth," I added, "when no one else does."

Oscar's tawny cheeks flushed darker. If ever a person was guilty of holding on to a secret, Oscar was the perfect example. He stood up in a rush. He patted his pocket and caught my gaze again. I felt Hector watching, and appealed to him in silence. He nodded in answer to the question I had not asked aloud.

"I am most fatigué," he said. "You will read to me,

Arthur? I would like to hear from Sherlock Holmes. *The Hound of the Baskervilles*, it is in my valise."

Arthur riffled the pages but Hector pointed to a spot in Chapter One where he should begin. Hector had memorized the complete novel, so I knew he'd chosen this passage on purpose.

"'Some people without possessing genius have a remarkable power of stimulating it,'" Arthur read. "'I confess, my dear fellow, that I am very much in your debt.'"

Oscar tugged on my hand and whispered close to my ear, "If you want to hear what I know, come now. Before it gets completely dark." We waved silent goodbyes so as not to interrupt the reading, and backed out of the tent.

"Well?" I said to Oscar, once we'd got a fair distance away.

"You've guessed correctly," he said. "I saw something that no one else knows. But we need to go to the cemetery for you to understand."

"But the cemetery is—" *So far away from my bed!* I managed not to say.

"Do you want to know or not?"

I asked fifty-nine questions and Oscar ignored me fifty-nine times. We slogged all the way back along the cliff path and arrived finally at the gravestone of Joseph and Mary Anning.

The evening breeze was soft but steady. I wished I'd brought a cardigan.

"I was meant to stay in town on Wednesday," said Oscar.

"But you came back to camp instead," I said. "In the dark. Without telling your father."

He licked his lips and looked toward the cliff. "You're not going to like this," he said. "You're not going to like *me*." He took a deep breath. "Before I came to the bonfire, I was here." He patted Mary Anning's headstone.

"You were *here*? When he—"

"It was windy that night, and I was . . . I was hiding. I didn't hear everything."

"But—"

"Just let me say it, will you?"

I pressed my lips together and nodded. *Listen!* my grandmother said, inside my head. *You never learn anything by talking.*

Oscar rubbed his hand along the top of the grave marker. "Look here first," he said. "Right here." His fingertip filled a small triangular gap in the edge.

"The missing bit?" I said.

"*That* is desecration," he said. "*My* desecration. I used my penknife and I took off my shoe and kept tapping until a chip came out."

"The stone!" I said. "In your pocket. That's from here?"

Oscar nodded. "Arthur thought I was stupid because

it wasn't a fossil, but I'd got exactly what I wanted. What I'd thought I wanted."

The gap was about as big as the top joint of his thumb. Hardly anything when considering the mountainous cliff we stood on, the billion pebbles that covered the beach, the pocketsful of rubble that visitors carried away every day from Lyme Regis back to their parlors or their classrooms in every part of England and even overseas.

But Oscar's bit had not been tossed up by a frothy wave, or dumped on the shore from an eroding rock face. He had purposely chiseled it from a monument to someone who had died. How would I feel if someone had done that to my Papa's grave?

"You hate me," said Oscar.

"Not hate," I said. But what? What *did* I feel?

"It's bad," he said. "I know it's bad. That's why I couldn't tell you."

"I suppose you wanted a relic no one else could have. Like your father."

He winced. "That's the worst part," he whispered. "I was thinking that this one time I could give him something he didn't buy for himself. A souvenir of someone he admired. Unique, you understand?"

I began to nod, but then decided to be truthful. "I can see that you wished for a way to please your father," I said, "but . . . you chose poorly, I think."

He opened his fist to show the small wedge on his palm. "I wish I could turn back the clock and not have taken it," he said. Tears welled in his brown eyes, and we both looked away. We said nothing for a few minutes, watching the peach-tinted sun slowly, slowly melting through a hedge of slate-gray clouds.

"But it turned out that you were not alone in the churchyard?" I said, after a bit. "Or did *you* kill Mr. B-C? To stop him from exposing your crime?"

Oscar barked out a laugh. "Of course not! I hope you're joking!"

"Is this why you think the killer was a woman?" I said. "Because you actually saw her? You know who it is?"

Oscar shook his head rather mournfully. "I didn't *see* either of them. I'd been preoccupied, you know . . ." He waved his souvenir before putting it back in his pocket.

"Desecrating a gravestone?" I said.

"Desecrating a gravestone." He rested a hand over the nick in the stone, hiding it briefly. "I heard a man's voice and a woman. I ducked down, over there. Behind that one." He pointed to a marker a little larger than the Anning one. *Peter Chandler, Eternally at Rest.*

"What did you hear?"

"Words I didn't catch, with the sea sloshing and the wind blowing. And me, well, scared . . ."

"Scared of being caught spying?"

"I wasn't spying on purpose!" he said. "My heart was pounding so hard I could feel it in my ears." He glanced over. "Do you want me to tell you or not? I felt horrible the minute I'd done it."

"I do," I said. "I'm sorry."

"I hunched into a ball when I realized I wasn't alone. I kept my head tucked down. Then the woman shouted, 'No! That's not true!' I didn't know what to do! Should I jump out and show myself? How could I explain what I was doing there? *'Here I am, desecrating a gravestone'*?"

This time I stayed quiet. Oscar rubbed his hands over his face and kept going.

"I caught hardly any of what B-C was saying. I heard 'sneaky' and 'robbing us blind,' but mostly his voice was low and growling. The woman said, 'Remember your wife?' but before that, 'my dad' and something about a choir. It didn't make sense, coming in snatches. B-C laughed a mean laugh and then the woman got fiercer. 'Don't you dare!' she said. What if he was hurting her? I knew I should get up. But suddenly I heard her sobbing, much closer than before, and I ducked down again instead." He chewed on his lip. "I'm a coward," he whispered. Then, "It was nearly dark by then, like now or maybe a bit later. She went crashing past, making choky noises. When I peeked around the gravestone, she was gone." He waved a hand toward St. Michael's.

"I waited about five seconds, then barreled off in the opposite direction."

"If you didn't see who she was," I said, "have you guessed since?"

Oscar looked out toward the rolling sea, dappled now with the ocher and silver of twilight. The sea was more changeable than humans, I'd learned. Any particular hour it might be green or gray or tangerine. It might bellow or ripple or lie utterly still.

"You've guessed too, haven't you?" Oscar said, very quietly.

"When you said before that it was a woman, my suspicions focused on Nina," I said. "She has the best motive of anyone to get rid of him, don't you think?"

"It wasn't Nina," said Oscar. "I told you that. It happened while you were having your bonfire, before I got to the camp. Nina was there with you and Everett, right?"

"Right," I said. "And your suggestion of Yvonne seemed pretty unlikely."

He waited, making me say the impossible words out loud.

"What I was trying to say before, when you ducked away . . ." Shivers ran down my arms. "Helen told a fib about where she was that night. Arthur thought the fib was yours." I remembered the paper passed from Cavalier Jones to Helen. "This is a guess, but I think that really she

284

was meeting someone else in the churchyard. Not Mr. B-C. Someone her father doesn't know about. A beau."

"I can see how her dad might be a problem," said Oscar. "Speaking as someone whose own father is not an easy one to live with."

"But *Helen*," I said. "Can *Helen* really have *killed* someone?"

"The trouble is," Oscar said, "that we don't want her to be bad. She's friendly and kind and looks out for us."

"Looks out for us," I echoed. A picture of Hector's wan face against the dead man's pillows leapt to my mind. "Oscar!" I said. "We've got to go back to camp at once! Grannie Jane told Helen to watch Hector especially tonight. His minder is a murderess!"

CHAPTER 28

A SORDID EXPLANATION

P.C. GUFF AND ARTHUR WERE on the cliff path as we neared Camp Crewe at a trot. Aided by the light of the policeman's lantern, they were pretending to have a boxing match, as young men were inclined to do for no reason that I had ever sussed.

"Why aren't you with Hector?" I said.

"He's sleeping," said Arthur. "Where've you two been?"

"For a walk," said Oscar.

"You're certain he's asleep?" I said. That was good. Helen had no reason to attack him in his sleep, had she? I'd suggested that Oscar tell Hector the whole truth, about what he'd heard in the graveyard and why he'd been there to begin with. Hector could be relied on to use his brain cells and his heart together in such matters.

"Where's Helen?" said Oscar.

Arthur didn't know where Helen was. P.C. Guff was on guard, he said, in case Miss Spinns tried to come back, or some reporter tried to sneak a look at the sea dragon. P.C. Sackett was stationed on the other side, by the trail to the main road.

"Who cares about a load of silly stones?" said P.C. Guff. "The sergeant's gone off home and left us on duty! With a murderer roaming about!" And why was P.C. Sackett suddenly famous just for owning a boat, Guff wanted to know. He hadn't even been rowing it when the big moment came! Sackett had been interviewed by two different newspapermen already, and here was Guff standing guard on the cliff well past his teatime. How was that fair? "You'd think it'd matter more who killed the old geezer than digging up a pile of bones. And what sort of woman spends her life looking at bones anyway?"

"A murderess, that's who," said Arthur.

"Arthur!" I said.

"What?" said Arthur. "It was Oscar who said the killer was a woman."

"Shut it," said Oscar.

"And why does Oscar think that?" P.C. Guff glared at Oscar. But then he smiled. "True or not," he said, "it's a good enough reason to get off this cliff. I'll go tell the sergeant a certain new claim has come to my ears, and then I'll go home to my Bessie." He clomped away in high spirits.

"Arthur!" I said. "How could you blab?"

"Aren't we all trying to find the murderer?" said Arthur.

"Have you never heard of loyalty?"

"I'm *being* loyal," said Arthur stubbornly.

"You're being a rat!" I said. "We're your friends! And so is Nina!"

"P.C. Guff is my cousin," said Arthur. "Blood is thicker than water."

Your head is thicker than a loaf of bread, I wanted to say.

"We do all want to catch the killer, don't we?" said Arthur.

"Yes, we do," I said.

"Hector," said Oscar, nudging me.

I started to run.

Spud had carried Hector back to the boys' tent to sleep in familiar surroundings. When we burst through the door flap, perspiring from the run, Helen was kneeling beside his cot.

"Don't touch him!" I said. Helen's eyes went wide. My fists went up, ready to fight for Hector's life, Oscar right behind me.

Helen screwed up her face and blew out a hefty breath. "I been expecting something like this to happen," she said. "But not from you." She edged her way past us and went out, without another word.

Hector pushed himself as close to sitting as he could on his own. "What is this about?"

I left Oscar to explain and raced after Helen, heart pulsing in my throat. What did she mean, she'd been expecting this? Was "this" an accusation of *murder*?

She was on her cot in the tent we shared, for where else could she hide?

"Go away!" she growled.

"Helen, please, I know you wouldn't hurt Hector, but . . ."

"I would never," she whispered, "and you of all people should know that. But, like I said, I been waiting. Someone was bound to accuse me."

I sat across from her. In silence, except for a fly whirring about. Helen chewed the cuticle on her thumb, staring at my knees.

"Were you there?" I leaned forward. "In the church-yard that night?"

"I didn't kill him. I'm almost completely certain that I—"

"But . . . you *pushed* him?" There. Her eyes locked with mine.

She nodded. And then she vigorously shook her head *no*. And then the tears spilled out.

"I pushed him," she said, sobbing the words, "but we weren't so close to the edge. I don't see how—it could never happen like that . . ."

"What *did* happen?" I whispered. "Why were you there at all?"

"You're not to tell my dad, you hear?"

I nodded, hoping with all my heart that I could keep such a promise. Though how could I, if she were hanged for murder?

"I went to meet my Ned." She spoke to the cup on the nightstand, not to me. "We hardly see each other in summer while the circus is touring so much. We meet in secret because nobody can know, see? Because of my dad."

"Nobody except Cavalier Jones," I said, remembering the paper that had exchanged hands.

"Excepting him," she agreed. "He helps us sometimes. Like for Wednesday, Mr. Jones gave me a note from Ned that said *Joy B, sunset*, so I knew Ned would come to the cemetery after the evening show." She squeezed her eyes shut and huffed out a big breath. "Only he weren't there. And he never did come."

"He was helping Oscar's father after Mr. Jones punched him," I said. "Ned took Mr. Osteda back to the Royal Lion."

"I know that *now*," said Helen, "but on Wednesday I waited next to the stone for *Joy Brownscombe, Our Mother, At Rest*, where we always meet. Things go wrong, you know? I can't get away, or sometimes Ned can't. We've agreed, we wait half an hour before giving up. Then we try again, next chance." She pushed a damp curl from her cheek and I saw that she was perspiring.

"My hair was under my hat, of course, so he didn't know it were me. And I didn't hear him, with the wind picking up and the tide coming in. Then suddenly, 'Hallo, sweetheart'—his voice out of nowhere, nearabout making my heart stop."

"Not Ned?" I said.

"Mr. B-C! Standing right behind me. I jumped up, and his face showed I weren't who he expected. I said hello, while inside I were cursing at being seen. I look around to warn Ned, thinking maybe he's late because he saw a stranger and tucked himself out of sight. 'Helen?' says Mister. It comes out 'Helllllen?' And I think, *Oi, he's drunk*. I say, 'Who were you expecting?'"

Helen reached for the cup and took a sip of water, making a face.

"Ugh," she said. "That's been there a while."

Keep telling, I thought. *What happened next?*

"He says, 'Never you mind who, and what about you? Alone in a graveyard at nightfall,' he says. 'You're up to no good, am I right?' 'No!' I say, raising my voice, in case Ned is close enough to hear and stay hid. 'No! That's not true!' Only he's getting stroppy now. 'I always thought you were a good girl,' he says, 'but you're every bit as sneaky as your dad.' 'My dad?' I say. 'What makes you say that?' And he says, 'His little temper tantrum today didn't fool me. He's hiding something. Robbing us blind, most likely. Or selling stories to the newspaper.' 'He isn't!' I say. 'He never would! He sings in the choir on Sundays, he does.' And the Mister laughs this nasty laugh, and I get prickles up and down my back. He already tried to fire my father in the afternoon, same as Everett, and now he's here, swaying drunk, and where's my Ned? But instead of leaving off and walking away, that's when I made my big mistake."

Helen put her face in her hands, and I saw the shiver go through her.

"What mistake?" I whispered.

"I could have shut my stupid mouth, but he were getting my temper up. I said, 'If anyone's sneaky, it's you, Mister, out here sozzled and waiting for someone named Sweetheart, instead of home with your wife.'" Helen looked over at me and lifted her shoulders in a helpless shrug, her eyes again welling with tears.

"See?" she said. "I could have made things better, but instead I made things worse. 'Remember?' I say. 'Your wife?' So, he gets all fiery-eyed and takes a step at me,

292

starting to rumble with that voice that claims how he's the only one who knows anything. 'How will your sainted father take the news that his daughter is loitering in churchyards after dark?' he says. 'How will he like being fired because of his precious little girl, eh?' He's threatening me! And that scares me silly. What if he *does* tell me dad? We need every penny! And what if I lose Ned? Now I'm trembling with fury, because how dare he? We work so hard! Mister takes another step toward me and I shout, 'Don't you dare come any closer,' and—"

She was really crying now, but trying so hard not to. She took in a deep, ragged breath.

"I gave him a great old shove," she said. Her arms shot forward, palms raised, showing me. "Quick and hard. Surprised him, I did. Surprised meself! He staggered backward, being legless with the whiskey, and that were my chance. I ran past the graves and all the way to the Cobb. The wind were blowing steady, spray from the sea near as strong as rain, and it cooled me down. I began to think, *Crikey, what happened to Ned?* But I knew I'd better get back to camp. I took the road, not the cliff path, praying Mister were drunk enough not to remember in the morning. I were sick with dread, walking back. What if I saw him along the way?"

But she hadn't seen him. No one had ever seen him again. Not alive.

A picture flashed in my mind of the balding spot on the back of his head. Not something I'd ever have noticed if he hadn't been lying facedown on the pebbly shore with his hat long gone.

"We weren't that close to the edge," Helen whispered. "I've relived it a thousand times. We were scarcely past the last gravestone. We—"

"Wait," I said. "Think again. You pushed him—"

"Hard," she said. "I admit. It were hard."

"You said he staggered. Did you see him hit the ground?"

She closed her eyes. She made a shoving gesture with her hands. She was remembering by looking at the picture in her mind.

"He fell on his arse." Helen opened her eyes and choked back a laugh. "One leg up in the air and his mouth round like a drain."

"Did he say anything?" I said.

"I didn't stop to listen," she said. "I ran like I never run before and hope never to again."

"I'm glad you got away," I said. "It sounds horrible from start to finish."

"I pray the Missus never has to know," said Helen. "Imagine looking her in the face and saying he was meeting a sweetheart." She covered her eyes again. "And my dad!" It came out muffled. "What'll *he* do if he hears about me being there?"

"I hope you never find out," I agreed.

She rolled onto her side and lay down. "I'm knack-ered," she said.

"Night, night, Helen."

Would anyone believe her story? I tried not to breathe until she began to snore. Was I a ninny for believing it myself? But I did believe her. She pushed Mr. B-C and she saw him hit the ground. The *ground*. Not the thin air over the edge of a cliff, followed by a harrowing wail. She had not killed him.

Had someone else been there to take advantage of the professor's inebriation? Other than Oscar? Oscar had no reason to rush out and push a man off a cliff. Had Ned been hiding nearby after all? I needed Hector! I pulled on a cardigan and retrieved my torch from under the cot. I slipped outside and darted toward the boys' tent, not bothering with shoes. I'd got halfway across the grass when the twin beams of a motorcar's lights jumped down the rutted trail and sent me scuttling for cover.

"Everett!" Nina emerged from her tent, calling his name in a low voice. I heard the click of car doors and the rumble of two men's voices as they approached. Nina thanked Mr. Osteda repeatedly, while I crouched behind the boys' tent. How could I explain if I were spotted in such a situation?

"Isn't it too late now to wake Oscar?" Nina said. "Leave him here till morning."

"I'll check on him." Mr. Osteda's voice came closer to where I was huddled around the corner. "Maybe he's awake." I heard the flap lift. I heard him murmur Oscar's name and get no reply. I held my breath as he withdrew and said good night and started the engine of his motorcar.

"Until tomorrow!" said Mr. Osteda, and drove away.

A half minute passed, with only crickets making noise.

"Welcome home," said Nina. "You look terrible."

I heard Everett chuckle, and risked a peek.

"I missed the big day," said Everett. "I could weep with frustration. I would pay good money to bop that policeman on the nose."

"Do you want to see Izzy? She's still wrapped, of course, so there's nothing to see except the size."

"You know I do!" said Everett. "Have you got a torch?"

"This way," Nina said. I froze as a torch beam danced on the dirt. She led him toward the shop yard, where the ichthyosaur lay in all its bundled-up glory. While they were out of sight, I crept around to the flap of the boys' tent and slipped inside.

Three voices gasped in unison. "Aggie?" They were awake! They'd been pretending to sleep so that Oscar wouldn't be dragged off by his father!

"What are you doing here?"

"You're lucky they didn't see you!"

"What happens with Helen?" said Hector.

"Ssh! Wait!" I said.

We waited. We'd done a lot of waiting this day. I sat on a heap of rumpled clothing near the door. Not too long later, we heard the returning murmur of voices, and then the words as well.

"You'll tell me everything tomorrow," said Everett, "but now, I must sleep. The bed last night was no more than a board."

"The snail-witted sergeant is running out of suspects," said Nina. "Spud, Mr. Osteda, Miss Spinns for a minute and then you."

"Your turn next," said Everett.

"Why didn't he start with me?" she said. "If he had an ounce of brain matter, he'd know I've got the strongest motive."

"Ssh," said Everett. "Don't say that."

We waited again, for the swishing of tent flaps, the steps of someone on the path to the backhouse, a gurgle from the tap. And finally, silence for long enough that we dared to speak again. Arthur, now asleep, mumbled occasional words and made odd lip-smacking sounds.

"You hear what we are suffering this week?" said Hector.

"Will you please listen and help think what to do?" I said. "Oscar was right—"

The tent flap whooshed open. A torch beam tried to blind me and I nearly fell over in surprise. Everett's whisper was as clear as church bells.

"If you are back in your own tent before I count to ten, Miss Morton, I shall *not* have seen a young lady consorting with boys after dark."

CHAPTER 29

A FALSE ACCUSATION

HELEN AND I AWOKE to a scuffling outside. The sudden arrival of unwanted company at tent doors was becoming a regular event!

"How does this blasted thing open?"

Helen's eyes widened in terror. I'd tied the cords last night after learning what might occur when taken by surprise. I fumbled them open now.

"G-good morning," I said, "Nina."

"Will you come out, Helen?" Nina peered around me. "Or will I come in?"

Helen whimpered. Her eyes were like those of a bunny trapped by a tiger.

"Out," she croaked. Having the tiger inside was more than she could bear. Nina waited while Helen and

I tugged on our dresses, not bothering with hair or stockings. As we slid into our shoes, Helen whispered, "Don't leave me alone with her."

Looking past Nina, I saw Arthur following Oscar toward the cliff path. Where could those two be going? And *together*? At this hour? The sun had not yet got its whole self above the horizon!

"I believe, Helen, that we have something of importance to talk about," said Nina, "though possibly not within your father's hearing?"

Helen made that mewing noise again.

"We'll walk around the little meadow," said Nina. "Follow me." She wore no shoes, but did not so much as blink as we set out through brittle grass and spiky stalks.

"Everett came back last night," she said.

"He survived his time in jail?" I asked. *While I was eavesdropping, you said he looked terrible.*

"Yes," she said, "and something he said got me thinking." We'd reached the far side of the open grassy area and continued around the perimeter. "I did nothing *but* think. All night."

I met Helen's worried eyes. Where was this leading?

"Everett commented that the sergeant had suspected everyone in turns. I joked that it would be my turn next because who else was there? My motive was stronger than anyone's, to escape an unhappy marriage. But I know perfectly well that I did not kill him." She glanced at us as if to check that we agreed. "So, who did?"

I dared not look at Helen.

"Who had he wronged so grievously as to provoke his own death?" Nina went on. "He'd argued with Everett, but that was not unusual. He'd upset Oscar's father, but to the point of murder? And there was the ugly scene with Spud, which I heard about afterward. I began to wonder, *How did that begin?*" She stopped walking. I paused too, as did Helen, who gave a little shudder.

"Howard overstepped the line of decency, is that right, Helen? And your father was rightfully outraged. But Spud is a softie, really, isn't he? He'd not harm anyone, would he, if it meant harming you as well?" Nina didn't wait for an answer. "But what if *you* . . . well, it occurred to me . . . I might not be the only woman who felt bullied. Was someone else braver than I am? Someone who took command when she felt threatened?"

Helen abruptly turned away.

"Are you feeling awkward because I was his wife?" said Nina.

"You've got the wrong idea," said Helen.

"Do I?" Nina did not wait for an answer. "Shall I first tell what happened to me? We're not so different as you might think. And Aggie should hear, because she's a girl about to be a lovely young woman. It is nice to be a lovely

301

young woman, but it cannot be the only thing you are. Do you understand?"

"Yes, ma'am," I said.

"Ma'am?" she said with a laugh.

I felt the flush in my cheeks as surely as I saw it in Helen's.

"My father was delighted that I should wed an eminent scholar," said Nina. "My mother felt I was too young. 'You will not see the world so clearly if guided by his eyes,' she said. But I married him the week after my graduation, and quickly learned another side of my new husband. He was content for me to continue my studies, but he would assume the right to present my work to the world. Suddenly his reputation became even more esteemed, thanks to my papers. A married woman has no standing in a court of law. He was a lazy opportunist. And still a flirt with every pretty student who crossed his path."

Helen kicked a stone.

"A picnic with Miss Pringle," said Nina. "A letter received from Miss McLean. A giggle from Daisy, who mended the linens. Oh, hell." We'd made a turn that brought the camp back into view. Nina stopped walking. "Is that the insufferable sergeant again?"

Yes, it was. The familiar bicycle weaved to avoid the ruts halfway down the track. Constable Guff was a considerable way behind.

"And look!" I said. "The patient is outside." Under the kitchen canopy, Hector lolled in a sling chair like those on the deck of an ocean liner. His injured leg was propped on one of the benches, next to where Everett was sitting.

"King Hector," I said.

Everett did not look concerned at the sight of the approaching policemen, just irked. Nina exhaled abruptly and strode toward camp.

"She's got the wrong idea entirely," said Helen. "I'd rather eat grubs than flirt with the professor. But Missus thinks I killed him and now she'll tell the sergeant!"

At that moment, the sergeant's bicycle toppled over, landing his bottom on the dusty track.

"Guff!" he shouted. "I've got a ruddy puncture!" He kicked his bicycle as he stood. Helen and I were far enough away to laugh aloud as he vigorously slapped at the seat of his pants to remove any marks. Poor P.C. Guff rolled to a stop to hear his sergeant's command. "Fix it!"

Spud appeared in the doorway of the cook tent.

"Dad's looking for me," said Helen. "I should be stirring porridge instead of listening to Missus suggest that I tossed her husband into the sea."

"Oi! Helen!" Her father had caught sight of us loitering in the meadow.

"Coming!"

Helen hurried into the cook tent and I knelt by Hector's chair. His pallor, in the brightness of day, made him ghostly and startling, especially next to Everett's brown face and bright eyes.

"You look as if you might faint dead away," I said, "like a damsel with consumption." *Like a rubber balloon with the air squeezed out. Like a vampire's victim drained of blood.*

"It is surprising that I do not expire," said Hector, "after so many hours sharing a confined space with—" His gaze jumped to something behind me. "With them."

Arthur and Oscar, back from their mysterious errand! They went straight past us and hurried to the tap beside the backhouse.

Everett laughed. "Boys are stinky," he said. "I'd avoid their tent if I were you."

I blushed, and did not allow him to catch my eye. Would Everett tell James where he'd found me last night? The boys came back, damp and cheerful.

"Where did you two go?" I said.

"Can't say," said Arthur, full of importance. Oscar, behind him, rolled his eyes and held up his hands. Under his fingernails, where usually a boy had grime—unless the boy was named Hector—was a telltale line of white plaster. I still was puzzled, until he patted the pocket where he'd been keeping his souvenir from Mary Anning's grave. Ohh! Now I understood. He'd replaced the stolen piece and affixed it with plaster! I hadn't even told Hector, but Oscar had confided in *Arthur*? Well, I supposed I'd been occupied with Helen, and Hector was down with an adder bite, so poor Oscar had been rather stuck with the one ally left over.

"We didn't make porridge this morning," Helen announced, "what with Mr. Jarvis and Mr. Volkov not being here." *And you not being on duty to make it*, I thought. "But we made a nice pan of scrambly eggs and there's bread and butter, of course."

We served ourselves and sat to eat, with the policemen grumbling too nearby.

"Let's pretend they're not here," said Nina. "It's a beautiful Monday and our ichthyosaur is safe and sound on dry land, waiting to travel to its next destination, wherever that ends up being. Isn't that all that matters? Whatever nonsense the officers are here to—"

P.C. Guff dutifully handed over his own bicycle so that the sergeant could arrive in a respectable manner. The constable picked up the useless bike and pushed it toward the shop yard. Helen abruptly retreated into the cook tent. It was not such a beautiful Monday the way she saw things, I imagined, expecting to be accused of murder.

The young woman's fluffy yellow hair was now matted and bedraggled as she huddled in a corner of the cold cement cell. Her rosy cheeks were drawn, eyes smudged with fearful shadows, hands manacled to an iron ring on the damp wall, and her heartbeat hollow and forlorn. Protests voiced by father and friends had been ignored. The paleontologist's claim was enough to satisfy the dim but comely officer.

"Your attention." The sergeant's voice banished my grim daydream, and prompted Helen to peek from the kitchen doorway. He wore his usual copper-buttoned uniformed and tall boots—as well as his usual smug expression. He held a collecting sack. Was it *the* collecting sack?

"Mrs. Blenningham-Crewe." Sergeant Harley lifted the sack. "You will recognize this as belonging to your husband?"

"I recognize it as one of a dozen that we have in camp," said Nina. "If it is the sack you snatched from my hands on Friday morning, discovered on Church Cliff by the children and holding Howard's flask but not a suicide letter? Then yes, it may have been used by my husband. Beyond that—"

"No letter," said the sergeant. "A flask with the victim's monogram, and two drinking glasses. One is now broken."

"*Two* glasses?" Nina said.

"Glasses?" said Helen.

"That's what I said, ma'am." The sergeant smirked. "What do you think of that, eh?"

Nina's eyes were resting on Helen.

Helen had become as still as a statue: *Girl with Tray and Teapot*. She must be thinking of the mystery woman named Sweetheart. I was certainly wondering where the glasses came from, as I'd seen none in the camp.

"My theory is that you and your husband had a little celebration planned, eh?" The sergeant was pleased with his deduction. "He went to the pub to meet the big American millionaire, to sell the fossil and make your fortune. Mr. Ostrid explained how you pretended to be reluctant about the sale so that he would offer a higher price to clinch the deal with your husband—"

Nina shook her head in disbelief.

"He had his flask filled up," said Sergeant Harley, "ready to raise a cup of good cheer."

Helen put down the tray ever so carefully, her hands a-trembling.

"Mr. Tobie claims you were with him in camp on Wednesday evening," continued the sergeant. "At first, we were fooled into thinking that he was using you to provide an alibi, while *he* dashed off to do the deed . . . but what if we look at the scene from the opposite direction?"

Nina was still shaking her head, as steadily as a human metronome. "If Howard had his flask and two cups in that sack," she said, "it was certainly not to celebrate with *me*. He was meeting someone who might appreciate his whiskey. There are several whiskey-loving men who wished to meet with Howard that night to conduct secret business . . . or, yes, I suppose it could have been another woman . . . but we don't need to be specific about such plans in front of children, do we, Sergeant?"

"We don't have glassware here in the camp," murmured Helen. "Breaks too easy."

"I do not hold you responsible for anything that happened on Wednesday night, Helen," said Nina. "You shall not hang."

"Missus!" Helen protested. "*Nothing* happened! I'm not—"

Nina turned toward the sergeant. "I want it noted," she said. "Going forward, I do not blame the girl. Howard could be overwhelming, I know that. I expect Helen felt crushed, as others have been. Including me. Mostly me. She may have done us all a favor."

CHAPTER 30

AN UNANTICIPATED TRUTH

A GASP FROM EVERY ONE OF US. Nina was condemning Helen! Tossing her into a moat with a snapping crocodile. A rather dull-witted crocodile, but one fond of making accusations.

"You've got it all wrong!" cried Helen. Spud stepped out of the kitchen to watch his daughter in alarm. Sergeant Harley's gaze fixed on her, and then flicked back to Nina.

"What makes you think—?" he said. "Do you have evidence to support this—?"

"It's a guess," Nina admitted. "It wouldn't be the first time that he—"

Spud made a growling noise. "Are you suggesting, Missus, that my girl was overly friendly with the Mister? Is that your claim?"

"Never! Dad, I swear."

"If you're trying to sway the sergeant's opinion," Spud thundered at Nina, "using some kind of trick to excuse yourself—"

"No!" said Nina. "I was here in camp! Ask the children! I did not kill my husband!"

"I didn't do it neither," said Helen.

"Who was it, then?" said Sergeant Harley.

"Because if you did"—Spud turned to his daughter—"you've cracked my heart like an egg on the edge of a bowl. Tell me straight, were you there on Church Cliff or no?"

"Good question," said the sergeant. "Yes? Or no?"

If Helen said yes, they'd all think the worst. If she said no, she'd be telling a lie.

"This is the time." Hector was looking at Oscar, prompting him, as if they had arranged this moment.

"*I* was there." Oscar's voice filled the trembling silence. "I heard what happened."

All heads turned to stare. He'd been so ashamed and nervous telling me, yet here he was making a declaration to anyone with ears.

"Speak up, lad," said Sergeant Harley. "I am terribly confused."

"You were *where*?" said Helen.

"When?" said Everett.

"You heard what?" Nina said.

310

Oscar waited for quiet. "I went to the churchyard," he said. "On Wednesday, when my father went to the pub. I heard them talking."

"You heard *who* talking?" said the sergeant.

"Mr. B-C," said Oscar, "and a woman, but—" His palm flew up to stop the instant flutter of questions. "I didn't see her. I know they were not there to meet each other. Mr. B-C was expecting someone else. He sounded drunk. There was shouting, but it was windy. I couldn't really hear. And then the woman ran away." He shifted his gaze from the buttons on Sergeant Harley's chest to face the girl with hair the color of yellow daisies. "Didn't you?"

A gulping sob from Helen, a groan from Spud and another chorus of gasps from everyone else.

"We were *nowhere* close to the edge," Helen whispered.

"She's right," said Oscar. "He—"

"What did you argue about?" said Nina.

I raised my hand. "An argument does not mean a murder," I said.

"What about the bruises on his chest?" said Nina. "*Someone* pushed him."

"A push *can* just mean 'go away,'" I said. "Isn't that right, Helen? Tell what happened."

Helen took a breath and did not look at her father. "I have a beau," she said. "His name is Ned Cleff and he plays a trumpet in the circus band. There's no cause for huffing, Dad. Let me tell it, now I'm begun. The whole reason Ned's a secret is your huffing. But he's a lovely boy and we've done nought wrong, I promise you that. So, I were meant to be meeting Ned on Wednesday evening, and when the Mister showed up it were a surprise for us both. He thought he had a tryst of his own. I'm sorry, Missus, but you were right about that. She didn't come, and I doubt she ever meant to."

"Wait!" I said, again plonking myself at the center of attention. All eyes suddenly turned my way. What had I meant to say?

"Excuse, please, the interruption." Hector came to my rescue, speaking softly. "Does not The Crow's Nest serve drinks in what you call half-pint glasses?" he said. "The professor's flask is full. He thinks he has made a conquest. He puts into the sack two glasses—"

"Yvonne!" I said.

"Yvonne!" said Spud. Relief spread across his face like butter on a hot griddle. "He was dead wrong, waiting for Yvonne. She gets chatted up by drunken louts five times a week and ignores them all."

Helen was nodding yes. "He had his hopes up, I suppose. But my Ned didn't come neither, thanks to Oscar's dad getting a shiner and needing help right then. The Mister didn't like me seeing him there, not one bit. He said I were fired, and my dad too, even if we work harder

312

than he does. Did. Mister were a bully and I were fed up with it."

Helen looked straight at Nina. "To answer your question about the bruising? Those were my handprints on his chest. I gave him a shove, to get him away from scaring me. But I swear before the Savior that I never pushed him over the cliff." She let herself meet her father's eyes at last. "I swear," she repeated.

"Oscar," said Hector. "Do you hear the agonized cry of a falling man?"

"No," said Oscar. "But I did hear him cursing like an old sailor! *After* Helen ran past me! There was grunting and bad words while he tried to stand up. I didn't wait around to see where he went, but I know for certain that she didn't push him off the cliff."

Sergeant Harley cocked his head to look at Oscar more closely. "And what was your own reason for being in the churchyard in the dark of night?"

"It wasn't all the way dark yet," said Oscar. "The sun was down, but the sky was still—"

"Answer the question," said the sergeant. "Why were you there?"

I saw a flash of panic as Oscar's eyes swiveled my way.

"Coming back to camp from the hotel for the bonfire, didn't you say?" I leapt in to help him, as he had done for Helen.

"I'd only ever gone by the cliff path," he said, shrugging. He shot me a grateful smile. "It was dumb, maybe, the long way around, but I—"

"It is best always to follow the path that you know," Hector said.

"It'd be scary going by road at night if you'd never done it," Arthur added.

"Hold on there," said Sergeant Harley. "I questioned the men, with no satisfaction. Mrs. Blenningham-Crewe says that she didn't kill him. Helen Malone says it wasn't her either, so what am I supposed to think? Who killed him? *Someone* must have done it! But who?"

But who?

"I have an idea of what might have happened," I said. The skeleton of a story was taking shape in my mind. Could I really say it out loud? I tried not to think of the crowd of faces watching me. I looked straight at Hector, as if we were having a Detection Consultation.

"A man succeeds in making everyone around him angry or frightened—or just wishing his bluster would stop." I heard the sergeant sigh, but I ignored him. Hector's green eyes were bright and reassuring.

"Nina and Everett try to brighten the evening by having a bonfire with us, the children. Spud and his friends have a pint or two to wash away the earlier clash with our victim. Also at the pub are Mr. Osteda and Mr.

Jones and Ned Cleff, the trumpet player. When trouble erupts at The Crow's Nest, not one person wants any part of it. The quarrel makes the men *less* inclined to follow the professor, not more. They steer clear and leave him to fend for himself."

Hector nodded, sending me courage to go on, despite exasperated noises from Sergeant Harley.

"Helen and Oscar were accidentally in the cemetery, but they both know that Mr. Blenningham-Crewe was alive when they left him there. Alive, but worse for the drink, and very much alone.

"Who did it?" I said. "I think . . . without meaning to . . . that he did it himself. After so much whiskey, he turned the wrong way. With no friend to hold his arm, he lost his step in the dark and blundered off the cliff. It's horribly sad, don't you think? Almost worse than murder."

The listeners were nodding. Each could probably recall a moment when they'd devised a way to avoid the professor's noisy presence. Or sat furiously hoping he'd disappear from sight. Sergeant Harley had a hand over his eyes, shaking his head as if to loosen an unwanted thought.

"I can see why you might all think . . . ," he began. "But this is my first murder case! My chance to be noticed! To qualify for Inspector! Don't you think that *someone* has to be the killer?"

"No!" we all said.

315

"It wasn't murder."

"Nobody killed him."

"Terrible bad luck."

"He just fell."

"You truly believe it was an accident?" Sergeant Harley looked miserable.

"Yes!" we all said.

CHAPTER 31

A PARADE OF FAREWELLS

THE SERGEANT HAD RUN OUT of suspects. He reluctantly admitted that we were likely right. The death of Professor Blenningham-Crewe had been an accident.

A blaring sound, like a flock of quacking ducks, announced the arrival of *two* motorcars bouncing down the track. Mr. Osteda drove the one in front and James was close behind, bravely disregarding the ruts. Grannie Jane, next to him, looked quite unnerved.

James had been unable to fetch along a doctor at such short notice, and was much relieved to see Hector sitting up. The arrival of a lord—not to mention a governor of the Natural History Museum— prompted a new fizz of elation at Camp Crewe. Everett and Nina were practically dancing in their eagerness to show him the ichthyosaur's body parts. And because lords and ladies were not common in America, Mr. Osteda was enchanted by meeting one for the first time. The only person disinclined to grovel was Sergeant Harley. He still seemed perplexed by having no one to arrest, and no reason to be standing about.

"He is the star of a show that does not end as he wishes," said Hector.

"As if he has forgotten his lines," I said, "and now must skulk away."

Skulk away he did, after looking around the circle of not-very-friendly-toward-him faces. Spud, Helen, Everett, Mr. Osteda and Nina had all been suspects, as far as the sergeant was concerned. Truthfully, Hector and I had considered most of the same people, but not with threats or jail time! He cycled away up the track and we soon stopped thinking about him.

"Are you packed?" James asked Hector and me.

"Alas, no," said Hector. "My leg does not permit—"

"We can help," said Arthur.

"Yeah, we'll do it," said Oscar.

"That's good of you, boys," said James. "Be quick! Are you ready, Aggie?"

I pointed to my case, trying not to laugh at the look of horror in Hector's eyes.

"This is most unsettling," he said. "I do not trust these hooligans to correctly fold my shirts."

"Luckily," I comforted him, "we are going to Owl Park, where there is a remarkable smoothing device called an iron."

James excused himself to fill his role as a museum governor for a few minutes, by following Nina and Everett, and Mr. Osteda, of course, to have a close look at our glorious ichthyosaur. Oscar's father, having permission from Sergeant Harley to depart, had agreed to wait for Hector and me to leave first. The Ostedas would then deliver Arthur to the cottage of P.C. Guff and his wife, where he would stay until his parents returned from Cornwall later in the week.

"Hector, may I abandon you for a moment?" I said. "I'd like to investigate the peculiar scene unfolding over there." I tipped my chin toward an unlikely pair sitting at the small table under the canopy. Spud seemed to have been telling the whole tale to Grannie Jane.

"Mr. Malone." My grandmother spoke with surprising gentleness. "What I know of Helen is that she is sunny, and reliable, and hardworking—attributes that any parent could wish for in a child. Young women are restrained by so many tethers, it is not surprising that occasionally they get themselves tangled. Is it so dreadful that a nice young man has recognized her shining qualities?"

Spud moaned, propping his lumpy head in his hands.

"She dared to push a university professor! And then he up and died! That's not good for a girl's reputation."

Grannie Jane *tsk*ed. "Helen defended herself and her family against dishonor!" she said. "Consider the anguish if she had *not* done that! Why not applaud such an act of courage? And perhaps this Ned Cleff will be worthy of her? She seems to think so."

Spud heaved a great sigh and managed to smile a small smile.

Grannie Jane noticed my lurking presence. "Are you waiting to speak, Agatha?"

"We're nearly ready to go," I said, "but I wished to thank you, Mr. Malone, for working so hard to keep us fed." Not for the first time since I'd begun writing poems, I silently marveled at how words could be usefully arranged to suit one's need. Almost, but not quite a fib. The alternatives in this case were socially unacceptable. *You are a better medic than you are a chef. The porridge had the flavor of paste. I may be five pounds lighter than I was a week ago—and it wasn't the shock of finding a corpse . . .*

The Izzy-gazers returned from the shop yard. James was suitably impressed with how very grand the fossil would be when reconstructed. "I must say, Aggie, those teeth have been very deftly wrapped! Well done."

"I have given Lord Greyson a full report," said Everett. "He was a bit dismayed to have left you in the care of a jailbird, but I assured him that apart from a small injection of venom, you're both fit and cheerful." He put a hand on Hector's shoulder and gave it a squeeze. "Thank goodness," he whispered. "Your composure in the face of death was admirable. I will strive to follow your example on the next occasion."

"The next occasion of corpse-stumbling?" I said.

"Should such an occasion arise," said Everett. "Which I rather hope it will not."

"Unless you are so lucky as to find another prehistoric marvel," said Hector.

"In which case," said Everett, "I shall be dancing on its bones."

Nina took my hands in hers and stared deep into my eyes, making the desire to squirm nearly impossible to resist. "If it weren't for you," she said, "I don't believe we'd know what happened to Howard. Not with that acorn-head of a sergeant running the show."

I smiled. "You might be another jailbird," I said.

"And instead . . ." She paused for only a moment. "I am about to find out what I can really do. All by myself." She turned away but came face-to-face with Helen. "Oh," she said, and then fell silent for an awkward minute, while Helen shuffled and went pink.

"I expect I should offer an apology," said Nina, "and I do, I do. I'm sorry to have made an assumption—and to do it out loud . . . But also, I hope . . . when Camp Crewe is all packed up and gone, and you're back to helping your mother wash sheets? I hope—for your sake—that it won't end there."

Helen nodded and went pinker and reached out a hand to me. She had another week to listen to Nina. For now she had us to wish farewell. She did not share wise words or gratitude, or even speak at all. She clasped me in her arms as fiercely as a green anaconda—and then did the same to Hector, nearly knocking him off his feet. That's when James extracted Hector and settled him into the back seat of the Peugeot, placing cushions to secure the injured leg in the most comfortable position.

Arthur bowed to me, though he lacked Hector's European flair. I responded with a curtsy, which made his ears blush. To Hector, he offered a smart salute with military precision. Ensconced in his nest, Hector could not bow, but he returned Arthur's gesture with gravity, and we were one step nearer to departure. Arthur stood stoically by, an English boy to his very toes, while Oscar hugged us, and wept, and even kissed me on the cheek before Grannie Jane put a firm hand on his shoulder to halt the display.

"This week has changed the course of my life," Oscar said. "I'll remember you forever."

"I'm starting the engine," said James. "Please, step away from the vehicle."

And away we went.

"God's nose," said James, "but that was an impassioned episode."

"Indeed," said Grannie Jane. "An American spectacle. Well meant, but best put behind us."

TORQUAY VOICE

MONDAY, JULY 13, 1903

Fossil Frenzy!!!!!!!
MISFORTUNE,
Not Murder!!!

by Augustus C. Fibbley

Two dead bodies on the beach at Lyme Regis have caused much speculation this week. One died more than a million years ago and the other died on Wednesday, shortly after sunset. Professor Howard Blenningham–Crewe fell from Church Cliff and was carried by the tide to rest on the beach between Lyme Regis and Charmouth. Children on a fossil-hunting expedition spotted the man's earthly remains on Thursday morning. Originally investigated as suspicious, his death has now been ruled as accidental by the Coroner's Court of Dorset, thus removing the onus of foul play.

Testing of the victim's blood indicated a high presence of alcohol. A witness in the vicinity of the incident declared that the man was alive some twenty minutes after the sun had dipped below the horizon. Evidence suggests that the professor lost his footing soon afterward, and followed the sun into the sea. A private funeral will be held in Tunbridge Wells, at a church frequented by the mother of the deceased. His grieving widow and several close colleagues plan to be in attendance.

As for the ichthyosaur, nicknamed Izzy by its rescuers, we have a happy ending. The specimen was unearthed on Sunday from its graveyard near the low-water mark by a small team led by paleontologist Mrs. Nina Blenningham-Crewe, who was responsible for the discovery. She was ably—nay, remarkably—assisted by Mr. Cavalier Jones, renowned circus impresario, known professionally as the Strongest Man in the World. As evidenced in the accompanying photograph, Mr. Jones single-handedly lifted each portion of the fossilized ichthyosaur into the waiting rowboat. This vessel, property of Police Constable Harry Sackett (and rented for a five-pound fee) was heroically rowed from Back Beach around Church Cliff to town by a young American visitor and prize-winning oarsman, Master Oscar Osteda (13).

A feud to own this magnificent fossil had been heating up between an American millionaire, Mr. Alonso Osteda (young Oscar's father) and Mr. Jones. Mrs. Nina Blenningham-Crewe was eager to have the specimen acquired by the Natural History Museum on Cromwell Road in London. The museum has expressed delight with this arrangement. Mr. Osteda was compelled to devise an alternative plan to enhance his collection. He will fund the reconstruction of two complete ichthyosaurs—as far as scientists can guess what these sea dragons actually looked like. Mrs. Blenningham-Crewe will advise upon, and the museum approve, the final design. The American collector will keep one model for himself and present one to the Cavalier Jones Cavalcade, where it will be exhibited in the Curiosity tent, alongside other marvels like a stuffed armadillo and a living snake that measures over fourteen feet in length.

After a week that held both devastating grief and ecstatic triumph for Mrs. Blenningham–Crewe, the new widow did not comment about her husband's death, but released a statement to the *Torquay Voice*. "Scientists are often thought to be bound by factual answers, but it is awe that inspires us to begin our exploration of the mysteries of the natural world."

"A surprising partnership," said Hector.

"They appeared ready to duel at dawn with pistols," I said, "but here they are best friends! Don't you wonder how many of Mr. Osteda's dollars it took to buy such a friendship?"

"Each gets what he most desires," said Hector. "The American has a sea dragon in the desert and the Curiosity tent of Mr. Cavalier Jones is full of people paying pennies."

"It would be a good story, would it not? Two people who seem to be the greatest of enemies turn out to be conspirators in a murder? Reluctantly they provide an alibi for one another, but their apparent loathing is all part of a devious plot!"

Several retorts seemed caught in Hector's throat but he said merely, "Not this time." And then, "I hope."

CAVALIER JONES
CAVALCADE

Rare Sights & Curiosities

Dancing Dogs, Bicycle Tricks,

Strongest Man, Fire-Eater

and newly featuring a mighty

SEA DRAGON!!!!

Wrenched from the depths of time

for your eyes only!!!!

Autumn Tour to include:

Exmouth September 7—11　❈　Torquay September 15—19

Paignton September 20—23

CHAPTER 32

A Tying-Up of Loose Ends

At Owl Park, James summoned the new physician, Dr. Weldon, to Hector's bedside. (Old Dr. Musselman was now a bit feeble in the head, according to my sister.) Dr. Weldon, among other accomplishments, had been in attendance at the birth of Baby Jimmy. But he had never seen an adder bite. This might have made us nervous, except that in his excitement he'd read two books, telephoned to three colleagues for consultation and gazed at Hector's puncture wound with scientific reverence.

Hector improved every hour, the medical attention no doubt enhanced by feather pillows and cotton bed linens, cups of chocolat and popovers with fig jam, as well as hours of Sherlock Holmes and *The Wonderful Wizard of Oz*. Baby Jimmy was much more awake than he'd been a week ago. Marjorie was sleepier, but happy nonetheless. She had Mummy as nursemaid, as well as Charlotte, my own hand-me-down nursemaid. And now she had Grannie too, to shield her from old Lady Greyson's opinions about mothering. Hector and I lay on the floor next to Jimmy's cradle, making silly sounds and blowing on his tuft of downy hair.

Grannie Jane had written to tell Mummy about Mr. B-C's death, but she had not shared any details beyond our discovery of the body. Telling the tale in person meant enduring Mummy's distress until she paused to let me soothe her.

"It was days and days ago, Mummy. We barely remember and have come back unscathed—except for the little matter of an adder bite . . . but Hector is near about as fit as a fiddle, is he not?"

We received from Arthur a postcard showing a picture of the Cobb seawall in Lyme Regis and his message, written in tiny script:

Dear Aggie and Hector, Camp Crewe is busy packing up and soon will be gone. The ichthyosaur will go to London, where it will take months to clean. BORING! Helen is now second barmaid at The Crow's Nest—permitted by her father because he's in there every night to keep an eye on her. I am applying to be a police cadet next summer, in a new program for boys. My cousin (P.C. Guff) says I will like it, but maybe not as much as the Young Scientists League.

Yrs truly, Arthur Haystead, prime-minister-in-waiting

Oscar sent a telegram from on board the RMS *Saxonia*. A telegram that remained private between Hector and myself, because of dubious language.

TELEGRAM

ALLS WELL THAT ENDS WELL STOP WILL SEND PHOTOGRAPH OF PRETEND IZZY IN TEXAS STOP HOPE ADDER BITE BETTER STOP BETTER THAN AN ANACONDA HAHA STOP BLAST AND DAMMIT STOP AFFECTIONATELY OSCAR

On the third day at Owl Park, the post brought a letter for Mummy from Mr. Cavalier Jones, and one for Hector from his mother.

"What do you think?" said Mummy. "He begins with, 'My dear Lady' . . ."

Hector and I laughed.

"Very forward," said Grannie Jane, tugging on the gray

wool that ran to her knitting needles from the muddle of skeins in her basket.

"He is inviting us to the circus!" said Mummy. "His Cavalcade of Curiosities is coming to Torquay, and he suggests . . . oh! The date he names is your birthday, Aggie! He offers us box seats . . . he says Grannie Jane should come, and Hector, of course . . . He thanks you both for your . . . Here it is: 'I wish to thank them for their part in securing me the greatest honor of my life, the opportunity to lift an ichthyosaur from the depths of time.' Shall we go?"

But then we saw Hector's face as he read his letter from home.

"Hector?" said Mummy. "Is there bad news?"

He folded the paper away and rested trembling fingers on the envelope. "The news, madame, it is most wonderful and most dreadful all at once." He swallowed and shone those green eyes directly into mine. "It is decided that I must return to Belgium. As soon as I am well enough to travel."

Thunder and lightning crashed inside my head.

"Return?"

Mummy and Grannie were quick to think of words to express make-believe joy on Hector's behalf. I was struck dumb, my own horror eclipsing any pleasure he might feel about returning to the embrace of his family. Why had I so recently claimed to Mummy that he was nearly repaired? If only he still walked with a limp or displayed less color in his cheeks! Could we not devise a setback that would forbid travel for weeks or even years? A lingering cough? A crusty rash? Except—and this was the hardest thing of all—except that Hector wanted to go!

I understood, I did. No, truly, I *did*. He loved his family as I loved mine. I'd had him all to myself for nearly a year! He must miss them most awfully, and I rarely cared to hear about Hector feeling lonely. I could never leave Mummy and Grannie Jane for so long. But still . . .

We passed two days of pretending that such a letter had never come. We surveyed the grounds of Owl Park from the terrace (as Hector now had an excuse to avoid hiking) and saw how summer transformed a place we'd seen last during the snowy winter. Swans idled on the pond, turning upside down to nibble reeds from the bottom and then fluffing themselves dry. A maze of privet hedges needed a clipping. Canes were required to hold up an abundance of raspberry bushes. The icehouse in the service courtyard held ice blocks big enough to hide the skull of an ichthyosaur—and were exquisitely cold to lick, once the sawdust packing was brushed away.

We crept along the secret passage from the morning room to spy on James in the study. He was speaking on the telephone, making arrangements for Hector's departure, a reminder that spying did not always benefit the spy.

The next day's post, delivered at breakfast with all of us gathered, brought a letter for James from Everett. He and Nina had relocated temporarily to London, where they now had access to a laboratory from which they would oversee the cleaning and reassembly of Izzy by the Natural History Museum experts. The B-C Ichthyosaur, as it had been dubbed, was expected to be on display to the public by next summer.

"Do you suppose," I said, "that the friendship of Everett and Nina has become rather friendlier?"

"It is a logical supposition," said Hector. "If I believed in supposing, or in guesswork."

"She's probably too busy being utterly free to do what she likes," I said, "with no time to waste on romance. Even if Everett is a top-notch character."

James cleared his throat. "'You'll be chuffed to know . . .'" he read from Everett's letter, "'and please pass the news along to Hector, that Nina has been invited to a town called Bernissart in Belgium, as part of the team recovering thirty-seven iguanodons discovered in a mine shaft.'"

Hector's face lit up. "Dinosaurs in Belgium!"

"'We can never thank you enough,'" James read on, "'for your generous contribution'—oh, never mind that bit. Let's see . . . Everett received a note of apology from Miss Spinns, but he does not forgive her for depriving him of witnessing Izzy's rise from the shale."

"Poor Miss Spinns will not be remembered kindly," said Grannie Jane, "and will be wise to remain incognito."

I looked sharply at my grandmother. Did she know more than we realized about the many faces of Mr. Fibbley? She gave no indication, but paused to count stitches along her knitting needle.

"Are you disappointed," I said to Hector, later, "that the professor's death was not a murder?"

"I trust," said Hector, "that you ask this question of no one else, chère amie. To be so despised that everyone assumes your fate to be murder, it is sad, is it not?"

"But he was *not* murdered," I said. "Only clumsy, as it turned out."

I asked myself the same question I had just asked Hector. Was *I* disappointed? We'd been the ones to discover a gruesome corpse, after all, and to dig out most of the clues. My Morbid Preoccupation was intact . . . and yet, I found it went further than fascination with a dead body. There was the surrounding spatter of people not behaving at their best—and our gratifying scrutiny through an imaginary magnifying glass.

"The demise of monsieur le professeur," said Hector, "makes me think of a quote most dismal from *The Hound of the Baskervilles.* 'Evil indeed is the man who has not one woman to mourn him.'"

"I expect at least that his mother is mourning him," I said.

"Let us hope this is true," said Hector.

"Despite not having a murder, we had a close-up view of a few dark secrets, did we not? Isn't that the best part?"

"Even better than gazing upon a corpse," said Hector. "Or touching one."

We grinned at each other, knowing he didn't mind, really.

On the next morning, the sun shone and the birds twittered wildly. I wished we might also have a sea breeze, but sadly, Owl Park was too many miles from the coast for that. Never mind. I cajoled Marjorie into letting us have breakfast on the terrace outside the library, to echo our arrangement under the kitchen canopy at Camp Crewe.

"A letter is come for you, Miss Aggie," said Dot, putting down the breakfast tray.

Though the handwriting on the envelope was familiar, I could not say for certain whether it belonged to Miss Sylvia Spinns or to Mr. Gus Fibbley. Inside was a newspaper clipping folded between the pages of a letter.

Dear Miss Morton,

You might be surprised to know how often I think of you. I hear from Constable Beck that you are visiting your sister in Tiverton. This news was relayed through his fiancée, Miss Charlotte Graves, who now is nurse-maid to your nephew. P.C. Beck told me that Hector was bitten by an adder in Lyme Regis. Please convey my best wishes for his swift recovery. I wish also to congratulate you both on your determined effort to reveal the truth about the professor's death. Your talent for crooked thinking is most admirable. I urge you to continue.

What will you make of the enclosed, I wonder?

Affectionately,
G.F.

The news article, written by Augustus C. Fibbley, was not from the *Torquay Voice*. Nor did it mention murder or excavating fossils. It reported on a demonstration outside the Digby Assembly Rooms, where more than two hundred women had gathered demanding their right to vote. The photograph showed four suffragettes holding up a banner that read DEEDS NOT WORDS!! VOTES FOR WOMEN!! The second woman from the left wore round wire-framed spectacles. She was identified as Miss Gussie Faraday.

"Gussie Faraday," I said. "Is that her real name?"

"It seems so." Hector leaned in to examine the face we'd known in so many guises.

"As a woman fighting for women's rights, she can go to all the meetings . . ." My thoughts skipped along Miss Faraday's path, and Hector sped beside me.

"And then report about the meetings as Mr. Fibbley," he said.

"And to be a writer in the newspaper, she becomes Mr. Fibbley."

"Women reporters cover mostly gardens and pies," I said. "When I grow up and have a job as a writer, I'm going to tell stories about science and murder."

"In ten years, or fifteen," said Hector, "much will be different, yes?"

"If Gussie Faraday and her friends have anything to say about it." I tucked the clipping into the envelope and the envelope into the back pages of my notebook. As often as I had been aggravated by Mr. Gus Fibbley, Miss Gussie Faraday was a person much like the one I aimed to be someday.

An Epilogue
(The Very End)

"THERE IS A NEW STEAMER FERRY across the channel," said James, later that morning. "It sails every day from Dover to Calais, in France, which is about two hundred miles from Hector's home near Spa."

I held my breath.

"I will accompany Hector to Calais, where he will be met by his father," said James. "Would you like to come along?"

"Yes!" I said. "When do we go?"

James put a hand on my shoulder. An I-am-so-sad-for-you hand. "Tomorrow," he said.

Tomorrow!

Time whirled after *that* announcement, leaving us no chance to moan. It was arranged that the vicar's wife would send Hector's belongings in a steamer trunk from the vicarage in Torquay to the ferry port. We departed early in the morning and endured a long, long drive to Dover. We dined on fish and chips in newspaper cones, heavily sprinkled with malt vinegar, and stayed that night in a hotel. The next day we boarded the *Queen*, the enormous steamer turbine ship that would take us to France.

James had brought with him a novel called *The Kip Brothers*, an adventure story taking place on a boat in olden days. He'd rather read about a harrowing mutiny, he said, than loiter about with children. Hector and I were free to roam but not to tumble overboard, was that agreed?

I did not wish to stand at the prow trying to spy France and what lay ahead. Instead, we made our way to the stern and gazed into the foaming wake—and everything else behind us.

Hector gripped the railing with both hands. "My insides are rolling like the waves," he said.

"Were you seasick on the voyage over?" I said.

"Then, I am sad to leave Belgium. Now, I am sad to leave England. Perhaps I mistake sorrow for the mal de mer." After a while, he took my hand. Salt water splashed across my cheeks, and where had that come from? "Might we say goodbye now?" Hector said. "I fear my family will be so overjoyed at saying hello that our farewell will be lost."

I swallowed the gravel in my throat. I did not, did *not* wish to say goodbye.

"We've become adept," I said at last, "at knowing what each other is thinking, have we not?"

"Telepathic," Hector said. "*Tèle* from the Greek for 'distant,' and *pathos* meaning 'perception.'"

"I hear you all the time!" I said. "I ask, what about this, Hector? What about that? More often, you tell me what to do whether I've asked or not."

"When *you* speak inside *my* head," said Hector, "I say, *Merci, this is too much imagination,* and I do the opposite of what you suggest."

We laughed, though mine was a little choked. And then we settled on silence, hand in hand until James came to find us. He had a Brownie camera, much like Everett's, and took four photographs of Hector and me by the railing, with the sea and a cloud-dotted sky behind us. Two we'd send to Hector and two were for my own album.

In Calais, we drew alongside the pier, lined with a crowd that cheered mightily as the *Queen* nudged her way to a stop. Some held banners to greet friends and relations, or held aloft rubber balloons tied in bunches. The docking of the boat was splendid, except that it was also my last hour with Hector.

"Can you see your father?" We leaned over the rail, scanning faces, though I did not know who to look for.

"There," said Hector, pointing. "My mother also is

here, and Genevie! You see there? The little girl with very black hair?" His cat-green eyes filled with tears as he began to wave.

We hustled with James into the line for disembarkation. The Perot family met us at the bottom of the gangplank and engulfed Hector so completely that I worried they would step back and find him dissolved. But no, they took turns laughing and crying and—in the case of Genevie— pulling down his stocking to see proof of the adder bite. Monsieur Perot wore a fine mustache with upturned ends. Madame had bright green eyes and a smile as warm as sunlight. Genevie chattered in French, barely taking a breath, sliding her arms around Hector's middle as if it were she who had come home.

The parting happened quickly in the end. James assisted Monsieur Perot in loading the luggage into the motorcar, borrowed for the purpose of collecting my best friend and carrying him far away. Hector's mother took Genevie to purchase a citronnade. Hector and I were alone for one more minute, looking at the channel from the other side. A whole new sea, really. We both had lead in our chests, I was certain of that. Lead or sawdust or bricks or fog—whatever weighty thing a writer might mention to describe the inability to breathe.

Next, we were waving, until even the face in the window disappeared.

James draped an arm over my shoulder. A warm, heavy arm that held me together as Hector was carried away. If he'd withdrawn his arm, I imagined that I would crumble to the ground in a thousand pieces, never to be reassembled in quite the same way.

But that was true, in any case, was it not? Aggie-from-before-Hector and Aggie-after-knowing-Hector were not the same person, were they? James did not withdraw the arm, not for ages. He seemed to understand about losing a friend.

There was the sky.

There was an elephant or an ichthyosaur.

There was a jungle or a sea.

And there was the most immense thing of all, the friendship of a whole other person.

When that was lost . . .

Oh, but I mustn't say it was really lost. Hector wasn't gone forever, not like Papa. I mustn't make it worse, because it was already terrible. Hector was still here in the world, and would be forever. He hadn't moved to Egypt; he had only gone home.

They had postboxes in Belgium, did they not? I tried to convince myself.

"They have pencils in Belgium, do they not?" I said to James.

"And sharpeners," said James. "Paper too. Made

from the very best trees. Entirely suitable for sliding into envelopes."

"Do you suppose they have postage stamps?"

"Very clever, the Belgians," said James. "I believe they've been using stamps nearly as long as the English have."

"And what about sealing wax?" I said.

"Made of chocolate," said James. "The Belgians are known for their chocolate. You simply bite off the seal to open the envelope." He produced a bar of Côte d'Or chocolate for us to share as we looked out at the rolling sea.

"If I haven't found another dead body before Hector's birthday," I said, after a while, "I shall write him a murder story in a letter, but I won't put in the ending. I'll write the clues and the suspects and possibly the weapon, but my present to him will be that he can puzzle it out all by himself."

"A fine present indeed," said James.

And so, I began to plot.

AUTHOR'S NOTE

There is no evidence that young Agatha Christie was especially curious about prehistoric bones—but she certainly spent many months of her life on archaeological digs in the company of her second husband, Sir Max Mallowan. Six of her novels feature an archaeologist character or a setting entrenched in the Middle East. Even one of her best-known books, *Murder on the Orient Express*, might be considered to belong in this category, because Christie's first trip to Baghdad was aboard that famous train.

Some of these stories were written while she participated in her husband's excavations, taking photographs and making records of the daily finds. Christie was familiar with sleeping in tents, and often set up her typewriter in makeshift conditions. She was most content when helping to restore ceramics, or cleaning items made of ivory using her own face cream. She paints a vivid picture of this alternate life in her witty memoir called *Come, Tell Me How You Live*, about time spent on a dig in Syria.

What if "my" Aggie's fascination with a buried past began when she was twelve, in the company of other young scientists? What if they were exploring the same Jurassic Coast in Dorset where young Mary Anning uncovered the first ichthyosaur in 1811? What if Aggie stumbled upon not only skeletons of creatures dead for millennia but also a newly deceased human body? These were some of the questions I asked myself while devising the backdrop for the fourth and final book in the Mystery Queen series.

I've come to know this character well since first creating her five or six years ago. We've had a few sleepovers, so to speak. She came suddenly to life during a conversation with Tundra publisher Tara Walker, and Hector appeared about a minute later as the logical and loyal best friend. The corpse Aggie Morton finds in July is her fourth such discovery in less than a year. Her world is otherwise safe and somewhat sedate, populated with family and neighbors—as Christie's was, in her homeschooled youth. Dropping the occasional corpse in the path of a shy Edwardian preteen seemed like a good fictional response to the question *Why did this particular person grow up to think about murder from morning until night?* The intention was to honor the real Queen of Crime, and to have fun with an homage that would include an imagined foundation for the observational acumen and morbid puzzling of the best-selling author-to-be.

This story's outdoor setting—so uncomfortable for Hector!—is a departure from the country houses and hotels of the previous books. Camping was becoming more popular in England at this time, and the first Boy Scouts gathered four years later (in 1907) only fifty-nine miles from Lyme Regis. I like to think of Arthur Haystead as a keen troop leader in his later teen years. (Arthur is my version of Hercule Poirot's sidekick, Captain Hastings. Athletic, loyal and always a step behind his friends.)

Although fossil-hunting had also become a trendy hobby, one of my challenges in this story was sorting out what present-day knowledge should be ignored and what might already have been accepted truth by paleontologists working in 1903. The ability to precisely calculate the age of a fossil using carbon dating did not yet exist. Darwin's theory of evolution had been published only forty-four years previously, and was still not universally believed. For scientists, though, the biblical tale of the world being created six thousand years ago, in six days, was not taken literally. But their estimates of Earth's origins being more than a million years ago fell far short of what we now know to be well over four billion years.

Not quite so old is Grannie Jane, my interpretation of the Miss Jane Marple who was composed by Christie with her own grandmother in mind. "She had this in common with my grandmother," said the famous author in an audio recording. "Although a completely cheerful person, she always expected the worst."

Being a pessimist myself (as well as a nosy parker), I strongly identify with the woman I created from Christie's anecdotes and from the fourteen novels and twenty short stories in which she is featured. My Mrs. Jane Morton holds high the bar she expects Aggie to reach on every occasion, but allows room for humor, missteps and macabre inclinations along the way.

Agatha Christie had a happy, if lonely, childhood. When the series begins, Aggie also spends much time in solitude—until she meets Hector and they both, rather suddenly, discover a best friend. Through subsequent adventures, Aggie and Hector collect several other young companions. Florence, Lucy, Stephen, George, Arthur, Helen and Oscar. They all expand Aggie's world a little further, and offer the first examples of the wide, wide cast of characters that fill the books she will someday write.

Sources

The best part of writing a book with an Agatha Christie connection is the opportunity to reread and relisten to many of her novels, and that I did—as well as dozens of other mysteries. All in the name of research, obviously. I consulted the library, the Internet and the podcast world.

Of particular use were the following:

Black, Sue. *All That Remains: A Renowned Forensic Scientist on Death, Mortality, and Solving Crimes*. New York: Arcade Publishing, 2018.

Brobeck, Catherine and Kemper Donovan. *All About Agatha* podcast. https://podcasts.apple.com/us/podcast/all-about-agatha-christie/id1155061645.

Brown, Lilian. *I Married a Dinosaur*. London: George G. Harrap & Co. Ltd, 1951.

Christie Mallowan, Agatha. *Come, Tell Me How You Live: An Archaeological Memoir*. London: HarperCollins Publishers Ltd., 1946.

Collard, Sneed B., III. *Reign of the Sea Dragons*. Watertown, MA: Charlesbridge, 2008.

Crampton, Caroline. *Shedunnit* podcast. https://shedunnitshow.com/listen/.

Doughty, Caitlin. *Will My Cat Eat My Eyeballs? Big Questions from Tiny Mortals about Death*. New York: W.W. Norton & Company, 2019.

Emling, Shelley. *The Fossil Hunter: Dinosaurs, Evolution, and the Woman Whose Discoveries Changed the World*. New York: Palgrave MacMillan, 2011.

Fowles, John. *A Short History of Lyme Regis*. Boston: Little, Brown and Company, 1982.

History of the Collections contained in the Natural History Departments of the British Museum, Vol I, The. London: Printed by Order of the Trustees of the British Museum, 1904.

Holding, Thomas Hiram. *The Camper's Handbook*. London: Simpkin, Marshall, Hamilton, Kent & Co. Ltd., 1908.

Shindler, Karolyn. *Discovering Dorothea: The Life of the Pioneering Fossil-Hunter Dorothea Bate*. London: Natural History Museum, 2017.

Valentine, Carla. *Murder Isn't Easy: The Forensics of Agatha Christie*. London: Little, Brown Book Group, 2021.

[Also, according to Carla Valentine, public engagement/
technical curator of Barts Pathology Museum in London,
Agatha Christie was credited (on the game show
Jeopardy!) as being the first author to refer to "the scene
of the crime." It appears in her third novel, *The Murder
on the Links*, published in 1923. This claim was my inspi-
ration for Aggie's use of the phrase in Chapter 17.]

ACKNOWLEDGMENTS

This book (like Aggie and Hector's previous adventure, *The Dead Man in the Garden*) was researched and written during a global pandemic. I was unable to travel to Lyme Regis to watch high tide flood the beach or to join a fossil hunt among the rock pools when the tide was low. Instead, I applied Internet ingenuity to spy on the town via satellite, as well as using historical maps. Happily, I also tracked down several experts who were remarkably generous with their wisdom and experience. Via Zoom, email and telephone, I soaked up whatever I could.

(Denizens of Lyme Regis may be horrified that—for the convenience of my characters—I allowed paths to exist where no cliff paths would be safe or possible. I apologize if this ruins the story for you! And I certainly claim responsibility if my scribbled notes misconstrued other facts as well.)

Thank you to Nigel Clarke, renowned fossil-walk guide, for a wealth of knowledge about the inhabitants of the ledges and the history of the town.

Thank you to Dr. Susannah Maidment and Andrea Hart of the Natural History Museum in London, who offered information on what was likely known about age-identification of fossils 120 years ago.

Thank you to Andy Robson of the UK Camping and Caravanning Club for a photo of "early tenting" and directing me to the 1908 edition of *The Camper's Handbook*.

Thank you to Harry May, a deep-sea fisherman based in Lyme Regis, who instructed me about tides.

Thank you to Chris McGowan, former curator at the Royal Ontario Museum, for explaining in wonderful detail how to make a field jacket for a fossil.

Thank you to Steve Davies, curator of Dinosaurland Fossil Museum, for setting me straight on some basic facts about prehistoric creatures.

Steve also introduced me to Brian Langdon, to whom I am indebted most of all. Brian sent a detailed narrative about the dramatic day he extracted an eleven-foot ichthyosaur from near the low-water mark off Back Beach, by Lyme Regis. This inspired a similar adventure in *The Seaside Corpse*, including the overloaded vessel that did not float until the very last minute. In honor of Brian's adventure, the *Touch Wood* in my story is named after his boat.

On the home front:

Thank you to Tara Walker for inspiring the series.

Thank you to editors Lynne Missen, Margot Blankier and Sarah Howden for your kindly, patient use of a hammer and chisel to be certain the story took the right shape.

Thank you to Isabelle Follath for the very loveliest portraits and illustrations.

Thank you to Sarah English for making Aggie and friends come so brilliantly alive in the audio versions of all the books.

Thank you to my stalwart literary agent, Ethan Ellenberg; to my screen agent, Rena Zimmerman; and to Evan Munday at Tundra Books, for boosting Aggie's place in the world.

Thank you from the bottom of my gnarled heart to Hadley Dyer for the lengthy and tender first readership.

And thank you, always, to my girls, for making me laugh.

More mystery,

more murder . . .

HAVE YOU READ THEM ALL?

AGGIE MORTON
MYSTERY QUEEN

MARTHE JOCELYN is the acclaimed author and illustrator of fifty books for young readers. Among her many honors, she has received the Mystery Writers of America Best Juvenile Book Award and the prestigious Vicky Metcalf Award for a distinguished body of work. She most happily composes that work in a hammock, or staring at water, or riding on a train. Even more than writing, Marthe likes reading books where someone is hiding a shocking secret. She lives in Stratford, Ontario. Visit her website at www.marthejocelynbooks.com.

ISABELLE FOLLATH is a freelance illustrator living in Zurich, Switzerland, with her family, where she creates art for books and many other things. She loves drawing all sorts of characters using her vintage pen and ink, and drinking an alarming amount of coffee. When she is not illustrating, you can find her searching for the perfect nib or reading mystery novels. Visit her website at www.isabellefollath.ch.